A VERY BAD BET

A GOLDEN RETRIEVER BLACK CAT ROMANTIC COMEDY

CIDER COVE SWEET SOUTHERN ROMCOMS
BOOK 2

ELANA JOHNSON

ISBN-13: 978-1-63876-301-7

CLAUDIA

I PAUSE TO WAIT FOR GENIE TO SNIFF THE TRUNK OF A tree, which is a huge mistake. The other two dogs I'm walking this morning think it's okay to turn our morning walk into a sniff-fest. I'm really off my game this morning, and it's all because of the announcement about the City Planner position with the city of Cider Cove.

The application packet is *in*-tense, and I need letters of recommendation, a portfolio, the experience, and it's at least a three-interview process. Application packets are due November fourteenth, and that gives the current City Planner and his team of people six weeks to find his replacement before his retirement begins.

"Come on," I say to Genie as I tug on her leash. "Walk. Let's walk." With dogs, you need to use short, easy commands. I take these three dogs on their morning walks every weekend, and Genie—a miniature poodle—looks up at me with her happy little smile on her face.

Yes, she's cute and she knows it.

"Walk," I say, tugging on the goldendoodle's leash, as well as the black, full-sized schnauzer who needs way more exercise than I can give him in an hour on Saturday and Sunday mornings.

Part of me wishes I could start and run a full-time doggy walking business, but that's only on pure, clear, somewhat cool Saturday mornings like today. I definitely love my job, what with all the cute skirts and slacks and blouses I get to wear.

I'm not like Lizzie or anything, who's started doing some plus-size modeling, but she's good with fashion, and she gives me plenty of items that I actually really like.

Right now, it's my job causing me to lose focus on the dog-walking. And it's *walking*. It's not hard.

The path we're on is one I've walked many times, the emerald green-grass on my right side opening up to a large field where several people have come to throw balls and Frisbees to their canines.

I'm not paid to do that, and it would make me a little nervous anyway. I have good control of my dogs, but Willie, the schnauzer, tends to bolt when he sees someone or something he likes. Even now, he's tugging on the leash a little too hard for my liking.

"Don't pull me," I say as I give his leash a hard tug. It pulls him back to me, and he looks over his shoulder as if

I've done him a horrible wrong. But he slows down and keeps pace with the other two dogs. If anything, Genie's the one working the hardest, her little tawny legs moving at twice the speed of the other dogs.

I make plans to work on my portfolio when I get back to the Big House, because I have plenty of experience in terms of events from my last several years as the Public Works Director.

The desperation to make sure every single thing is exactly right with my application claws at me, and I round the bend in the path, now turning into the sun. Some people complain about the heat in South Carolina, but I personally love it.

It's not as bad as South Texas, where I grew up, and it's got the beach instead of the border of Mexico. I love the beach, and sometimes, if I'm feeling particularly peppy, I walk the doggos on the sand instead of through this park.

It's a harder walk for all of us, as the sand shifts in mysterious ways beneath our feet, and Lucy, the golden-doodle, is a little bit psycho around water. But I determine that tomorrow, I'll take the dogs to the beach to do our morning walk.

"I'm going to get this job," I tell the trio of canines. "I managed the clean-up of Discovery Park, and that place was a mess." Now, it's one of the most-reserved pavilions and the pickleball courts there are impossible to get on.

I've been working on that layout in my portfolio for a week, and I think I've about got it done. Right.

As they often do when I'm stewing over work, my thoughts move to the only person I think could get this job over me.

Beckett Fletcher.

He's the Deputy Director in the Public Works Department for the city, and he does a lot of work with private investors and businesses, using their donations to improve public lands. He's done some incredible projects too—including a riverwalk improvement that I sometimes take the dogs to—and I know his portfolio will be as flawless as mine.

I scoff under my breath, because there's no way he can put together a double-page display that shows the before-and-after the way I can. For once, my scrapbooking skills have come in handy, and I never thought I'd say *that*.

My phone rings, thankfully distracting me from the downward spiral of my thoughts. Ry's name sits there, and I swipe on the call with my thumb while maintaining control over the three dogs with my left hand. They trot along on my left side like the good puppers they are, and I say, "Hey, Ry," as I lift my phone to my ear.

"Hey, are you out walking the dogs?"

"Yep."

"Emma says she could use some help at the shop today, and I got the task of calling everyone." Her voice slows on the last few words, almost turning into a question without becoming one.

I suppress my sigh, because I don't mind helping Emma at her florist shop. "What's she got going on?"

"She has a wedding tonight," Ry said. "And someone just came in, begging and crying for flowers for their company party."

"A company party?" My eyebrows go up toward the sun.

"You know how Emma is," Ry says with the sigh I wanted to make a few moments ago. "She can't say no."

I've been walking at a brisk pace for half an hour, and my breath scoffs out of my mouth. "It's a company party. Not a last-minute funeral."

"Is that a no?" Ry asks.

"No, of course not." I spot a man jogging toward me with two dogs on my side of the path, and I need the use of both hands for this. "I'll be there, but I won't be home for another hour or so."

"We're going to go over at ten," Ry said. "I'll have Tahlia make you a breakfast sandwich. Emma said she'd order us pizza."

"All right," I say. "I have to jet." I slide the phone in the side pocket of my stretchy pants, and I tug all three dogs closer to my side as Shirtless Jogger continues toward me. He's wearing a visor and a pair of sunglasses and the shortest shorts I've seen on a man—and I've seen plenty jogging around the city, the beaches, and on this very path.

He's got muscles from here to the West Coast, and I'm glad my own eyes are shaded behind a pair of sunglasses, so he can't tell how I'm ogling him.

His dogs—both brown canines that look like mutts—are on leashes, which are connected to a belt around his waist. He's got earbuds in, and I see the slightest movement of his head toward me as he gets closer and closer.

His dogs' tongues hang out of their mouths, and it sure looks like they're going to trot right past us. I'm not sure who moves first. It could've been Willie, who definitely crosses in front of me. Genie follows him, and in the next moment, I'm trying to high-step over their leashes while the guy slows and pulls on his dogs' leashes.

Both of them are tail-waggingly sniffing Willie already, and all five dogs have decided their greeting chain is happening right in front of me.

How they stop so fast, I don't know, because I feel like my momentum is still propelling me forward—right on top of them.

"Move," I bark at the same time I'm trying to find a place to put my feet that isn't dog flesh. They move like snakes, and just when I see a spot of open cement, it disappears under a bushy, brown tail.

I'm going to fall, and I know it. I look up into a face I recognize, and it's not until I'm descending backward that I realize the muscular, two-dog owner behind the shades is Beckett Fletcher.

Then I'm down, pain smarting through my tailbone

and up into my spine. I only hold one dog leash, which means my other two are loose, and I'm not sure if my pulse is panicked because of that or because Beckett has A Body.

And two dogs. And jogs in this park where I walk my canines.

"Whoa, whoa, whoa," Beckett says, and he's instantly on his knees in front of me. "Are you okay?"

If he knew it's me on the ground, he wouldn't be so nice. I feel put together wrong, like everything that's usually straight is all askew, from my sunglasses, to my ponytail, to every stitch of clothing on my body.

"I've got the dogs," someone says, and I look to my left, where the dog pile was. The dog pile I'm now part of. Only Genie sits there, and I don't see a stitch of black anywhere. Great. Willie's gone.

"I have—" I try to say, but my voice feels stuck behind my lungs. Until I can get a proper breath, I won't be able to speak. I have to try. "A schnauzer," I manage to say.

"I've got him," that someone says again, and Beckett looks over to them.

Then back to me. "The dogs are right here," he says. "Can you get up? Did you twist or sprain something?" Beckett puts his hand on my shoulder, and the touch burns partly against my bare skin and partly through my tank top strap.

In this moment, with him looking at me with concern, and touching me, I realize—he has no idea who I am.

I never wear my hair up at work. I don't wear

athleisure attire. I don't have dogs, or wear sunglasses, and Beckett and I never talk about personal things. I don't know where he lives, or that he has dogs, or anything about him really.

Now, I see the little bit of scruff on his face that indicates he hasn't shaved today. It's the color of the rich brown floors in the living room at the Big House, and he's got a mouth full of white teeth as he flashes me a smile.

My heartbeat clangs strangely in my chest, and I know this feeling inside myself. If he was anyone but the annoying, obnoxious, arrogant, grumpy Deputy Director who works next door to me, I'd be interested in him.

I'd get to my feet and try to flirt with him enough for him to ask for my number. The thing is, Beckett already has my number, and he would never, ever use it to ask me out on a date.

"I'm okay," I say, my voice lodged down in my throat. I'm relieved I don't sound like myself, and with Beckett's hand in mine, I get back to my feet.

I straighten my tank top and take the leashes back from the second man who'd stopped to help. I recognize him too, because he comes to this park all the time. My heart drops to the soles of my feet as Landon smiles at me. He's asked me out before, but there's no fizz between us.

Not like there just was when Beckett put his hand on my shoulder.

"Thank you," I say to him, adjusting the leashes in my hand so I'm holding them the way I like.

"Sure thing, Claudia," he says, and I press my eyes closed.

So close.

"Claudia?" Beckett asks, his voice pitching up into a near-screech.

Oh, so close.

BECKETT

I CAN'T BELIEVE WHO'S STANDING IN FRONT OF ME. Claudia Brown.

I can't believe I didn't recognize her, but she's wearing clothes I've never imagined her to even own. Her dark-as-midnight hair is pulled up into a ponytail, and she doesn't have her bangs. Her forehead is more like a fivehead, but I think it's kind of cute.

I can't believe I think my nemesis is *cute.*

But as she sprawled on the ground because of Duke, because the silly dog can't stay in his own lane, I had definitely thought she was cute enough to try to talk to. You know, once I'd determined she wasn't hurt badly. Duke thinks all other canines came to the park just to see him. He's sitting right at my side, panting like I've run him ten miles today when we've only gone four.

In front of me, Claudia pushes her sunglasses up onto

her head, and yep, there are the deep pools of beauty. They've never looked at me with anything like softness or attraction or even tolerance.

I always get the defiance and disgust she currently wears in her expression, and I've never felt my blood running so hotly through my veins. It's from all the running, I'm sure. I'm out later than normal today, as I'd normally be done with my Saturday morning workout by now.

The sun has fried my retinas, that's all.

I mean, any man with even one working eye can see how gorgeous Claudia is. I've never entertained those thoughts for long, because it's clear the woman dislikes me greatly. I can admit I've never made it easy for her—for anyone—to like me, but the know-it-all, arrogant grump has kept my heart safe for a long time now.

It's a persona I'm comfortable with, though even I can admit I'm growing tired of putting up such a strong façade for everyone.

"Sorry about my dogs," Claudia says, and I jerk back to attention. I can't just stand here in the park, staring at the midnight beauty.

I clear my throat and nod at her. "I didn't know you had dogs."

"I don't."

I raise my eyebrows, and even behind my mirrored sunglasses, I'm clearly asking her about the three very real dogs whose leashes Claudia holds.

She startles and looks down at the dogs. The littlest one has laid right on down, taking shade from the shadow of the huge black schnauzer. "I mean, yes, I walk these dogs. They're not mine. It's a...side gig."

I can't help the way my mouth curls up. "A side gig."

"We're not at work." She brings the leashes closer to her. "I don't have to talk to you. Come on, guys." She looks down at her dogs, and adds, "Walk. Let's walk." She practically barks at them, and they go right with her.

She strides away in those skin-tight leggings, her high ponytail bobbing with the movement, all three dogs falling right into line at her side. So she's a good dog trainer. That doesn't mean we're going to become friends.

"Or frenemies. Or anything at all." I look down at my dogs, and Duke and Rocky look back at me. "Let's go." I don't have the sexy dogwalker bark down, but my dogs get going again without an issue.

We finish our run after I cut it short by a couple of miles and open the back of my king-cab pickup truck for the dogs to get in. They do, and the annoying sound of panting accompanies me all the way home.

As a city employee, I decided I have to live in the community I serve, so I've got a quick drive from this park that was built on the border of Cider Cove and Charleston to my place on the border of Cider Cove and Sugar Creek.

Everything about my life feels stale, from the way I run every morning, to how I clip my grass on Saturdays, to how neat everything is in my house. I do my dishes after every meal, because I hate the smell of leftover food. I'm obsessive about taking my trash out, and I do it every morning before I go to work. That way, my house won't smell when I walk in after work.

Somehow, I manage to allow the dogs to live in the house, and their scent doesn't bother me.

"You need therapy," I mutter to myself as I hang the leashes on their appointed hooks in my garage. The dogs trot off to drink out of their fountainous water bowl, and I go back into the garage to fire up the lawn mower.

I have a square little house, in a common little neighborhood, for my fits-inside-a-box life. By the time my grass is exactly the right height and I'm scrubbing the sweat from my skin in the shower, I can't hold back the sigh anymore.

I don't need therapy. I need some color in my life. Some spice. Some...something. The talk of the town is Matchmaker, and I get out of the shower, pull on a pair of gym shorts, and go join the dogs on the couch.

The three of us fill it up, and I commit to filling out my profile all the way. I put in my name; I use a real picture from my gallery; when it comes to the two hundred characters I can use for my description, I pause.

This is where I'd make up something totally outlandish that somehow sounds real. Like, that my favorite food is chicken gumbo, and I love holidays with my family, and there isn't a mountain I don't want to climb.

I like gumbo just fine, and my family knows me better than anyone, and I do like spending time outdoors. So it's not entirely untrue, but it's definitely not true either.

City government. Dog lover. Outdoor enthusiast.

That's what I put down, because those three things do sum up my life. They're generic and vague, but honestly, so am I.

With all the pieces in place, I submit my profile for approval, and I get a notification that it could take up to twenty-four hours for it to be live. I look over to Rocky, who only moves his eyes toward me. His eyebrows are so expressive that it looks like his whole face moves.

"What do you think, boy?" I reach over and scrub his face. His eyes close in bliss as I ask the second half of my question. "Should I start dating again?"

My phone makes a noise I've never heard before, and I look down at my lap. A heart icon sits in the top notification bar, and I swipe down to see what that's all about. It's Matchmaker, and it says my profile is approved and live.

Another heart pops up, and then another. "Husky pups." I'm too old for this, and I can't believe I let my insecurities get the best of me.

I'm getting matches already, and my profile is only five minutes old. The women in this town and surrounding suburbs of Charleston must smell fresh meat, because wow. Some of them simply tap on the heart-match, but a couple of them do that and then message me too.

I don't know how to do this type of dating. I failed at the in-person kind too, and I feel like I need to take a George-Constanza approach.

"Opposite George," I whisper. In one of my favorite episodes of *Seinfeld*, one of the characters—George—does everything the exact opposite of what his natural instincts are.

I need to do the same.

So no, I normally wouldn't even be on this app. I wouldn't message women who probably have fake profile pictures and probably have these half-truths on their personal descriptions too.

"Maybe I should start tomorrow," I tell myself. After all, I've gone jogging this morning, and I've mown my lawn. Those are Normal Me things, not Opposite Me things.

I sag back into the couch and close my eyes. When it's just me and the dogs, the ceiling fan moving air around my house, I can be the Real Me. And at this moment, I ask him what he wants.

An image of Claudia Brown enters my mind, and she waltzes in real slow, like she wants me to see all of her before she gets too close. I have the woman's number, because we work together. Closely.

My office is right next door to hers, and no, I haven't been the picture of Prince Charming or anything like that. I hate it when she closes her office door, because it makes the air conditioning in the ancient building where we work malfunction. My office grows hot within a minute, though that might be because I get irritated that she's talking to someone about something I'd like to know about too.

I lift my phone up in front of me and start sliding and tapping. I start a new text and type in the first few letters of her name. It comes up, and all I have to do is tap it. My pulse starts to race, and I'm sweating as if I'm still outside pushing the mower back and forth in neat, trim lines.

I tap on Claudia's name, and the text has begun. I leap to my feet, because I don't even know what I'd say to her. "Complete opposite," I mutter to myself, and the next thing I know my thumbs are flying.

> Hey, Claudia. Just checking to make sure you're all right and made it home okay. Duke sometimes just gets excited around other dogs, especially those smaller than him. They're like dognip to him.

I don't even read over it again, and I always, *always* read over my texts before I send them.

This time, Opposite Me simply hits send. I smile as the message pops up and I see I used the word dognip. I know it's not a real word, and I fully expect Claudia to correct me on it.

But while I have hearts flying into my phone and messages popping up on the Matchmaker app, Claudia doesn't answer right away.

I let my eyes drift closed as I sit down again, and Duke snuggles his part-golden-retriever self into my side. I cuddle him close and stroke down his side. My dogs are my best friends, and I do talk to them throughout the weekends and evenings when I'm home.

But I need more than a couple of dogs to chatter at.

My phone makes a normal noise, and I yank my eyes open to see who I've gotten a text from.

"Claudia." I sit up straight, my dog suddenly too hot against my side. She's said:

> I made it home fine, thank you.

Hardly an invitation for me to text her again. I opened the door, but she's practically kicked it closed again.

Still, I start texting again, abandoning all reason and praying I can face her on Monday morning.

CLAUDIA

My phone bleeps over and over and over, to the point where I glare at it and then Ry in my passenger seat. "Can you silence that?"

"Who is it?"

I don't answer her, because I think I know. And it's super confusing to me. I'm not sure why Beckett has decided that a random park sighting means that we can now talk outside of work.

My phone bleeps again while Ry has it in her hand, and my stomach feels like someone has force-fed me menthol. It's cold and radiating a chill through my whole body. "It's Beckett From Work," she says, her voice awed. "What's his real last name?"

"Fletcher," I bite out.

"He's..."

"Irritating?" I supply when she doesn't say more. "Obnoxious? The fastest texter on the planet?"

Gorgeous, my mind supplies in the most traitorous of ways. I can see him in those tiny shorts and no shirt, and I can't help the way my pulse picks up its pace. Great, now my whole body is betraying me.

I'd told him I'd made it home fine, thank you very much. I don't need him to check up on me. He's not my father—or my boyfriend.

"Just silence it," I say. "I'll talk to him at work on Monday."

"He's asking if you can get together with him to go over something."

"He's delusional," I mutter as I turn into the parking lot where Emma's flower shop sits. Well, it's not really hers. She's trying to purchase it outright, but she's waiting on her loan to be approved.

She works here full-time with a part-time assistant— and her besties and roommates whenever big orders come in or she falls behind.

I practically ram the flower shop as I pull into a parking spot behind it. "This brake pedal is a little finicky," I say in my defense.

"Yeah, totally," Ry agrees with me, though she knows I'm a crazy driver when I get upset.

"Let me see the texts." I hold out my hand for my phone, but Ry doesn't give it to me immediately. She cocks her right eyebrow at me—a feat only she can do out of all of us at the Big House—and then slaps my device into my palm.

> Hey, I know you've been working on your application for City Planner.

> I have been too, and now we've got this Christmas Festival on the docket.

> I'd love to meet with you to go over a few of the high points for that before I pitch anything to Harvey.

> Maybe we should come up with a plan together?

> I'd love to sit down one day soon and hammer a few things out.

I want to hammer his thumbs flat, because every single one of those came as a separate text.

And then,

> I have to head over to my aunt's to help her with a few things, but then I'll have my phone handy.

"Chantilly Lace," I swear as I look up.

Ry laughs and says, "That's the best you've got? Chantilly Lace has been the most popular paint color for a long time, Claude."

I can pick a paint color for any room, and I actually

adore paint samples with my whole soul. Thus, I have quite a few of their names memorized, and since I work in small town city government and need to watch my tongue, I've taken to using them for my curse words.

"Balboa Mist," I say next, and Ry tips her head back and laughs.

"That's better," she says through her giggles. "Now, come on. Bring all those texts, and let's go see what Emma's advice about Beckett-From-Work-Fletcher is."

"I don't want her advice," I gripe as I get out of my car. "I'm not going to work with him more than I have to." I frown over the top of the sedan at Ry, who gives me this all-knowing look, like maybe she's been able to peel back part of my skull and see my traitorous thoughts about how good-looking Beckett is.

Impossible.

She is a manager at an office supply store, and she does have a BS-meter that can register any time anyone is lying to her. But me?

I really *don't* like Beckett, his body notwithstanding. Someone can be beautiful on the outside and absolute poison on the inside. I know, because I grew up with a father like that, and I will not—I *will not*—have someone like that in my life again.

"Okay," Ry says in this irritating way that says I'm wrong and she knows it. That I'm just dying to work more with Beckett.

But I'm not, and I'll prove it to her.

Beckett has left me on read plenty of times, so I make sure the device is silenced before I shove my phone in my pocket and follow my roommate into the flower shop. The complete chaos in front of us makes both of us pause, and I mutter to Ry, "Not a word about this to Emma today. Ten bucks says she's already crying."

Vines hang down from the rafters. Flowers lay everywhere, in random order. Glass vases and metal buckets and baskets wait for their arrangements. And the baby's breath. Holy Boothbay Gray, the baby's breath.

It's *everywhere*, like an invasion of the stuff has landed here at the shop and will soon cover the entire town of Cider Cove, bringing us all to our knees at any moment.

"I'm not taking that bet," Ry says.

"You know I'm going to win."

"You usually do." Ry takes a breath and reaches out to touch the velvet petal of a white rose that's been discarded on a nearby shelf with dozens and dozens of others. "We're here," she calls, and she bravely takes the first step further into the shop.

Emma comes out of the back, wiping her hands on her green apron. "Thank goodness," she says, and yes, a round of tears starts rolling down her face.

That so was a bet I would've won, and I silently give myself the victory as Ry and I move to embrace our friend. "Okay," I say after giving Emma a moment to cry. "We've got this, Em. Give me your lists, and I'll start organizing."

After all, right behind knowing all the most popular

paint colors for the past several years, I'm also an organizational queen. I even have a crown and everything. Yes, Tahlia made it for me, and yes, I display it proudly on a shelf in my bedroom. Doesn't matter that it was a roommate award from three years ago.

Organizing things is a specialty of mine, and I take Emma's rumpled papers from her and say, "Okay. They're just flowers. We've got this," though I have no idea how Emma takes flowers and turns them into art.

I just know I need the distraction, and while I wasn't super-jazzed to come help her in the flower shop today, now I certainly am. Because it means I won't have time to answer Beckett.

Pro.

The con is, I do have time while I'm sorting flowers and putting them into bins for Emma's arrangements to think about him. And think about him. And think some more about him.

Caliente—which is a popular red for accent walls.

————

Yes, the Christmas Festival needs a lot of help this year.

I STARE AT THE TEXT, wondering why I had to wait through the floral arranging to come up with those words.

Then I went to a late lunch with Tahlia, Ry, and Lizzie. Now, I've sequestered myself upstairs on the third floor, where I live alone now that Hillary's moved to LA for her documentary.

I expected to miss her, but how much is unfathomable. Being up here all alone, it feels...weird.

I don't like being alone, I think, and somehow my fingers type that out.

Horrified, I mash my thumb on the delete button, which takes the first sentence with it too. And I'd labored over that for fifteen minutes.

I sigh and look up from my device. The sun has started to set, and I haven't turned on any lights. I reach over and flip on the lamp, and soft, cheery, yellow light fills my bedroom.

Everyone in the Public Works Department got an email on Friday night right around closing time about the Christmas Festival Director.

She'd quit. Suddenly.

"That, or she got fired," I mutter to myself. No matter what, Beatrice Dees isn't running the festival this year, and it's already been announced to the public. Now, since it's only the beginning of September, you might think that's plenty of time to put together a Christmas Festival.

But Cider Cove is like *The Hallmark Channel* on steroids. The mayor even pays for that fake snow they use in the movies. She puts it all around the square, and there are more twinkling lights on every building than the whole rest of the state. It's like the North Pole met Times Square, and they had a baby and dropped it in the South. That's Mayor Garvin and her love of the Christmas Festival.

So someone is going to need to step up and take on the Festival in a big way—and that someone will then have something pretty darn amazing to put on their City Planner application.

My brain misfires, because the two events don't line up. The Christmas Festival isn't until Christmas, obviously. The City Planner applications are due November fourteenth.

Still, if it's on Beckett's radar, then it's on mine. I don't want him having more meetings over in the main government building, and I certainly can't have him riding in on some white reindeer to save the town's Christmas Festival. Then everyone will have his name on the tip of their tongues, and that matters when being considered for a big job.

My desperation for the City Planner job coats the back of my tongue like glue. It's suddenly not easy or pleasant to swallow, and I feel like I'm choking.

My only way out is through texting, and my fingers fly as I type a text to Becket. Just one, thank you very much, because it's totally okay to put more than one sentence in a text.

> The Christmas Festival is going to be a disaster unless someone steps in. Sybil and I have met to discuss a few things, and I have a short list. I already have a meeting with Winslow next week to go over a few things, and I don't really need to hammer out anything.

I don't use our boss's last name the way Beckett did. I don't want or need to meet with Beckett. I have my ideas, and I don't have to share them with him just because I can't stop thinking about what it might be like to see him outside of work.

That's just crazy-thought anyway.

> Oh, and you really should check your use of the phrasal verb in that last text.

I send the message all as one, the tension in my shoulders off-the-charts-high.

> You should check your double usage of "a few things."

The text pops up, and I blink-blink, blink-blink at it. I re-read my text, and blast Beckett, he's right. I so doubled up on that phrase, and I can't take it back now.

> I'd love to go with you and Sybil to see Winslow.

My own fingers fly now too. I'm so going to beat

Beckett at some sort of world record in texting speed. *I'm sure you would.*

> We can't have a united front on this thing? I just want the Christmas Festival to be amazing for the townspeople.

I scoff, because if Beckett is anything, it's not philanthropic.

> Tell me your ideas for the Festival.

> I'd love to. Over dinner?

I drop my phone as if it's caught on fire. Fortunately—or unfortunately, as a series of bleepity-bleeps come in—it doesn't break.

Bleep, bleep, blee-bleep.

"How in the Vintage Wine does he text so fast?" I gripe as I lean over and retrieve my device from the floor. And why is my heart pounding so hard? "Has he really asked you out?"

My fingers close around the hard plastic case of my phone, and I'm sure the letters will have rearranged themselves into something reasonable and rational when I look again—and not a dinner invite from Beckett-Has-A-Body-Fletcher.

> Tonight?

> Tomorrow?

Monday?

Wait, I can't Monday. My aunt has an
appointment in Columbia, and I
drive her.

When's your meeting with Winslow?

I can also do lunch any day in the
foreseeable future.

The texts finally stop, but my eyes roam over them again and again. I somehow manage to pull my attention to the top of my phone, where the time shouts at me that it's only five-forty-two. Definitely still dinner-date-able, despite my late lunch. Maybe now's a great time to eat with Beckett on purpose—when I'm not hungry, so I won't make a fool of myself in front of him.

Before I can decide what to say or do—my stupid pulse is seriously attacking my body from the inside out—more texts pour in.

Brunch tomorrow?

Sunday brunch, Claudia!

Wait, what time do you walk the dogs?

Is that an every-weekend-day thing?

Do you always go to Riverside Park?

I could meet you.

Do a doggy-walking power meeting.

A pause, finally. Well, long enough for me to take a breath and press one hand to my chest like a proper Southern belle who's been overwhelmed with the male attention she's received today. I actually feel kind of sweaty and woozy, like I've simply been twirled around the dance floor too many times by too many handsome suitors.

> Okay, I'll stop now. Just let me know when.

He really does stop, but I stare at the dog emoji. I say, "He sent me a—dog—emoji." I look up like someone will be there, listening. Like someone will be able to tell me what the heck to do. Like someone will know what all of his texts mean.

In times like these, when I'd already isolated myself from the rest of the Big House, I'd scurry down the hall to Hillary's room and ask her advice. Another keen sense of missing hits me, but I still get to my feet and stride for the door.

"Guys," I yell as I enter the hallway, though none of my current roommates will be able to hear me. I fly down the steps, calling again, "Guys, I need help! It's a man-thing! Come quick!"

Ry comes out of her room on the second floor. "A man-thing?"

Lizzie meets me at the bottom of the steps in the kitchen, with Ry hot on my heels. "What kind of help?"

I simply thrust my phone into her hands and pace away from her. Tahlia has started on her Sunday baking early, bless her soul. I bite my thumbnail while Ry and Tahlia peer over Lizzie's shoulder and the scent of snicker-doodles fills the air.

Emma isn't here, because she had two major deliveries to make for the events tonight, and she'll hate being left out. But I feel like I'm going to throw up. She'll have to get caught up later, that's all.

Lizzie looks up, her eyes like big blue moons.

"Well?" I ask. "Someone tell me what to do."

Tahlia finally pulls her gaze from the phone too. "Is this Beckett, the guy who works next door to you?"

"Mm hm," I say, unable to form words.

Ry falls back from Lizzie, who's still holding my phone with a tight grip. "Well," she says while everyone else stays silent. "You *did* flirt with him, so...maybe you should go out with him."

I scoff and then choke. Then cough, and choke, and scoff again. "I did not—*I did not* flirt with him."

Lizzie hands me back my phone, her eyes dazzling and sparkling like sapphires now. "Claude, honey, you kind of did."

"It's *Beckett*," I say, as if that will explain everything. It always has before. But as I look down at my device and see all those texts with his name on them...nothing makes sense.

And I still have no idea how to answer him.

BECKETT

I know Claudia was just looking at her phone. She was texting me back quickly, a real exchange that actually has my blood pumping harder through my veins.

Now, she's gone silent.

I look away from my phone and over to my aunt. She's just had a knee replacement, and I come every day to help her. Especially at night, she needs company, and she needs help cleaning up, bringing things inside, and getting in bed.

She'll watch TV, read, or crochet from there, and Aunt Jill looks over to me too. "Ready to head out?"

"Whenever," I say though my stomach growls mightily. My aunt has been eating whatever her neighbors bring, or what I show up with in a brown bag after work. I can't really blame her, because I'm like Jerry on *Seinfeld*.

There's food in my cupboards and fridge, but it's more for show than eating.

I don't know if I'm a good cook or not, because I don't even try. I stop for coffee and scones on the way to work. I go out to lunch every day, and I pick something up on the way home. It's a good thing I run every day, or I'd probably look like the bacon cheeseburgers I eat several times each week.

"I'm ready." Aunt Jill sighs as she scoots to the edge of her chair.

"Wait, wait, wait." I jump to my feet to be there to steady her, and her little chihuahua nearly trips me, which would send *me* to the hospital for a knee replacement.

"Cocoa," I chastise. "Get out of the way. I'm helping her." I steady my aunt's hands in mine as she stands, and her eyes meet mine.

"You're such a good man, Becks."

I wish she'd tell Claudia that. Instead of suggesting my disabled aunt talk to the woman at my office who doesn't like me—a total stranger for her, and nearly one for me—I just smile at her. "Tell my momma that, would you?"

"I do," Aunt Jill says. "Every single day, when she calls me."

I keep my smile hitched in place, because I don't talk to my momma every day the way her sister does. She loves me; I know she does. She simply has another life now, one that's taken her across the country with a new husband and new adventures.

"Don't trip on this rug now," I say, though I taped it down extra-secure just two days ago.

"Oh, you." Aunt Jill fake-swats at my chest, which nearly sends her off-balance on the perfectly flat floor.

I chuckle at her and keep us both on our feet. Unbidden, my thoughts wander to Claudia toppled on the path in the park this morning. Why, I don't really know. I haven't spent much time thinking about her outside of work, though she does have a nickname. That's mostly because I like giving everyone a nickname.

When I was growing up and all through college, I couldn't actually remember people's names very easily. So I made up nicknames for them simply so I wouldn't look stupid when I couldn't remember.

I've come up with tricks to remember names, and the more I'm around someone, the easier it is. Of course. But Claudia wasn't always in the office next door, and until I moved into the one beside hers and really knew and remembered her name, I called her Midnight Beauty.

She'll probably sock me in the mouth if I ever tell her that. I vow silently that I'm never going to tell her as I follow my aunt into her bedroom. I help her get in bed. I make sure she has all the things she needs within arm's reach—a cold drink, her bag of crochet, the TV remote— and then, the softie I am, I bend and get Cocoa and gently toss her onto the bed.

She gives me a little doggy sniff, a chihuahua-glare over her shoulder, and goes to circle near Aunt Jill's hip.

My aunt has two cats not much bigger than the chihuahua, but they can jump on the bed themselves. They haven't come down the hall with us, because they both love Rocky to death, and they've been snoozing on him since we got here.

"Thank you, Becks," she says.

"See you tomorrow," I say, giving her a small salute before I turn and leave. My phone hasn't made a single sound, and that only makes me sigh in frustration as I walk down the hall alone.

I roll my neck as I do my aunt's dishes, and my thoughts grow thoughts of their own as I take out her trash and make sure she's got everything set out next to her coffee maker for tomorrow morning.

Then, I go back through the living room and look over to my dogs curled up on my aunt's couch. "Come on, guys," I say, ignoring the cats as they ignore me. "We're not staying here tonight."

Duke moves first, but Rocky stays absolutely still, like he's a gargoyle who can't move until he's released by the princess's magic. His eyes do move, and he's so expressive in his eyebrows that I can't help smiling at him.

I dig in my pocket and pull out my keys. "Come on, Rocky. I'm going, and I'll leave you here if you're not in the truck."

He yawns. Actually yawns, and I roll my eyes as I head for the door. Duke trots along with me, and sure enough, I have to wait for Rocky to make his way over to us and out the door. He looks up at me like, *What? I came, didn't I?* as he hurries by.

"Yeah," I say. "You're a slow poke is what you are." I follow the dogs to my truck and let them jump up into the back seat. I've got a net to keep them back there, or Duke would try to hitch a ride on my lap.

They pant the whole way home, though I haven't made them run tonight, and I pull into the driveway and stop. I don't usually sit here and stare at my house, but I can't bring myself to get out and go inside textless.

"You texted her back too fast," I mutter to myself. I'd just been so excited to hear from her, to get more than one message from her.

"You *are* excited to hear from her," I mutter as I open the back door for my dogs. I need dinner, but there's no way I'm taking a bite of anything until I hear from Claudia.

If I ever hear from her again.

I groan as I follow the canines through the garage and into the backyard. I make sure the gates are closed and the door behind me, and then we all find a patch of shade to settle into. It's still really nice in the evenings though autumn has started to arrive, and if I had a glass of lemonade, I could be fifty years older, toeing myself back and forth on a swing-seat-built-for-two and complaining about the weather.

Oh, and the beautiful woman who still hasn't texted me back.

I look over my texts, and yeah, I'm over-eager. "You're a mess," I say, and both of my dogs look up at me. Duke pants, but Rocky just lays his head back on his paws and sighs, like I've committed some horrible crime by making him leave my aunt's house to come do this. Rocky turns part-feline whenever we go over there. I swear, sometimes he purrs and everything.

I growl, my thumbs zipping across my screen as I start another text to Claudia. I can practically hear my sister telling me to *stop it! Delete it all, Beckett. You literally threw out every rope you have. Let her grab onto one.*

So I delete it all and I tap away from Claudia's name to get to Liv's. Her phone rings twice, and she says, "Hey, little bro. What's up?"

"I am in so much trouble, and I need you to talk me off the ledge." This is not the first conversation I've started this way with my sister.

So it's unsurprising when she says, "Work ledge, relationship ledge, friend ledge, or family ledge?"

"Kind of a combo of both?" I groan-slash-growl again. "Let me send you some screenshots." I quickly put her on speaker and navigate back to Claudia's messages. Fine, they're mostly my messages with a bump here and there where Claudia has said a couple of things.

"I threw too much out there, didn't I?" I ask before the screenshots have even gone through.

"This sounds relationshippy," Liv says.

"It's part that," I say. "Part work."

The pictures go through, and Liv—an extraordinarily fast reader—says, "Ohhh." And not in a good way. Not a *this-is-fine-Beckett* way. But in a *you-pulled-a-George-Costanza-move* way.

George is forever messing up his relationships. I think it's one of the reasons I love *Seinfeld* so much. I'm not stocky, or balding, or living with my parents. But I feel like I sink every relationship I try to have too, usually within the first few dates.

Not even being able to get one? Because I can't control my fingers? Because they spew out every thought that comes into my brain?

Pathetic.

"Who is Claudia?"

"A co-worker," I say miserably. "I ran into her in the park this morning, and well, I don't know. We've never gotten along, but there was this fizz. You know? This bubbly, bright feeling between us. I don't know, I—"

"Okay, Becks," she says. "Breathe for a second, bro."

I do that while Liv lets me do that.

"You've never gotten along?"

"Not particularly," I say, my mind suddenly flashing all the times I've yelled at her through the walls to open her door. I've knocked on the wall separating our offices. I've loitered near open windows to eavesdrop on her. I've deliberately made sure she knows about my meetings over in the main building, just to watch her face turn a tomatoey red.

I hang my head, though my sister can't see me. This is how this goes. She gets to ask a question; I answer it truthfully and slowly, calmly and succinctly. My mouth really runs as fast as my feet sometimes. It's a blessing and a curse.

"You don't like her? Or you do?"

"I mean, I never have all that much before today," I say. "But outside of work, I...don't know."

"But these texts are about work," Liv says. "Are you trying to use work as a way to see her outside of work?"

"Duh," I say. "Was that not obvious?"

"No, it was," Liv says. "I just wondered if it was to you."

"If it is to me, then it is to her."

"I'd think so, yes," Liv says.

"So I've messed up."

"Depends," Liv says. "I mean, you're obviously eager. She has to know it. She hasn't answered?"

"It's been about thirty minutes," I say. "And no. She just went silent."

"You work with this woman. What does silent mean for her?"

"It means—" I cut off, because I work with Claudia. I know her better that I think I do. "It means she's confused. Or she's trying to come up with the perfect response."

"Maybe she's talking to her sister too."

"She doesn't have a sister," I say. But she has a house full of roommates, and I groan again. She's probably showing them all of my insane texts right this second. I'm never going to be able to go to her house and pick her up for a date. Never, ever—and not because she won't answer me. But because I'll be too embarrassed to face her room-mates—and her.

How am I going to see her at work on Monday?

I heave a sigh and decide my humiliation for the night is complete. "I have to go, Liv. Thank you."

"Beckett," she says sternly. "Do *not* text this woman again. Swear to me."

"I swear," I say dutifully.

"That did not sound like you mean it." Liv sounds like the momma-drill-sergeant she is with her kids. Toddlers. "You've said enough. Let her come back with something first, and if you need me to look at it, text it to me. Do you hear me?"

"Yes, ma'am," I say in my most Southern-boy accent. "Thanks, Liv." The call ends and I gaze into the sky as it starts to bruise. I tell myself mentally that I won't even look at my phone for the rest of the night. I'll silence it and order in my favorite foods, and me and the dogs will enjoy our Saturday night together, the way we have dozens of times in the past.

Then my phone zips at me, and my eyes are on it like lightning to a rod.

Claudia.

Relief sings through me.

> Lunch sounds fine.

"Lunch sounds fine," I repeat slowly, trying to quell the excitement trembling through my fingers. She certainly doesn't sound super excited to go to lunch with me, but then again, why would she?

We are not friends.

So why am I thinking about her as *more* than a friend?

My stomach pinches at me as I take a screenshot and send it to Liv. *#help* I send with the pic while my own brain comes up with a pity response.

"I don't want pity," I tell myself. "I'm trying to get her to go out with me and like it."

Then maybe you shouldn't have made it sound like you wanted to mine her for her ideas on the Christmas Festival.

So, completely disobeying my older sister, I start to text Claudia back.

> We don't have to go over the Christmas stuff.

Send.

> I mean, we can if you want.

Send.

> But it's not required.

Send.

Great! Liv texts. *So you tell her you're thrilled, and ask her where she'd like to go. Her favorite place. Your treat.*

I can type that in my sleep, but Claudia responds before I get more than two words in.

> Then why would we go to lunch together at all?

What a great question—one I suddenly do not have an answer for. I can't snap screenshots and send these to Liv. She'll fillet me alive with one of her toddler's spoons, and that won't be pleasant.

I'm on my own here, and instead of texting, I do the unthinkable. I tap the phone icon at the top of the screen and call Claudia Brown.

CLAUDIA

"Oh, Bird's Egg Blue," I say, my phone flying from my hands again. "He's calling."

"Answer it," Lizzie says, lunging after my device. "I swear, Claudia." She comes up with the phone, but it might as well be a snake. "I'm answering it."

Before I can protest, she slides on the call and chirps, "Claudia Brown's phone."

I want to die. Just right there, wither up and die for a moment. Then, the sun will come out tomorrow, and I'll roar back to life, and nothing that's happened today will matter.

"Oh, sure, she's right here," Lizzie says, and she pulls the phone from her ear and extends it toward me. After I'd texted that lunch sounded fine, me, Ry, and Lizzie went into the living room while Tahlia finished up with the cookies.

I really need some cinnamon and sugary goodness before I can talk to Beckett. But he's right there...

I snatch the phone from her and say, "Hey," in a curt voice. It's one I'm well-versed in using with Beckett, and it just comes naturally to me.

"Hey, there she is," Beckett says like he's a real party animal and there's a deep bass beat behind him. But there's not. It's just his overly cheerful voice and all my roommates staring at me as Tahlia brings a plate of snickerdoodles into the living room.

No one even takes one, which is how serious this phone call is. Tahlia extends a cookie over the back of the couch toward me, and I take it while Beckett says, "Lunch would be really great. What are you doing tomorrow?"

"Tomorrow?" I squeak, and then I take the biggest bite of cookie any woman on the planet has ever taken.

"Yeah," he says. In front of me, Ry's eyes have gone wide, and Lizzie is making slashing movements across her throat.

Tahlia nods with a smile, and she even says, "Lunch tomorrow, huh?"

"She just needs to go out with him," Ry says, her gaze returning to normal. She even looks away from me and takes a cookie from the plate. "Rip off the Band-aid, you know?"

"Can you imagine them in the same booth for longer than four seconds?" Lizzie actually looks gleeful at the thought of getting to watch that.

We so would make it longer than four seconds. I mean, I work with the man, and I've had longer-than-four-second conversations with him tons of times. And Lizzie won't be able to witness my lunch date with Beckett.

"So you tell me where your favorite place is," Beckett says. "And I'll buy."

My brain kicks back into gear, and I swallow all the cinnamon and sugary goodness. It does nothing to settle my nerves, and I remind myself that I've bested Beckett several times. "But you don't want to talk about the Christmas Festival."

"I'll leave that up to you."

I turn my back on my roommates and lower my head, as if I'm about to say something super controversial. Or secret. For some reason, my chest grows warm at having a secret between me and Beckett.

Dead Salmon, I think, picturing the paint color in my head. It's actually a really nice, creamy, light chocolate color that goes perfectly in some kitchens.

"Are you asking me out?" I ask. "On a date? Or a work thing?"

Beckett clears his throat, and I have my answer. My blood feels like Tahlia's poured cinnamon and sugar into it, and I actually bounce on the balls of my feet once. Fine, twice.

Behind me, Lizzie squeals, and I know she's seen the ball-bouncing. But Beckett's saying, "It's a date, Claudia," in a really quiet voice. One I've never heard him use at the office. One I didn't even know he was capable of speaking in.

I lift my head and come face-to-face with the TV. It's off, thank goodness, or I'd probably be blind. For some reason, my mouth says, "Okay."

"Okay." Beckett breathes out like he's just finished drinking an entire can of soda. "One o'clock?"

I think of my dog walking, and I should be home by eight-thirty, which leaves me plenty of time to shower and primp for my date. "Okay," I say again. I swear, has my brain gone on vacation? "I like Better Than Butter, and you might need a reservation on a Sunday afternoon."

"Consider it done."

I almost scoff, because it's so Beckett to act like he can get a reservation for *tomorrow* at a popular place. He has less than twenty-four hours, for Dead Salmon's sake.

"Are you going to come pick me up?" I ask as I turn to face my roommates. I lower the phone and tap the speaker. "I can meet you."

"Make him come pick you up," Lizzie says.

"Wait," I say, smiling. "Lizzie says you have to come pick me up."

I swear Beckett audibly swallows. "Then I'll come pick you up."

"Perfect," I say, feeling a little bit like I have the upper hand again. For whatever reason, I need to feel like this with Beckett, and alarm bells ring at me. Why do I want to go out with him again?

"See you at one," Beckett says. "'Bye, Claudia."

"'Bye," I say, my bravado all gone. I tap to end the call, and then I sink onto the couch, my body suddenly boneless. I look over to Ry, whose eyebrows go up. On my other side, Tahlia says, "Give her a minute. You know how she likes to process things."

But Lizzie asks, "You're going out with him? *Tomorrow?*"

I look over to my two roommates on my left. I wish Hillary was here as my smile slowly grows and grows and grows. I tame my mouth back into a straight line. "There's one good thing about this date," I say, slowly surveying everyone.

"Oh, spit it out," Lizzie says.

"I know Beckett doesn't have another girlfriend in Atlanta." I allow my smile to curve back up again, but Ry scoffs.

"Please," she says. "You didn't know he had a body, so how can you be sure of anything?"

A moment of silence fills the Big House, and then we all start laughing. Well, they do. I'm reciting paint colors in an attempt to stay calm, because I have a date—a real *date* —with Beckett Fletcher tomorrow.

———

"LEAVE IT," I say crossly the next day. "Ry, he's going to be here any second."

"Lizzie's got the door handled," she says as she tries to tame my thick hair into a second French braid. She's tried it twice now, and she claims the third time will be the charm.

"Yeah, she and Emma better not have a booby trap set." I roll my eyes, but my stomach has been a ball of wound-up yarn that refuses to untangle since I woke up. I childishly avoided Riverside Park and took the doggos to the beach, though I rationalized every step on the shifty sand by telling myself that I'd already planned to go to the beach that morning.

Beckett-With-His-Body hadn't been on the beach, and I told myself not to text him all morning. I can ask him where he normally runs at lunch. We have to have something to talk about, don't we?

Dogs, I tell myself. He has dogs, and we can talk about them.

Work. A mental block flies into place, because I don't want to talk about work on my date. If I do, then I'll spill my guts about my ideas for the Christmas Festival.

"I can't do this," I say at the same time Ryanne finishes my hair. Oh, and the doorbell rings.

I pull in a breath; Ry pulls her hand back and says, "Done." Though we're on the second floor, the clucking and warbling sounds of Emma and Lizzie reach my ears.

"Breathe," Ry says. "It's lunch at your favorite place. You're the prettiest woman in the state of South Carolina. *He's* the lucky one."

"*He's* the lucky one." I focus my gaze on the two of us in the mirror, and Ry squeezes me in a side hug.

"Claude?" Emma fake-calls up the stairs, and we turn from the mirror together. I take a deep breath and smooth my palms over my stomach, wishing it were a little flatter. But only for a moment, because I love my body and think I look amazing in this pair of black capris and a flowered blouse. It's got blue and white and pink flowers on it, and it makes me feel fun.

By definition, most people who work in small town city government aren't fun, and I own more skirt suits than anyone under fifty ever should.

Ry goes downstairs ahead of me, and I swear my vision goes to Ice Mist when my foot reaches the bottom step. I blink, and color rushes back into my retinas.

I turn, and there's Beckett with his Body. He's wearing a pair of shorts the color of denim, but they aren't denim. They're made of khaki material, and he wears them like they've been stitched thread by thread just for his form.

I've never seen him wear shorts—except for those super short things in the park yesterday. And the polo stretching across those broad shoulders? It's so Not Beckett and Totally Beckett at the same time.

It's blue, white, and green striped, and I swear, the blue is a perfect match to the not-really-denim shorts. He's wearing sneakers and a smile, and oh, he knows how charming that thing is.

"Hey," he says in a totally easy-going way—again, a

tone I've not heard him use before. His eyes dart down to my feet—I'm wearing sandals with my capris and blouse—and rebound back to mine only a moment later. "You sure look amazing."

"Thank you," falls from my lips before I can second-guess the compliment. I tell myself not to be stupid. Of course he's going to compliment me on a date, and if he was any other guy, I wouldn't second-guess it at all.

Something foams and fizzes in the air as I walk toward him. I'm not sure if I'm supposed to kiss his cheek in the typical Southern greeting way, and I decide against it at the last moment. He's not my elderly aunt I haven't seen in a while, and I've literally never gone in for a cheek-kiss at work.

You're not at work, I tell myself. *You're not at work. You're not at work.*

So then I think maybe I should kiss him. I end up stutter-stepping and tripping over something—I have no idea what. I lurch toward Beckett, and his eyes round slightly.

Still, he has the reflexes of a ninja, and he manages to brace himself to absorb my weight and move his hands to grip my shoulders. Impressive, but he is a runner, so I tell myself not to be too impressed.

We stand chest-to-chest now, and while Beckett is taller than me, I'd have to be dead not to feel the way his pulse flutters in his chest and a complete zombie not to feel the heated zing of his skin on mine.

He's got big hands, warm, and he doesn't remove them from my shoulders right away. Someone outside of my awareness clears their throat, and Beckett and I jump away from each other like two teenagers caught doing something naughty by their parents.

"Hey, so here's your purse," Emma says in a loud voice, each word enunciated as if no one else in the room speaks English.

I take it from her, my eyes leaving Beckett's beautiful face but not seeing anyone else. "Thanks," I manage to say, and then Ry and Lizzie herd me out the door ahead of Beckett. The click-bang of it closing shakes me out of the strange funk the last five minutes have brought on. I take a breath and look over to Beckett.

"Hey," I say.

He smiles, seemingly at ease again. "Hey." He darts ahead of me and opens the door on his truck, and I climb in. I watch his every move as he rounds the hood and gets behind the wheel. "This is weird, right?"

"The fact that I haven't thrown an insult at you, and we've been in the vicinity of one another for at least five minutes? Yeah, that's weird."

He chuckles and starts the truck. "So Better Than Butter, huh?"

"They have the best lobster in the world," I say.

"You are not seriously going to make me pay for lobster on our first date." He looks at me with a stunned expression on his face. A moment later, that melts into resignation. "Of course you are." His fingers grip the steering wheel. That delicious jaw jumps.

Then he flips the truck into reverse to pull out of the driveway. "All right," he says. "Go big, or go home."

BECKETT

LOBSTER, I THINK. SHE'S GOING TO ORDER LOBSTER. Then I mentally scoff. It's a good thing I'm fiscally respon- sible, or this Sunday lunch date would break me. Then I tell myself never to even think the words *fiscally respon- sible* again.

I pull up to Better Than Butter before I realize it, and as I swing into a parking space, Claudia in all her dark- haired, dark-eyed beauty says, "We don't have to do this."

I look over to her. "We don't?"

"We haven't spoken one word on the way here." She half-throws her hands up into the air. "I don't know. This is—this is just—maybe we're just not meant to be more than co-workers who throw jabs at each other."

"You literally told me you were going to order the most expensive item on the menu," I say, because she might be right. I have plenty to say when I'm throwing some pointed words in her direction. "So no, I didn't feel like conversing on the way over."

"Please, I know how much you make." She rolls her eyes.

"Yeah, but you don't know *me*," I say. "You don't know anything. Maybe I have massive student loan debts or an ex-wife and child I'm paying an exorbitant amount to in the city."

"The city?" she fires back at me, punctuating it with the folding of her arms. "What city?"

I sigh, because this so isn't what I hoped today would be. "No city," I say, deflating the same way the air leaves my lungs. "I don't have an ex-wife or any kids."

"There," she says without missing a beat. "Now I know more about you than I did before."

"Fine," I say. "What about you? Got an ex-husband somewhere?"

"No." She uses that biting tone I'm used to, and I suppose I shouldn't have hoped for anything else. "My last boyfriend had another girlfriend—a serious one—in Atlanta." She deflates too, and it's not a sight I like to see. Which is so confusing, because I've always loved beating Claudia in a verbal throw-down.

"I—" My brain catches up to my mouth before I say too much. Praise all the stars in the heavens, because I certainly don't need to pile on that. "Wow, that's just wrong."

"Yeah, it wasn't pleasant." She looks over to me, her arms un-cinching. "What about your last girlfriend?"

I shift in my seat, suddenly ready to run inside Better Than Butter for that lobster. And I don't even like lobster. "It's uh, been a while for me."

"A while since you had a girlfriend?"

"Yeah." I switch off the ignition, sort of wishing I can pull the plug on this date. Sort of. Not really. One look over to Claudia, and all the chemicals in the world mix together. They foam and bubble and spark, and I don't want to cut any of the electricity flowing between us. "Should we go in?"

"You're deflecting on the girlfriend thing." But she unbuckles her seatbelt and opens her door. I hurry to copy her, and I meet her at the front of the truck. Part of me wants to reach for her hand and feel her skin against mine again, and the other—louder—part of me wants to keep my hands attached to my body, thank you very much.

"I am deflecting on the girlfriend thing," I say as I turn so we're walking the same direction—toward the restaurant. "For now." I glance over to her to find her with a half-smile on her face. Before, it used to drive me to the brink of insanity. Now, I find it kind of cute. "It's the first date. Cut me some slack."

"Okay," she says in a mock-casual voice. "You get some slack this time."

I reach for the door and open it for her. She enters ahead of me, and big surprise, the scent of butter fills the air here. Claudia takes a deep breath of it, which makes me smile, and we move together to step over to the hostess stand. "Two," I say, and we get seated immediately.

It takes a couple of minutes to settle in, move my chair, look at the menu, glance at how close everyone else is to the table. When I'm finally comfortable, I look over to Claudia. Both of her eyebrows are up. "What?"

"You're like my three-year-old nephew. He always has ants in his pants."

I blink, sure she didn't just compare me to a toddler. "I like being in control of my environment," I say. "It's not a crime." I look at the menu, and I'm irritated by all the butter puns within five seconds. I set it back down. "What's good here? Besides the lobster, of course."

Claudia doesn't move her head; only her eyes come up to meet mine over the top of her menu. "I didn't mean anything about the nephew comment. Are you comfortable?"

"Yes," I say simply. I am now. "But I haven't eaten here before, so I need help."

"You hate puns," she says with a knowing smile.

"I suppose you know me better than I thought." I put both arms on the table and lean into them as a perky blonde appears.

"Hey, you two," she says like she's about to start a high school cheer and lead a crowd of football fans to scream their team to victory. She tosses a couple of cardboard coasters on the table with, you guessed it, plates of butter printed on them. Bright yellow, shiny, silky butter. I don't know why I can't look away.

"Have you been in before?"

"I have," Claudia says as I shake my head. She nods toward me. "He hasn't."

"Well." Cheerleading Captain smiles at me like I'm about to have the adventure of my life. "Our drink menu is a little different."

"You don't say," I say.

"Beckett," Claudia growls out, and while that usually gets me all lit up in a competitive way, today it has fire burning in my chest for a completely different reason.

The cheerleader looks at Claudia and back to me. "We have a lot of hot drinks with butter," she says, her chirpiness down a notch. "Hot chocolate, coffee, tea, butterbeer. We have some Italian sodas, and then a regular fountain as well."

"What would you recommend to a butter virgin?" I ask.

She blinks. "You've never eaten butter? Like, ever?"

"In a drink," Claudia clarifies, her dark eyes burning with flames. I'm not sure if she's about to laugh or lunge across the table and throttle me. I kind of want to see and experience both.

"Oh, in a drink." Cheerleader laughs. "Uh, do you like coffee?"

"Yes," I say simply.

"I'd get our Golden Churn Mocha," the waitress says,

pointing to my discarded menu. "It's our rich, dark, in-house roast, with plenty of richness from the butter."

"Can I get cream too?" I ask.

"Of course." She starts writing on her pad. "And for you?" She looks over to Claudia, who doesn't look away from me.

"You're going with the Golden Churn Mocha?" she asks me.

I nod. "Sure. She recommends it."

"Hm." Claudia has made that noise before, and it always made a shot of red flash across my vision. It sort of does today too, mostly because I don't know why she's judging me for getting the buttery coffee. "I want that too." She looks up at Cheerleading Captain. "And can I have the marshmallow cream with mine?"

"You got it." Cheerleader beams and beams. "I'll give you a minute with the menu."

"Thanks," I call after her before I look at Claudia again. "What was that humming noise for?"

"Nothing."

"Come on."

"Come on what?"

"I get you wouldn't want to tell me when I'm just the irritating man who works in the office next to yours." I lean back in my chair, and oh, Liv is going to fillet my muscles from my bones. She told me to be cool today. Go along with whatever Claudia wants. *That's how you get a second date, Becks,* she'd said.

"But we're on a date," I say gesturing between us. "You're supposed to tell me personal stuff about you."

"Ask me a personal question then."

"I just did. I want to know what that humming was for. You do it around the office too." I reach for the glass of ice water that was on the table when we arrived. "It sounds super judgey—but then, you ordered the same coffee as me."

Claudia rolls her whole head, as if just her eyes aren't enough. When she looks at me again, it's with a measure of weariness. That expression, I've seen plenty of times. "I found it interesting," she says, biting on every syllable of the word. "That one, you went with her rec. And two, that it's the same coffee I happen to love."

I search her face, trying to find any hint of dishonesty there. I can't. "So you're shocked that we might have something in common."

"It would be shocking," she says. But her arms aren't all buttoned up over her chest, and she actually gives me another half-smile. I'm so going to get a full one before this date ends, and I make that my new goal.

"I'm sure we have plenty in common," I say. "For one, we have the same career."

Shutters close over Claudia's eyes, and that sends another shock of irritation through me. She blinks, and she's back to normal, and I calm down just as quickly. "I do love my job," she says.

My phone rings, and I practically topple out of my

chair in how fast I whip it from my back pocket. "Sorry, it's my aunt..." I tap to dismiss the call, and I quickly fire off a text to her to remind her *I'm on a date. I'll call you back in a bit.*

Aunt Jill isn't a speed-texter like me, and I manage to silence my phone and start to flip it over before her response comes in. *A date? With whom?* still registers in my vision as the phone turns and lands face-down next to my napkin and silverware.

I scoff. Out loud. Claudia appraises me like I have plenty of explaining to do. "My sister lives in Columbia," I say. "My mom got remarried a few years ago and moved to Cali. So it's just me and my aunt here, and she just had knee replacement surgery." I roll my shoulders, because wow, this right one is so dang tight. "So I'm helping her a lot right now is all."

"You are?" Claudia asks like I've just told the biggest fib on the face of the planet.

"Yes," I clip out. "Why is that so unbelievable to you?"

"It's not."

"It is." I nod over to her, my eyes dripping down the top half of her body until the table conceals the rest. When she'd stumbled into me at the house, I'd caught plenty of her perfume. Lotion. Shampoo. Skin. All of her. Claudia-essence, and it's fruity, soft, powdery, and pure femininity all in one breath. I want it in my nose, in my chest, in my life again.

"Let's talk about the Christmas Festival," she says, and even her eyes go wide.

"I don't even have my coffee yet," I tease.

Claudia just looks at me, and I have no idea what she wants from me. I know I'm not going to start laying out my ideas before she does. Cheerleading Captain arrives with our drinks, and Claudia orders her lobster. I once again ask the waitress for her recommendation and go with it, and she flounces away, leaving Claudia and I to go back to our elementary-age staring contest.

She blinks; I smile. "I win," I say.

"You win what?" she asks.

"You blinked."

She scoffs and looks away too. Double win, but I keep that to myself. "Listen," I say. "Why don't we do like, dating things? Tell me where you're from."

"South Texas." She folds her arms as she says it, though.

"Why'd you come here?" I try anyway, because I know she doesn't want to talk about the Christmas Festival. She only said that because...well, I'm not sure why. I take another peek at her, trying to look closely at her without seeming like I'm looking. She swallows, and oh my heck. She's nervous.

That's why she brought up work. Work is easy to talk about. We can bicker and snipe about work. Personal things...not so much.

"My brother moved here," she said. "He's older than

me, and I came for college. My mom got remarried and..."
She trails off, and this time I do know why. Liv will be so
proud.

"Ah, another thing in common," I murmur as I stir my
hot coffee with a shiny layer of butter floating on the
surface. That so has to be mixed in before I can take a sip
of it, and I reach for the cream too.

"You should try the marshmallow," Claudia says into
the café noise surrounding us. I look up at her, and she
nudges the cute little tin of marshmallow cream the waitress brought for her closer to me. "It's sweet. It cuts
through the richness of the butter and the bitterness of the
coffee."

"I'm not a super sweet guy," I say.

"You don't say," she says, her voice even dropping to
mimic mine when I'd said it to Cheerleader Cathy.

I pick up the tin and peer into it like it'll have vipers
inside instead of marshmallows. "I just meant I don't love
super sweet stuff."

"And I literally just named why it's good with butter
and coffee," she says. "Neither of which are sweet."

I meet her eyes. "Fine," I say as I start to tip the marshmallow cream without looking at it. "But I'm trusting you
on this."

She says nothing, and I drop my eyes to watch the
cream slide through the butter and into the depths of my
coffee. Neither of us say anything, and my last words ring
in the air between us. I stir and stir, liking the way the

liquid lightens and seems to come together better instead of being a separate pool of fat on top of my coffee.

I lift my cup to my lips and take a small sip, expecting to immediately spit everything right back out. Instead, my eyes widen as my brain realizes we actually like what's in our mouth. It's hot. It's rich. It's...full in a way only butter can achieve. And it's sweet.

I moan, and Claudia rewards me with that full smile—and I didn't even have to work very hard to get it. Satisfaction slides right down my throat with that delicious sip of coffee, and as I lower my cup, I say, "Well, you're right, okay? That's the single best thing I've ever tasted."

She laughs lightly, stirs some cream into her own coffee, and takes a delicate sip. I have never been more jealous of a lump of clay in my life, but that coffee mug gets to touch her mouth, and I don't.

Yet, I tell myself.

Get a second date, I hear Liv say in my head.

"So," I say as I lean into my arms on the table again. I stare into the depths of my coffee mug, hoping I won't want to drown myself in it after speaking. "I was thinking for the Christmas Festival that we should hire that company that does mobile ice rinks." I do the same thing Claudia did a few minutes ago—I only raise my eyes to look at her.

She's blinking like someone has just blown a handful of sand into her face. "That's...That's...That's actually a great idea, Beckett," she says.

"I don't appreciate the use of the word *actually* in that sentence." I lift my coffee and take another drink. "This reminds me a little of the birthday cake coffee at Legacy Brew. Have you had it?"

She shakes her head. "I've been there, but I haven't gotten that."

"It's my favorite coffee shop," I say, going for more personal things. "I stop by there every morning before work. I'll bring you some."

Claudia nods, and I score that as a victory too. I'm shooting and scoring all over the place so far. Sort of. The ride here wasn't all that great, and I'll just omit that part of the story when I call Liv later.

"I was thinking that we should try to rent out the theater for a throw-back Christmas movie as part of the festival," Claudia says, and that has my eyebrows going up.

"What movie?" I ask.

She lifts one sexy shoulder in a half-shrug, her eyes dropping to the table. "I don't know. I haven't gotten that far."

"There are licensing things for stuff like that."

"Gee, I didn't know that," she says dryly, all the fire flaming right back into her expression. I can't decide which version of her I like more. The vulnerable, unsure Claudia Brown, or the self-assured, in-charge Claudia Brown.

Both, I tell myself. I like both of them, and I'm glad I know she even has two versions of herself. Three, if I'm counting the sexy dogwalker I ran into—literally—yesterday.

"I have an idea," she says.

"Shoot."

Those eyes burn at me, but this time it's not with irritation or anger like it usually is. There's something else there. Something deeper and softer. Holy New York City sidewalks, it's desire.

And mischief.

The air in Better Than Butter is smoking hot, and I feel like my next breath will char my lungs. It doesn't, but man, this thing between me and Claudia is *hot*.

"We work together on the Christmas Festival," she says. "But submit two different proposals. Whoever wins gets bragging rights and..."

"And?" chokes out of my throat, because I'm so going to win this bet, and I want to know what the real prize is. My eyes drop to her mouth, and I can't believe myself.

"And the loser has to write a letter of recommendation for the other for the position of City Planner." She sits back in her chair, those arms coming across her chest now. Pure satisfaction streams across her face, and I'm left gaping like a fish out of water.

"I..." I even sputter, not sure how to form English words anymore.

CLAUDIA

I'm not only an amazing organizer and pro-picker-of-paint-colors, but I can make—and win—bets with the best poker players in Las Vegas. Fine, I've never actually played poker, but I'm really good at making bets I know I'm going to win and making them sound like I might lose.

I honestly wasn't sure what today's lunch would be like, but it's been one constant up-and-down roller coaster with Beckett. He's mad at me, and I'm irritated at him. Our emotions ebb and flow easily, morphing and changing as fast as someone can turn on and flip off lights with a switch.

I've stunned him now, and our waitress chooses that moment to arrive with our lunches. My lobster takes up a whole platter, and my heartbeat cheers with several extra beats as another man slides it in front of me with the words, "B-utterly in Love with Lobster," and a wide smile.

I look over to Beckett, and he's rubbing one hand down both sides of his beard as he watches the blonde waitress put a legit plank of wood in front of him, chirping, "Butter Basted Bliss."

The board—which has to be something like ten-inches by ten-inches—is holding a whole chicken. A whole, gloriously golden, glistening-with-butter, chicken. As we both stare at it, a glob of butter melts off the top and slides precariously down the side of the chicken breast.

A plethora of potatoes, carrots, roasted onions, and two cobs of corn—drenched and swimming in butter—rest on the right side of the board.

"Enjoy," the two waiters say together, and they make an exit.

Beckett looks up at me, and I can't help it. I burst out laughing. His expression... I can't even. It's part shock, part stupefied, and part intrigued. All rugged handsomeness. I can't believe we have anything in common, but I do love the butter coffee with marshmallow cream here, and my mama did get remarried and leave town, so I have no reason to go back to Texas. With Luke here, I simply stayed.

Beckett stayed for his aunt. His mom got remarried too, and as I start to quiet and look over to him again, I wonder what else we'll have in common.

"This is more food than I can eat in a week," he says.

"Oh, come on," I say. "You have two dogs. They can scarf this in under five minutes, I bet." I pick up my lobster fork and look down at my crustacean.

"Where'd you walk your dogs this morning?" he asks.

I crack into a lobster leg and look at him. "I took them to the beach today."

"So you don't go to the same park every time."

"Nope." I smile at him and shake my head. "Let me guess—you do."

"You like routines too," he shoots back at me. "You've told me that more than once."

"At work," I clarify. "I like procedures and routines at *work*, Beckett." I dunk my lobster meat into my clarified butter, my mouth watering for want of this buttery goodness. "It makes things predictable."

"You mean boring," he says. He hasn't touched any of his food, and he actually looks a little afraid of it.

"Are you going to eat?" I ask before I stuff another bite of drippingly delicious lobster into my mouth.

"I don't even know where to start," he says, his voice still a little bit awed. He looks at me. "This is a whole chicken."

I giggle again. "She said that, Beckett."

"Did she?" He picks up his fork like he'll carve the bird that way.

"Do I need to come cut up your food for you?" I tease.

He shoots me a death glare. "No."

I take another bite of lobster while he shreds off a piece of chicken, buttery-crisp skin and all. "You didn't say anything about the bet," I say delicately after he's put a bite in his mouth.

He glares at me, but he's not nearly as menacing and annoying as he is in the office. Something about his beard and how it softens him. Or maybe it's because he's been open and vulnerable with me today. Maybe it's that he takes care of his aunt, or that he misses his momma, or that he now seems like a human when before he was just something to be endured.

"We can go over my proposal to the T?" he asks.

"You betcha," I say. "And we'll do the same to mine. And we'll submit them. Fair and square." I take another bite, careful to maintain eye contact for an appropriate amount of time. Not too long, but definitely not too short, like I'm being shifty or *can't* hold his gaze for some reason.

"Bragging rights," he says. "What do those entail?"

"Total gloating," I say. "Whoever loses can decorate the Public Works building and they have to come out of their office and applaud and cheer for the other whenever they walk in." I grin at him, and there's something about laughing and smiling with a delicious man that makes a woman happy.

He smiles back at me, and this time, it's not the arrogant gesture that says he knows so much more than I do.

It's just a smile, and it sits on his face nicely. "How long does the letter of recommendation have to be?"

"Professional length," I say. "Everything has to be true, and the other has to approve it before it's submitted." My eyes do dance away then, and I have a difficult time pulling them back to him.

He's watching me closely while cutting into a full-length carrot at the same time.

"Those are candied," I say. "Butter and brown sugar." I nod to the carrots, because Lizzie's gotten the Butter Basted Bliss before, and all six of us in the Big House shared it. Beckett clearly didn't know it was going to be so huge, because he really didn't look at the menu for more than two breaths.

He puts a chunk of carrot in his mouth. Surprise and delight coats his expression, and I have to admit I like it. "See?" I ask. "You don't hate this place as much as you were expecting to."

"It's higher-end than I thought," he admits. "But I can't abide the puns."

"Oh, I b-utterly believe that," I say.

A beat of time passes in complete suspension. Even the noise from the other diners around us goes *butterly* silent.

Then Beckett tips his head back and bellows a laugh toward the ceiling. I have never felt such a supreme sense of satisfaction and joy in my whole life. I join him, and that's saying something, because I don't think I've ever even smiled in Beckett's presence. Well, besides the Evil-Queen type of smile. The one that says, *I've got him right where I want him.*

Somehow, I'm having the same thoughts, but in a much less menacing way.

He's still chuckling, his head shaking back and forth slightly, when he looks at me again. "All right, Claudia," he says. "You've got yourself a bet."

"It's a bet," I say, hoping this doesn't turn out to be the worst bet I've ever made in my life.

————

AN HOUR LATER, Beckett groans as he picks up the toaster-sized to-go box, pretending like his muscles aren't big enough to carry it out of the restaurant. But the way they bulge in those polo sleeves tell a different story, and I roll my eyes at him.

I leave Better Than Butter ahead of him and completely satiated with how much lobster I ate. He comes to my side and my skin prickles. Shockwaves travel from him to me, and in the next moment, his hand slides into mine.

He says nothing, and I actually look down at our hands to make sure they're touching. Mine feels discon-nected from my body for a reason I can't name, but when I see my fingers intertwined with his, all feeling in every

nerve ending there roars with life, with desire, with satisfaction.

Beckett takes me to the back driver's door and holds
my hand while he opens the door and sets his box on the
floor. He faces me, smiles in a timid way—something I've
literally never seen him do—and takes me around to the
passenger seat.

"Claudia," he says after I've climbed into the truck. He
stands in the doorway and looks at the floorboards. Then
up to me. His jaw tightens, like he has to work up courage
to say whatever he's about to say. "I had fun. This was fun,
right?"

I imagine those as two different texts, and I smile at
him. "Yeah," I admit. "I had a good time. I mean, after we
got here."

"Right, yeah." He backs out of the doorway and closes
the door. I once again watch him as he rounds the hood
and gets behind the wheel. "Would you go out with me
again?" He looks over to me. "Like, that's a hypothetical
question. I'm not asking you out again. I just want to know
if you *would* go out with me. You know how you'd have
those teachers who'd be like, 'You don't have to answer. I
just want to know who thinks they know the answer. Just
raise your hand if you know the answer'? It's totally hypothetical."

Oh, Beckett Fletcher has a runaway tongue. He swallows and presses his lips together, all signs that he knows it

and is trying to stop. I find him so...cute, and I do what feels natural.

I reach over to him and cradle his face in the palm of my hand. Holy Iguana Green—the color we painted the door on the Big House the year I moved in—his beard is soft. He melts into my touch, and he's so Perfectly Beckett in that moment.

He's relaxed and real. Sweet and savory at the same time. His eyes even drift closed for a moment and then pop back open. I drop my hand and look at it as it travels to my lap. I clear my throat.

"You don't need to answer that," he says as he starts the truck.

"Yeah," I say anyway. "I'd go out with you again. You know, if you were really asking." I twist and reach to pull my seatbelt across me, and I only glance at him briefly while I snap the two pieces together.

I take a breath. "And I always raised my hand when teachers would say stuff like that."

Beckett stares at me as we sit there in the parking spot at Better Than Butter. I keep my gaze out the windshield. "Even if I didn't know the answer. Then, when they'd say, 'Okay, so now who wants to answer?' I'd just put my hand down." I look over to him, and he's staring at me with that same *stunned-by-the-whole-chicken-on-a-two-by-four* look he had inside the restaurant.

"I used to do that too," he says, his throat working with a hard swallow again.

I nod, and that somehow lightens the mood. He puts the truck in reverse and gets us moving back toward the Big House. His tongue seems to have used up its allotment of words, because the return trip is just as silent as the drive to the restaurant was.

He pulls up to the Big House and looks at it. "I was so embarrassed to come pick you up," he says in that real, authentic way he's used with me all day today. Well, when I wasn't throwing darted phrases at him, that is. He switches his gaze to me. "You showed all your roommates my texts, right?"

"Uh, yes," I say, reaching up to play with the bottom of one of my braids. Ry told me not to do it, and I've made it through the whole date until now. I force my hand down and simply look at him. "I needed help."

"I called my sister," he says with a smile.

"Liv?" I guess at the name, because he never told it to me outright, but he mentioned her during lunch.

"Right." He turns off the truck and unbuckles. "I'll come get your door."

I let him play the Southern gentleman, though I know how to open my own door. Something magical and mighty plays in the afternoon air between us as I slide to the ground in front of him. He's given me almost no room, and he slides both of his hands into both of mine.

"I'm asking you out for real this time," he says. "On a second date." He drops his eyes to the ground as he smiles. "What do you think?"

"I think you cheated," I say, and that brings his gaze right back to mine.

"How so?"

"You felt me out first," I say. "You didn't want to ask until you knew I'd say yes." I bump him with my hip to get him to back up a little, which he does. We face the Big House together, but I don't really want to go back inside yet.

It's a lazy Sunday, and Tahlia will have something baked and delicious waiting—and all of my roommates will be circling like sharks to get the bloody news about this date. I'll give it to them too, because I don't mind talking about the men I go out with.

"I call that going into a situation with confidence," he says.

"Call it what you want." I take the first step toward the Big House. "It's still cheating."

"Is that a no?"

"No," I say.

"So we should sit down and go over our proposals tomorrow. You never did say when your meeting with Winslow is."

"Thursday," ghosts out of my mouth before I can silence it. I don't even want to silence it, and that is still so confusing.

He puts his foot on the first step leading up to the porch. "So we'll meet tomorrow in your office, but that's not a date." He looks over to me, his expression open and hopeful. "That's work."

"You said all of your lunches were open for the foreseeable future."

"Ah, so she does read my texts." A smile blooms to life on his face. "I'm driving Aunt Jill to her doctor's appointment tomorrow afternoon, and we always stop at this Thai place on the way back." He reaches the porch and faces me fully again as I take the last step up to join him.

I reach out and fiddle with the bottom button on his polo. "Dinner on Tuesday, then," I say, letting my eyes slide right past that perfectly framed mouth to his eyes. "Because stepping out for a quick bite of lunch at work feels very...work-y."

He grins at me. "Work-y. Yeah, it does." He isn't awkward at all as he envelops me in his arms and hugs me. "Go talk to your girlfriends. We've got a work-date and a date-date set up."

I take a deep breath of his shirt, getting cotton and fresh air, butter and musk, and the Scent That Is Beckett is the best thing I've ever inhaled. "Okay," I say. "Thank you, Beckett." I step out of his arms and move the couple of steps to the door.

It swings open and in easily, and I imagine myself like a perfectly quaffed princess, stepping back into her secluded tower until the handsome prince can come rescue her again. Instead, my heel catches on the four-inch step up into the house, and I stumble clumsily into the house.

No less than three roommates gasp, and behind me, Beckett goes, "You okay?"

My face burns like lava. "Fine," I bite out as my fingers smart from how hard I had to grip the door handle to keep myself upright.

I'm always so close.

I glare at him as I close the door between us, and that's so not how I wanted to end this date.

So dang close.

CLAUDIA

"Wait, wait, wait-wait-wait-wait," Hillary says, her face getting closer and closer to the camera on her phone. So close, I swear I see right up into her brain. "Beckett Fletcher? The horribly annoying guy next door to you at the Public Works office?"

"Yeah," I deadpan.

"Yeah, like Liam," Emma says pointedly, and Hillary yanks the camera back.

Surprise covers her whole face, and then it all dissolves into a smile. "Yes, well, he was annoying."

"Until he wasn't," we all chorus with her. Now they've moved to Los Angeles together, and while she's not wearing a diamond yet, she could be. Hillary doesn't want to be engaged for very long, but that doesn't mean she and Liam haven't already started planning their wedding.

"He's going to be here in half an hour," Hillary says,

setting her phone on the coffee table in front of her, an appropriate viewing distance. "So get talking, Claude."

The weight of all of their eyes lands on me, and I don't normally hate it. I don't really today either, but I also don't want this to be too big of a deal. I always make my relationships into something bigger than they are, and I need this to be small until it isn't anymore. If it ever isn't.

"I had a good time," I admit. "I mean, we almost didn't go in, because he didn't say a word to me the whole way there, but once we got the ice broken, it was pretty fun."

"This is the guy who only wears white shirts and ties, right?" Lizzie asks. She's got a smorgasbord of brownies on a paper plate in her lap, and she's already made it abundantly clear she's not sharing. It's fine; Tahlia has pans and pans of them in the kitchen, and even Hillary has a brownie in her hand from across the country.

I miss her so much, and I'll text her privately later.

"Guys who dress professionally for work can be fun outside of work," I say.

"If you say so," Lizzie says. "All the guys at my work are just as fuddy-duddy outside of work as they are inside it."

"They're *chemists*," Ry says. "What do you expect?"

"*I'm* a chemist," Lizzie says as she picks up a mint brownie and spears Ry with a glare.

"I'm just saying," Ry says. "They're scientists. I'm not sure they're born with a sense of humor at all."

"They're not as bad as accountants," Emma says. We

all look at her, and I'm not sure who starts giggling first. Probably Hillary, and that sends us all into fits. Emma's dated an accountant or two—or three—and none of them have been all that special. I'm not sure why she keeps attracting them. Probably because she's awful with money, so she'll call someone to come help her with her finances at the flower shop, and one thing leads to another in cramped quarters...

I think of the size of my office, then Beckett's. Neither of them are huge, but neither of them can be classified as "cramped" either. Plenty of room for us to walk around each other there. No accidental touching.

I pull my attention back to the group when Hill says, "Claudia. Claudia!"

"What?" I give her a nasty look and look over to Tahlia. "He asked me out again. I said yes."

"Oh, wow," Ry says. "What's the paint color for that?"

I shake my head, but my smile won't disappear. "I don't know."

"You don't know?" Tahlia scoffs. "Come on, Claude. You can do better than that."

"Something purple," I say quietly, yet they're all listening. I look at the screen, and Hillary's staring right back at me. "Lilac Haze, maybe."

"Oh, someone's hazy, all right," Hill teases.

My pulse skips a beat, but I made the bet. Now I need help winning it. "I made a bet with him."

"Here we go," Ry practically yells.

I give her my best *Really?* look and go back to Hillary. "He wanted to go over the Christmas Festival."

"I thought you weren't going to do that," Lizzie says.

"I didn't," I say. "I mean, we did talk about it for a minute, but I'd love to know what's on his list. So while I was sitting there, the delicious scent of butter making my thoughts slow, and that marshmallow coffee in my gut, I had an idea."

"It's that marshmallow," Tahlia says in her Mom-Voice. "I told you not to order that until *after* you ate." She shakes her head and pinches off the corner of a double-fudge brownie. She bakes and bakes, but she's the thinnest of all of us. She usually only eats a bite or two of her desserts, while I can't stop myself from eating half a pan of brownies, especially the mint ones.

"It's not the marshmallow," I argue back. "It was a good idea. I'm totally going to win the bet." Then I remember his idea to bring in an ice skating rink. We don't really have those in the South, and certainly not outdoors, where all the garland, Christmas lights, and Santa's reindeer can loiter nearby.

"Then why do you look like you're going to throw up all that lobster you ate?" Hillary asks.

"He's not a stupid man," I say. "This way, I get to see all of his ideas, and I can modify mine if necessary."

"Okay." Emma drags out the word, telling me to get to the point. To the bet.

"So I said we can help each other with our Christmas

Festival proposals. They're due this week. And whoever wins gets full bragging rights, and...the loser has to write a letter of recommendation for the other for the job of City Planner." I rush over the last several words, and they all flow into silence.

My roommates are never just silent. For the first time since I thought of this bet, I think maybe it's a bad idea. That maybe I won't win.

I look at Ry and Emma on my right and Tahlia and Lizzie on my left. Then back to Hillary on the screen. "Well? It's a good bet. I'm so going to win." I nearly choke out the last word, though.

"Yeah," Hillary shouts. "You so are." She smiles at me, and she's never been anything but supportive and amazing.

"I'll be the bad guy," Lizzie says, and I look at her. She's blonde and petite and an amazing chemist-slash-model. She's definitely the best-dressed and cutest female in her company, I can guarantee that. "I mean, we chemists usually don't hold back." She dusts her hands of any brownie crumbs.

"Claude, honey, it's a bad bet."

"A very bad bet," Ry murmurs.

I whip my attention to her and back to Lizzie. "Why?"

"What if you lose?" Lizzie asks.

I swallow, because such a thing is unthinkable. "Then I'll write him a letter and decorate the office and give him all the—bragging...rights." I'm whispering by the last word.

Tahlia covers my hand with hers. "What if you fall in love with him?"

I stare at her while my pulse zigs and zags through my whole body. "Well, I—"

"Just because you've never fallen in love before doesn't mean you won't with Beckett," Hillary says from thousands of miles away. She offers us all a small, soft, somewhat-sad smile. "Trust me on this one, ladies."

I swallow, because no, I haven't been in love before. I dated in college. I've dated after college. Nothing serious for a while, but that's okay. Not every date has to turn into an ultra-serious relationship. "Maybe—" I start, but I hate maybe's and what-if's as much as anyone.

"You said yes to a second date," Tahlia says in a quiet voice. "You already like him, even if you don't think you do." She looks at me. Really looks, and I let her. I look right on back, feeling more and more vulnerable by the moment. I literally think my heart is going to bust through my ribs and run up to the third floor without me.

Tahlia squeezes my hand, and I blink my way back to reality. "What if I win?"

"What if you do?" Ry asks. "And it upsets him? And he can't be with you for whatever reason?"

"What would that reason be?" I don't speak harshly, and I can't believe I didn't see how very bad this bet would be. At the restaurant, it had glowed with butter, and it had flowed from my mouth easily. Beckett had even seemed interested in the wager.

"Pride?" Ry guessed. "I don't know, Claude." She lays her head against my shoulder. "But I do know one thing about bets: There's always a winner...and a loser."

"And there it is," Emma says into the silence that follows, and Hillary is nodding from her apartment in California.

I don't like to lose, and I don't want to lose this bet. The problem? Beckett doesn't like to lose either, and he won't want to lose this bet.

And no matter what, there *will* be a loser.

"Great," I huff as I fold my arms. "I've issued a very bad bet, and he's accepted it." I survey my friends, a new kind of desperation clawing its way up my throat now. "Is there anything I can do about this?"

"Maybe just talk to him," Lizzie says. "Say you've been thinking about it, and you've decided it's a bad idea."

"See if he'll let you call it off," Emma says, and I start nodding.

But when I meet Hillary's eyes, we both know that won't happen. I'll either be too big of a chicken to actually admit I did something wrong, or Beckett will be so into the bet, he won't allow me to void it.

"Well," I say with another hefty sigh. "I'm seeing him tomorrow to go over the Christmas Festival plans, so I'll... talk to him then."

"Sure you will," Hillary says. "Now, Liam is going to be here in a minute, and he wants your opinion on a wall color for this house he's working on right now..."

BECKETT

"Morning, Becks," Macie Cochran says to me from behind the register at Legacy Brew. She owns it with her now-husband, though they weren't always together. "Your usual?"

"Yes," I say. "Times three."

Her eyebrows go up, and she taps on the pad in front of her. "Times three?"

I can't stop myself from grinning. "I'm taking coffee to the office today."

"And there's only three of you there?"

"In my immediate department," I say. "My secretary is still on maternity leave, so I thought I'd take coffee for the two others picking up her work while she's gone."

"Sure," Macie says, and she's not second-guessing me. She's never been to my office, as I make the drive into the city for this coffee, and then back out to the drab building where my office is in Cider Cove. She has no idea where I live or how far I drive here for my morning coffee. Just because I come five days a week and she knows what I do for a living doesn't mean she knows about the strange way my pulse jigs when I think of walking into Claudia's office and setting down one of the three cups of coffee I'm paying for right now.

Macie runs my card and when her bright eyes meet mine again, she says, "Did you hear about Tara's grand opening?" She swipes up a piece of paper from beside the register, where all the little straws and sticks and napkins are.

I take the quarter-sheet flyer and see the announcement of a restaurant grand opening. An idea starts to percolate in my head the same way the coffee here at Legacy Brew does. "When is this?"

"Tonight is the soft opening," Macie says. "Tara's trying things out on a weeknight. The big gala is Friday, but she's doing special opening specials every night this week."

I look up, ultra-interested in taking Claudia somewhere nice for our date tomorrow night. I haven't come up with a solid plan, and with someone like Claudia, I need a cemented plan A, and a solid plan B, and then a rock-hard plan C.

"Is she full for tomorrow?" I ask, looking back at the flyer.

"I don't know," Macie says. "Call her." She looks to the

next person in line, and that's my cue to move down and wait for my order. Since I'm all about multi-tasking, I whip out my phone and dial the number on the flyer. There's no answer, and irritation seeps into me with every ring that stretches out.

"This is Flavor," a voice mail message says. "We're only opening for dinner this week, and if you'd like to make a reservation, our hotline for that opens at noon each day. We're currently taking reservations in the next four-teen-day window. If you'd like to—"

I hang up, because I have the answer I need. It's barely seven-thirty in the morning, and as usual, I'm a little overeager to do something. I tuck my phone away, grab the to-go cup carrier with my three coffee cups and the fourth one filled with three lemon blueberry scones. My mouth waters, and I go through my usual routine of eating and drinking breakfast on the way to the office.

When I walk in, I'm carrying my briefcase in one hand and the coffee and scones in the other. Sybil looks up as I walk through the doorway that separates my department from the Transportation Department and the Physical Facilities Department.

Larry Schenman works in the office on the other side of Claudia, but he doesn't have a secretary. As the Public Works Director, Claudia has a full-time secretary, and as I'm the Deputy Director over City Development in Cider Cove, I have one too.

But Tabby is out, as she's just had her first baby only a

couple of weeks ago. I smiled and congratulated her when she'd brought in the little girl, but I really need someone to do all the tasks she does. The Public Works Department provided a part-time substitute secretary, but she actually quit last Friday. I'm not sure why.

"Good morning," I chirp to Sybil. I set down the coffee on her desk, my pulse thrumming in a strange way.

"Good morning," she says, and the surprise in her voice isn't lost on me. I wonder if I'm not friendly when I come into work. I'm fairly certain I say good morning... Don't I?

"I brought coffee and scones," I say, plucking a cup out of the holder for her. "Have you had the birthday cake coffee from Legacy Brew?"

"No," Sybil says slowly, and she's got her blonde hair all swept up into a bun today. She only wears her hair in one of two ways, and the bun is her typical Monday hairdo. I know that, so I surely must look at her and say good morning when I walk by her desk.

"It's really good," I say, picking up the last cup of coffee and the final scone. There's no way I can walk into Claudia's office with this. But as I glance down to the cup holder, there's clearly *two* cups of coffee left. I mean, mine is almost gone, but Sybil doesn't know that.

"Uh..." I look toward the open door of Claudia's office, praying she'll appear there and save me. She doesn't.

I clear my throat and walk around Sybil's desk. I don't have to give her an explanation. My office is to the right.

Claudia's is behind Sybil's desk, and I need to veer left. I can't seem to make my feet do that, and instead, I go into my office.

I sigh as I sit down behind my desk, and I glare at the extra cup of coffee. I could scarf that scone, but I ate way too many rice crispy treats at Aunt Jill's last night. I could barely get myself up to go running this morning, but I did it. Maybe I didn't run as fast, but I went.

The office is too quiet, especially because I know—I just know—Claudia is in that office next door. I fire up my computer, my mind scattered. It's Monday, and I'm sure I have tasks. I just can't think of what any of them are.

"Mister Fletcher?" Sybil stands in the doorway with a clipboard in her hand. "I'm headed over to the inter-department meeting. Did you have your bullet points?"

"Uh, yes," I say, shifting some papers on my desk. I can just hear Claudia shrieking about how unorganized I am. "I've got them here somewhere." I locate the sheet I'd worked on last Friday, and I rush toward her with it.

Sybil can't weigh more than a hundred pounds, and I'm maybe a little hopped up on birthday cake coffee. Her eyes widen just before I practically slap her with the sheet of paper, and Claudia asks, "Are you headed out?"

Our secretary flinches away from me, and I press one palm into the doorjamb, knowing I'm standing way too close to Sybil. Claudia's wearing a black skirt that wafts around her legs until halfway down her calf, and a red blouse with black rose patterns woven through it. She's tucked it in at the waist, and my mind goes completely blank.

Sybil's voice sounds as she turns away from me, and she and Claudia have an exchange while I stare.

"Stop it," Claudia hisses just before she stomps—as much as any woman can in heels—back into her office.

I lurch after her. "Stop what?"

"You're practically drooling," she says, shooting me a glare as she sits behind her desk. "We've been out one time, Beckett."

"You look fantastic today," I say in my defense. I start toward a chair in front of her desk, then remember the coffee. "Oh, I brought you some coffee."

"You brought me coffee?" she asks as I leave her office. I hurry to grab the extra coffee and scone and bustle back into her office. I feel like someone has stuffed Energizer batteries into my bloodstream, and I tell myself to calm the heck down. I can even hear it in Liv's voice, as she'd told me the same thing last night during my lunch date report.

"Birthday cake coffee," I say as I set it in front of her. "And my favorite scone from Legacy Brew." I smile like I've just presented her with a gift fit for the Christ child.

Claudia looks up at me in disbelief, and then she reaches for her mug of coffee. Not a to-go cardboard cup of coffee, but a real mug in a pearly blue color. My whole morning deflates in front of me, and I sink into the chair in front of her desk.

"You don't want the coffee?" I ask.

"I'll give it a try." But she doesn't. She's really cool this morning, and I'm not sure why. I'm like a bouncing golden retriever hopped up on caffeine, and she's sitting there in all her elegance and sophistication, looking at me the way my aunt's cats do when they want to exert their dominance over me.

"Are you okay?" I ask.

"I'm great," she says as she lowers her coffee cup.

Confusion riddles through me, and I really don't have time for games. "What are you working on today?"

"The usual."

"What's usual?"

"You know, the usual."

"No, I don't." I lean back and fold my arms, my own eyes feeling hot and lasery. "Tell me the usual. What's the usual for Claudia Brown on a Monday morning, when her maybe-could-be-boyfriend, or at least the man she went out with yesterday and agreed to a date with tomorrow, brings her his favorite coffee and she refuses to try it."

"Beck—"

"I have work to do." I get up and spin away from her the way I have during our arguments in the past.

"Beckett, come on," she says behind me.

I turn back at her doorway. "Give me usual, then."

She sighs as she stands, and she leans into both palms against her desk. "If you must know, I was going over bullet points for Sybil's meeting, and then I sent an IDM to Richard in the Public Relations Department, because they completely messed up the article I sent for the Chronicles, and he was arguing back with me, and then I heard you shuffling around in your office."

"So you're just in a bad mood."

"I am *not* in a bad mood."

"You won't try the coffee."

"I had just made myself some of the, uh, a fresh cup from my Keurig."

"Oh, the Keurig," I say, teasing now. My moods go from high to low like a roller coaster. "What pod did you put in this morning?"

"One of my favorites."

"Which is?" I press though she takes a step toward me that doesn't feel like she wants to get closer. More like she wants to push me out of her office. I hold my ground, every nerve ending starting to tingle.

She crowds right into my space, and I don't mind that at all. She was cool sixty seconds ago, and now everything feels too hot. "You're really nosy."

"It's called getting to know someone. You know, have you heard of it? Maybe I'll want to get you a really thoughtful gift one day, and it'll be your favorite Keurig coffee pod flavor." I've said so much, and my tongue feels like it's grown fur.

"If you're going to get me a really thoughtful gift, it better not be Keurig coffee pods."

"No matter the flavor?"

"No matter the flavor," Claudia confirms.

"So, uh, what would someone get if they wanted to get you a really thoughtful gift?"

"Claudia?" Larry asks, and she grabs me by the knot on my tie with one hand and starts to close the door with the other.

"I'm in a meeting, Larry," she says as the gap closes more and more. "Give me a minute." Then the door slams closed, sealing me and Claudia inside her office.

It's gonna get hot in here in less than a minute, especially with the way Claudia is looking at me with her non-meeting face.

CLAUDIA

I HAVE TO GET BECKETT TO THINK THE BET IS A BAD idea. I simply have no idea how, and he smells like coffee and sugar and lemons all got together in the pine tree woods and danced around a fire.

He's smoky, and sweet, and I want a bite of him so badly my mouth is actually watering.

I yank on myself and get my mind back where it belongs, and it's not on kissing Beckett. Not only have we not even been out to dinner yet, but I certainly do not want my first kiss with him to take place in my office, with the only other man who works in this department hovering outside my door.

"You're acting strange today," Beckett says, only lighting up my irritation further. "Is this because of lunch yesterday? I was kind of hoping we'd get along better, not worse."

"We're getting along fine." I realize I still have ahold of his tie, and I release my grip on it quickly. "Sorry about the tie." I move away from him, the vents in the ceiling above doing nothing to blow in the air conditioning.

"Claudia," he says, and holy Barbie Dreamhouse—one of the brighter pinks in the world, really only good for a tween girl's bedroom—I'm never going to be able to hear my name any other way. Throaty, almost desperate, deep, and needy. Perfect Boyfriend Voice—and it came from Beckett.

I turn and face him. "What?"

"Just tell me what's going on."

I can't hold back the words as they surge out of my mouth. "I think the bet is a bad idea."

He blinks a couple of times, and his hands, which he'd been using to fix and straighten his tie, fall to his sides. "You think the bet—which you issued less than twenty-four hours ago—is a bad idea." He's not asking, and I hate the lack of a question mark on his statement.

"Yes," I say.

"Because you think you're going to lose?"

"Because there *will* be a loser." I don't know how much to put out there between us. This feels like a pivotal moment, as if we didn't have at least a dozen of those yesterday too. "And I don't know. We're starting to get along a little better, like you said." I lean back against my desk and brace myself with my hands beside my hips. "I don't want either of us to lose."

He takes a step toward me, his gaze searching mine with an intensity I've only ever gotten from Beckett. "I'm sorry, I didn't have my phone recording. Are you saying you don't want *me* to lose?"

I give him a half-smile. "I said I don't want *either* of us to lose."

"But that includes me."

"You're the one with two college degrees," I say. "I think you know the definition of the word *either*."

He grins at me. "I still think we should work together on the Christmas Festival. Are you taking that away if the bet goes away?"

I hesitate, because I do want to know what's going on inside his head.

"I want to work on it with you," he says. "We could submit just one proposal. No winners. No losers." He's talking fast, in short, clipped sentences—the way he texts. I can see him building up steam, and if I don't cut him off fast, he'll let that tongue loose and who knows when I'll get him to stop talking. "We don't have to compete, Claudia. Maybe we both do a great job on the Christmas Festival, and we both turn in a stellar portfolio and application for the City Planner job." He's still advancing toward me, and I wonder where he'll stop.

"It won't be best man wins," I say.

"It might be the best woman wins."

"It might just be luck."

He reaches the chair in front of my desk and puts both hands on the back of it. "Or seniority."

"Or maybe Mayor Garvin will have just eaten her favorite sushi roll, and some of the sauce dropped over my stellar résumé, so she didn't see how I cleaned up Discovery Park without going a dollar over budget." I shrug like the City Planner job doesn't matter to me. But we both know it does. It glows inside me like the moon, but the problem is, I know Beckett wants it just as badly.

"Or how I've cleared more than four miles along the river and turned it from nothing into usable city park and business space," he says. "Without costing the taxpayers a single cent."

I nod to him, my way of conceding that he's good at his job. I know he is; he knows he is. I clamp my teeth around the offer to write him a letter of recommendation. If there's no bet, I don't have to do that. I don't have to be *that* nice.

"I found the perfect place for dinner tomorrow night," he says, changing topics on me rapidly. We kind of seem to be that way—like a dog sniffing out a squirrel. There's one over here. No, over here. Nope, up there! We flit all over the place, and yet, I always know right where we are in the conversation.

He nods to me, his chin dipping down toward my heels. "You really look amazing in that. Might you wear something similar tomorrow night?" He swallows as his eyes travel back to mine, and oh, the desire swimming in his eyes is plain as the nose on his face.

"So somewhere that requires a dress?" I ask.

"It's a brand-new restaurant," he says. "They're doing soft grand openings all week. It's a bit more upscale, but not like tuxedo level."

"Do you even own a tuxedo?"

"Of course I do," he says without missing a beat. "I had to walk my momma down the aisle a few years ago." Pain flashes in his eyes now, and I want to know that story. I can't believe I want to know that story, but I do.

"I have something similar to this then," I say.

"Mm, great."

"Claudia?" Sybil walks into my office. "Why is this door—?" She cuts off as Beckett twists to face her. She comes to a complete stop, the sheets of her yellow pad of paper on the clipboard still swaying slightly with how abruptly she stills.

She looks from Beckett to me, and I swear she's checking to make sure my lipstick isn't smeared. It wouldn't be anyway, because I don't wear lipstick. Too sticky. Too many color names to memorize, as my brain is stuffed full of all the best paint colors.

"Should we go over the IDMs?" she asks crisply. She enters the office more fully and takes the other chair in front of my desk. The one Beckett isn't standing behind. "Is there a reason Larry is standing at my desk, eating all my M&Ms?"

I meet Beckett's eye too, and then I say, "Larry, grab a chair and get in here. Sybil has our weekly notes from all the departments." I sit behind my desk, noting that I have four windows up with IDMs now. The Interdepartment Direct Messaging system for the city of Cider Cove is awesome—until I get so behind and-or have so many messages that I can't keep up. Like this morning.

I sigh as I reach for my coffee, and I'm not paying attention as I lift it to my lips. My first hint that I've picked up the cup Beckett brought for me is the touch of the plastic lid against my lips. The second is his gasp. The third is the absolutely delicious taste of coffee and birthday cake in one single sip.

My eyes widen as I lower the cup. Beckett is watching me with ninja stars in his eyes, like my reaction will make or break his day. Since he's so stinking good-looking, and he wants this so badly, and he brought me this coffee for free, I decide to be the nicest I've ever been to him.

I say, "Wow, Beckett, this is amazing."

He crows like he's Peter Pan, startling everyone in the office. Which is bad for Larry, who has to lug in his own seat. He's so startled, he drops the chair, and it clatters on the thin carpet covering who-knows-what underneath in this portable trailer building.

"Mister Fletcher," Sybil says, one bird-like hand pressed to her chest. She frowns at him, but he's laughing now.

"You have no idea how hard I worked for that," he says among his chuckles and Larry's efforts to right the chair. His eyes meet mine, and I swear the neatly stacked and filed papers on my desk nearly catch fire with the flames between us.

Sybil pulls in a breath, and I say, "Okay, let's get this show on the road. I have a million things to do today, as I'm sure we all do." I avoid my secretary's eyes, a tactic that will work until this meeting ends. Then she'll want to know what's going on between me and Beckett.

I wish I knew what to tell her. I wish I knew if Beckett and I still had a bet or not. He never did agree to cancel it. I wish I knew why seeing him outside of work skewed everything so completely.

Then I wonder: Perhaps this attraction between us has always been there, and we've simply built walls around it. And bam, with the smallest of cracks, it's all come spilling out.

Either way, I keep sneaking looks at him during the meeting, something I never would've done before. I imagine him in a tux. I wonder what he'll wear to dinner tomorrow night. I think of him taking his aunt to the doctor in Columbia this afternoon.

But most of all, I think about us being a real couple, and what meaningful gift Beckett As A Boyfriend would bring me on my birthday, and how exciting my life would be with him securely, and maybe even permanently, in it.

BECKETT

"Thanks, Sybil," I say as she sets a white plastic bag that smells like lunch meat deliciousness on my desk.

"Yes, Mister Fletcher." Sybil turns and I see the hesitation as Claudia looks up to her. She nods slightly, and Sybil continues toward my door. She doesn't close it, and I stand up and take off my jacket.

I drape it around my chair and turn to get the food out of the bag. Claudia stands to join me, and her eyes skate past me as I take out the first container. "I think this one's yours." I set it on the edge of the desk, because she came into my office to work on the Christmas Festival, toting her shiny green folder with her. It even has a label—a legit label—on the front that says *Christmas Festival Ideas* on it in red Sharpie.

"This one must be yours then." She hands me the

clear plastic clamshell container, and I take it from her, spotting the roast beef.

"Yes," I say, and I sit down in my chair. It's one of those really nice ones, with a soft seat and the ergonomic back.

Claudia looks down at me, something in her gaze that I can't quite identify. She lifts one eyebrow and asks, "Is that a custom-tailored shirt?"

I look down at my baby blue dress shirt. "It's a...Keisman," I say. "I bought it at the mall."

"What size?"

"Large?" I guess, wondering what this line of questioning is about. I'm wearing a tie in varying shades of blue, with yellow and orange accents. My pants are navy too, as was my jacket. I don't always wear a jacket to the office, but I did today for some reason. I always do when I go to the City Center for meetings, and though Claudia's office door was only closed for ten minutes or so earlier, the whole building still feels too hot.

"Hmm." Claudia sits down and reaches for her food.

"You're doing that humming again." I unsnap my clamshell and inhale the scent of freshly baked bread and avocado and beef. I tear my attention from the food and focus on the woman across from me. "You're judging my shirt? Or where I shop?"

"Just the fact that you shop is strange."

"Men need clothes too," I say. "I'm not like, donning a hip pack and hitting the mall every weekend or anything."

"Just the fact that you know what a hip pack is alarms me a little."

"So are you offended by my shirt, where it's from, or just me?" I pick up my sandwich and take a bite while Claudia opens her container.

"I just think—it's like perfectly formed to your body, that's all."

I finish chewing and swallow. "So my body offends you." I'm not asking, and I'm not smiling.

"No," she says, her dark eyes glittering like diamonds in the night. She ducks her head and leans over her container as she takes a bite of her sandwich. She ordered turkey and provolone, which is about as normal as you can get.

"I run about twenty miles a week," I tell her.

"Which is why your body doesn't offend me," she says.

Heat flames down my throat. "So you're saying—"

"Can we just eat, Beckett?" Claudia's face carries a shade of red skin never should, and she takes another big bite of her sandwich.

I do the same, wondering if I should give her some sort of compliment. Then I remind myself that I've already complimented her on her clothes this morning. I brought the coffee—which she liked, miracle of miracles—and as long as I don't embarrass myself or let my mouth run away from me during this meeting, the day should end with a win.

After all, I'm leaving early to take Aunt Jill to her

doctor's appointment, so I just need to make it through the next couple of hours.

It's two hours, I tell myself. How hard can it be?

But then I look across the desk to Claudia Brown and remind myself that she and I have never gotten along about anything at work. Literally not one thing.

She finishes her sandwich after me, and as she tears open her chip bag, I say, "Okay. Let me get my file open." I start clicking around on my computer, but I don't want to tell Claudia that I've literally just typed out some sketchy notes in an email I never intend to send. It doesn't even have an email address in it. It's just for me.

The green folder gets flipped open, and I glance over to the pages as Claudia lays them out in front of her. She stands and then pulls her chair closer to the desk, so she can sit up to it and write. She clicks a pen into action, and that does steal my attention from my screen.

"That's a four-color pen," I say.

She beams at it. "It's my favorite." She turns it around to show me the black, green, blue, and red buttons. She's activated the red one, and I find myself smiling.

"You're doing everything in Christmas colors." I nod to the folder and then meet her eye again.

Hers drop to her folder, where she's hand-written all of her notes in red ink. "It puts me in the right mood," she says.

"Mood?" I ask. "Or mode?"

"Christmas mode?" she questions, but I think she's

asking herself. She looks up again and smiles, and oh, that thing is glorious. It makes her eyes turn into stars and brings her to life in a way I've never seen before.

Because she's never smiled at me like this at work before.

"Yeah," I say, my voice a little soft. "Christmas mode." I clear my throat and spin in my chair to get a piece of paper out of the printer. When I turn back to her, I rifle through my desk drawer to find a pen, and then I push everything else from the middle of the surface in front of me and look at her.

She wears a look of mild horror, but blinks and recovers quickly. "Okay," she says. "Ice skating rink?" She turns her papers over in an organized way until she reaches a clean one. She starts to write while I watch.

"Yeah," I say. "The company is Mobile Adventures. I have contact information for them, and they book about three months out. So we need a date for them to come set up and tear down. The rink can be up as long as we want it, but of course, every day costs more."

"Of course," she murmurs. She finishes writing and lifts her head. "I still think it's a great idea. We can charge for skating to help earn back some of the cost."

"Definitely," I say. "And do a family movie night one night if you're going to rent out the downtown theater."

"I've already called the Myriad," she says, and talking to her in work-mode is somehow sexier than ever. Just thinking it's sexy at all is a first for me. "We can do a single day, or even just a four-hour timeframe." She pushes her hair over her shoulder. "I was thinking of a family matinee and a couples date night."

"So a whole day."

"Yes," she says, and I make a note though I don't need it and probably won't even look at my chicken-scratch handwriting again. "And if we do that, then we can do something for breakfast too."

"Yes." I lean back in my chair and gaze up at the ceiling. I've gotten a lot of answers and ideas this way, and I take a deep breath. "Like Moms and Muffins or Dads and Doughnuts."

"And we can serve those things for breakfast."

"This would not be a free event, then," I say. "Doughnuts for hundreds? That's expensive." I look over to her, and she's nodding. She's *agreeing* with me. "I don't know what the Christmas Festival budget is, but I'm imagining we'll have to be careful with the spend."

"I'm planning to submit a budget with the proposal," she said. "Mine, anyway."

My heartbeat races. I've got an accounting degree in addition to my bachelor's degree in Public Administration. "I was just going to submit what I thought I'd need to pull it off."

"Similar," she says, but somehow, I'm imagining Claudia with pages and pages of spreadsheets, with a budget down to the penny. She's organized, tenacious, and detailed like that. I shove papers anywhere they go to make room for one I don't really need.

She finishes her note-taking and sighs. "But no, not a free event. So the morning event—and we could have two, if we're going to have the theater all day—would have a charge."

"Something for single moms and single dads," I say.

"Then a family showing," she says.

"And a couples event in the evening."

"You know," she muses. "That could have a fee too, especially if we make it this romantic evening."

"Yeah?" I ask, telling myself not to look back at the ceiling tiles for inspiration. "What would that look like for you?"

"Chocolate dipped strawberries," she says, her pen scratching and her attention on it. "We can't serve alcohol at the theater, but we can do sparkling cider..."

"I meant for you," I say.

She stops writing and only moves her eyes to look at me, not her whole head. "Me?"

"Yeah." I fold my arms, suddenly self-conscious about the size and fit of my shirt. "If we were going to be enticed to go to this couples movie night, what would be the deciding factor for you?"

Claudia simply looks at me for several moments. Then another. And another. I tell myself not to move. Not to clear my throat. I asked, and if I give her any sense of weakness, she won't answer. My throat feels like a sandbox, and my heartbeat sounds like a big bass drum in my head.

Then Claudia finally says, "It's not about what's there, Beckett."

"No?"

"I wouldn't care about the movie, or the strawberries, or the offered blankets, or any of the extras."

Then how are we going to come up with them? I wonder, but I say nothing. I'm maybe not the most romantic person on the planet, but I've been known to impress a woman or two with flowers, gifts, and fancy dinners.

"It's about who you're with," she says.

"Who you're with," I say.

"Yes." She looks at her paper again. "Who *I'm* with."

Thunder and lightning could boom through the office and strike my desk, and I wouldn't move. I can't look away from her, and finally—finally—Claudia looks at me. "Would you go with me?" I ask, breaking my own rules for my mouth. Stupid tongue. Sometimes I just can't keep what I'm thinking contained beneath my vocal cords.

"We don't even know if this is going to happen."

"Why are you always so cool and collected?" I reach up and loosen my tie. "I'm so dang hot." I get to my feet and turn away from her, pure humiliation dripping from the top of my head to the soles of my shoes. "You just make me...crazy." I face the windows, things really off the rails now.

"I make you crazy?"

"I don't even know how to face you," I say, wishing I could melt through the glass and just walk away from this building. My view isn't of emerald green grass and a swing set with children playing, but a train yard. Fine by me, though this view has always bothered me. But now, I want to hop on the next locomotive and just...go.

"Beckett," she says.

"I don't know what happened yesterday," I say. "But I have this huge crush on you, and I just want everything to be perfect between us. But why would it? You've never liked me, and you're not going to start in one day."

She comes to my side, which startles me and sends my adrenaline shooting through my veins like sparks flying off a wildfire. "Beckett."

"My friends and family call me Becks."

She glances over to me, but I refuse to look away from the railroad. Claudia takes her time answering, the same way she usually does. The silence drives me toward madness, but I sternly tell myself over and over and over not to say another word.

I've already word vomited all over this office, and that's a lot of alphabet splatter to clean up.

Her hand slips into mine, and she says, "Come sit down, Becks. Let's keep talking this through, okay?"

I turn and look at her, really enjoying the way her hand feels like a cool, delicate anchor in mine. "Chocolate-dipped strawberries, huh?"

A tiny smile appears on her face. "Who doesn't like chocolate-dipped strawberries?"

"Fruit purists," I say.

She scoffs, and her smile grows. And grows. Then she starts to laugh, and that somehow covers up all the things I said that she hasn't addressed. I let her lead me back to my desk chair, and I swallow as I watch her re-take her seat across from me.

"All right," I say, hoping I can learn how to be as cool as her. "So I hate—absolutely *hate*—the fireman's breakfast after the five-K on Saturday." I glance over to my email. "The pancakes are always cold, and the bacon is always burnt."

"I agree," she murmurs.

"I've talked to the fire chief, and they still want to sponsor it, because it's a great fundraiser for them."

"Of course."

"But I've proposed teaming up with a couple of professional chefs I know." I finally find the courage to look right at her. She nods at me with a measure of encouragement I've never seen from her. "It's the same people whose restaurant I'm hoping to take you to tomorrow." I reach for my phone. "I need to call and see if they have a reservation for us. They didn't open until noon."

"What are their names?" She sits with her pen poised, her legs crossed, and everything female about her calling to everything male inside me.

"Tara and Alec Ward," I say. "I'm going to just step out and call real quick, okay?"

"Go ahead."

I leave my office, ignoring Sybil as I go by, and head out of our department. I just need some fresh air to clear my head, and then I can try to forget about all the embarrassing things I've said.

Claudia seems to handle me well enough, just like she always has, and that only makes me like her more. I sure hope I haven't messed up too badly, and I look up into the sky as the line for reservations at Tara's new restaurant rings.

"Please let there be room," I mutter, and then someone says, "Flavor, do you need a reservation?"

"Yes," I say in my cool, crisp, business voice. Where's this when I'm talking to Claudia? Jeez. "I'm hoping you have room for two for dinner tomorrow."

CLAUDIA

I BEND AND GET THE SHEET OF COOKIES OUT OF THE oven. They look brown enough on the edges, and I slide the tray onto the stovetop. Tahlia's not home from work yet, but I expect her at any moment, and I figure if I leave enough cookies, that'll buy me some time with my roommates.

See, I don't normally leave work early to come home and bake cookies for a man who I don't know that well. But I don't have a guy who runs twenty miles a week tell me he has a crush on me every day. Or ever.

So I left the office only ten minutes after Beckett. Becks. I can't believe I called him that, and I'm still not sure that nickname fits him. I don't know him in that context, and as I spatula the cookies off the sheet and onto a cooling rack, I tell myself this is why I'm taking him cookies tonight.

"To get to know him better," I say. "Or to see where he lives." I mutter the last part, thankfully none of my room-mates are home from work yet. I borrowed his address from our department directory, and I probably should text him and let him know I'm stopping by with dessert for his Thai meal.

I mean, I have no idea how long he'll be in Columbia, or how long dinner will take, or how long he'll stay at his aunt's house after he drops her off. I don't have to work on my portfolio tonight, but I still want to.

"Hey." Tahlia enters the kitchen from the front of the house without her briefcase bag. She's probably deposited it on the bench in the short hallway that leads to the master suite on this level. She lives in there, and she usually doesn't spread her stuff out around the house. I don't either, but Ry is the worst offender of that.

Tahlia takes in the kitchen, though I clean up the ingredients as I use them. "You're baking?"

"Yes," I say coolly. "I'm going to take a leaf out of Liam's book and take dessert to Beckett." I meet Tahlia's eyes. "Is that desperate?"

"Are you going to climb up on the roof?"

"No." I shake my head though my smile appears. Liam really was cute as he and Hillary dated. "But is this desperate?"

"I don't think so," Tahlia said. "I've been taking cookies to the history department for weeks, so I hope

Beckett isn't as dense as Andy." She sighs as she sits up at the counter.

"I can't believe he hasn't asked you out yet."

"It's like I'm invisible," she says. She pushes her hands through her blonde hair and comes up with a smile for me. "But you and Beckett got along at work?"

"We managed," I say.

"Did you call off the bet?"

"I told him I wanted to," I say, turning back to the cookies. "He didn't actually confirm it." I open the lazy Susan cabinet and turn it until I find the paper plates. "I'm going to talk to him tonight, after I give him these cookies." I pick up one and turn. "You want one?"

"Double chocolate peanut butter," Tahlia says with a kind smile. "A woman after my own heart."

I get my own cookie and sit down next to her. "Milk and semi-sweet chips," I say.

"You seem a little reserved." Tahlia glances over to me and then takes a bite of her cookie. "Mm, Claude, he's going to love these."

I hope so, and I pull out my phone. "I should text him, so I'm not sitting in his driveway like a creeper." I meet my roommate's eyes. "Right?"

"I'd let him know, yes."

I tap out the message quickly and send it. Then I lean my head against Tahlia's shoulder and we sit there together. She's only a year older than me, and we lived together for a couple of years in college. We made fast friends, and we even lived together in another apartment before Tahlia inherited the Big House from her aunt.

My phone zings at me, and both me and Tahlia look at it. It bleeps again. Then again. Then again. "That's Beckett," I say as I lift my head from her shoulder.

"I know. I'm staring right at it."

"He texts one sentence at a time." I look at the phone and then her. "It's irritating."

My phone bleeps again.

"Yeah," Tahlia says with a giggle in her voice. "I can tell it really bothers you." She pushes my phone closer to me, though it's practically in front of me. "Answer him, and maybe he'll stop."

"If I encourage him, he just texts more," I say dryly.

Tahlia laughs, and then says, "Yeah, and you like flirt-texting with a man."

She's not wrong, so I pick up my phone to see what Beckett's said.

We're just leaving now.

We'll stop for Thai, but they're fast.

I'll have to be at my aunt's for a little bit, helping her get ready for tomorrow.

I should be home by about seven?

I'm gonna guess by seven.

You know what, I WILL be home by seven.

"Six texts to tell me he'll be home about seven." I tip my phone toward Tahlia, but I don't give her long enough to read them.

"That gives you some time," she says. "Since he lives literally down the street."

"There are a couple of turns," I say. Seven o'clock feels impossibly far away, and I get to my feet. "I'm gonna heat up a bag of ready rice and then work on my portfolio before I go."

"You better plate up the cookies and take them with you. Emma can't resist peanut butter."

———

WHEN I PULL up to Beckett's, the sun maybe has thirty minutes left in the sky. The sky is Monticello Peach, Orange Nectar, and Citrus Blast. Corals, oranges, and golds.

Beckett's house boasts a bright white, and I don't have all the outdoor paint colors memorized. But his door is a dark blue I'd label Midnight Sapphire, and his shutters match. "His shutters match," I tell myself. That feels like such a Beckett thing to do while also being so far outside my understanding of him.

The yard is neat and trimmed, and I totally expect that from a man who shows up to work in a suit coat and tie every day, with a dress shirt that looks like it's been built on a mannequin his exact size. Although, his desk is a mess, so I expect the inside of the house to have some clutter, but the overall picture is perfect.

His garage sits open, with only his truck inside. A lawn mower waits on the other side, along with a few other yard tools. I don't see a ton of clutter the way I expect, and I figure I better get out so Beckett doesn't think I don't want to be here.

I collect the cookies and head for that dark blue door, and I ring the doorbell. Ice fills my chest as I breathe in, and then Beckett opens the door. He's still wearing his slacks and that light blue shirt, but the top few buttons are undone, and the tie has been dropped somewhere.

His throat calls to me, and I stare at it for an extraordinary amount of time. When I finally move my eyes up a few inches, Beckett's wearing a wide grin. "Are you okay?" he asks.

"Yes."

"I said your name twice." He's leaning into the door-jamb, and he folds his arms, that grin only growing wider.

I don't know what to say to him, so I lift the paper plate with his cookies on it. "You said you didn't have a peanut allergy."

"I don't." He backs up a little. "Come on in."

I step up, mercifully without tripping. I planned ahead and wore my ballet flats, but Beckett doesn't give me much room. In fact, he puts his hand on my waist and slides it along as I move past him. I shiver, because the nearness of him makes me hot, but I still have that ice in my lungs.

"Where are your dogs?"

"I put them in the backyard," he says. "We can go sit out there with them." He slides past me and into the kitchen, pausing just past the couch. I go with him, and I see his dogs standing on the deck just beyond his sliding glass door, their canine noses pressed against the glass.

They both pant, and for some reason, they make my heart so happy. "Look at them." I turn toward Beckett. "Do they live outside?"

"They have a door that allows them to come and go," he says. "I just locked it so they didn't rush you on the porch." He steps closer, the scent of his skin, his clothes, Simply Beckett enters my nose.

My eyes drift close, and I have no idea what will happen next. His lips brush across my cheek. "It's great to see you," he says in his husky voice. Then he's gone, and I feel completely unanchored from the earth.

"I'll grab us something to drink," he says. "I've got a porch swing in the backyard."

My eyes finally come open about the time his fridge closes, and he's got two bottles of sweet tea and the cookies. I look at my hands, surprised he relieved me of the plate of cookies and I didn't know it.

"Let's go," he says, and he opens the sliding door.

All chaos breaks loose. A dog barks. Claws slide on the hard floor. Another bark. Beckett saying, "Rocky, don't you dare."

Rocky arrives in front of me and jumps up, putting his

front paws on my torso. I stumble a little against his weight, but then I brace myself and bend down. "Hey, buddy." He starts to lick, and Beckett pulls his dog off me.

"Get back," he tells Rocky, and he's holding his other dog back with his leg. "Sorry, Claudia. Sorry. This is why I put them in the backyard. They'll settle down."

I smile as he wrangles the two dogs and holds the plate of cookies. Rocky barks again, and Beckett growls at him. "Stop it," he says. "You guys act like you never see human beings." He looks up at me. "I take them running every day. On paths with lots of people, I swear."

I grin at him. "I like dogs. They're fine."

"They'll take every inch they can get."

The dogs settle down a little as I move in close to him and start to give them a scrub along their backs. "They can sit by me." I look up to him while I'm still bent down patting his dogs, and I add, "You bring the snacks, yes?"

"Yes, ma'am." He leads the way out the door, saying, "Come on, guys. Leave her be. Let's go. Let's go outside."

He must've spoken the magic word, because his dogs go with him. I follow them too, and all the ice in my chest melts by the time I reach the end of the sidewalk where Beckett's porch swing waits.

But now I'm presented with a whole new problem: the two-seater porch swing. He tells the dogs to sit down, and they actually go do what he says, finding a spot of shade on the grass in front of the swing.

Beckett sits down, the swing pushing backward as he

does. I stare at it, because I'm going to have to sit down beside him. The swing is going to pitch wildly, and he'll throw the cookies which he's now removed the tin foil from.

"These look great," he says, looking up at me. "You made these?"

"It's my roommate's recipe," I say.

He picks up a cookie and takes a bite while I stand there, wondering if I can fake an emergency and somehow avoid sitting on the swing with him. Beckett's no dummy, and he's not even done with the first bite when he looks pointedly to the spot next to him.

"I'm not going to bite," he says. "My dogs don't either."

I see no way out of this, and I take a step toward him. "I'm going to make that thing sway a lot."

Surprise crosses his face. "I'll hold it for you."

I scoff and decide to go all-in. I turn and grip the armrest while he slows the swing and holds it with his foot. No matter what, this is going to be a wild ride, and I just commit to it. Sure enough, the swing pitches backward, and Beckett can't hold it.

Humiliation runs through me, but I take the cookie Beckett hands me without comment.

"Sometimes I sit out here, and I think I'm an eighty-year-old watching the sun go down," he says.

"Do you sit out here a lot?"

"Usually just on the weekends." He toes us back and forth, and my pulse settles back to its normal rhythm.

"How was dinner?"

"Amazing." He glances over to me. "Do you like Thai food?"

"Yes."

He reaches over and takes my hand. We sit there as the sun goes down and the sky turns from corals, oranges, and golds to pinks, purples, and blues.

"Tell me something I don't know about you," I say.

"Tell me what you already know."

"Let's see," I say. "You like to run with the dogs. You have two bachelor's degrees. You like birthday-cake-flavored coffee. You don't cook. You like dogs and have two of them. You've got good ideas for things around the office. You shop at the mall for your Keisman shirts, which are like a second skin, by the way. You don't have any allergies, and your mouth runs away from you sometimes."

"You're the one who's said like fifteen sentences in a row," he says.

"You send way too many texts," I fire back. "You know you can put more than one thought in a text." I glance over to him. "Right?"

He smiles and shakes his head. "I like to send one thing at a time. Then things don't get lost."

"I can read more than one sentence at a time."

We move forward and back, back and forward, forward and back before he says, "I do that because of my momma. If I put more than one thing in a text, she misses them." He's speaking in a less-confident voice than usual, and I realize he's peeled back the Confident Beckett skin and he's showing me himself.

He lets another healthy pause go by. "I'm left-handed," he says.

"You are?"

"I wrote in front of you today. You didn't notice?"

"First, you wrote maybe three words," I say. "I think you got that paper out for show."

"I did not."

"Where is it now?"

"On my desk."

"You have no idea what's on your desk."

"I have some idea."

"You need a three-tray organizer. I'll get you one."

"You don't need to do that. I have my own system."

"Are you going to bring me coffee every morning?"

"Not if you don't want me to."

"I really liked the blueberry scone."

"Am I hearing you didn't like the coffee?"

I lean against his bicep, glad when he picks up on my body language and lifts his arm around me. "I liked the coffee, Becks," I say, his nickname rolling off my tongue a lot easier than earlier. "I'm just saying you don't need to bring it for me every day."

"Because you have that single-serve coffee-maker in your office."

I really like sitting here with him, with twilight falling and his dogs nearby. I like how comfortable I am, and how he's not stuffing the silence with that runaway mouth of his.

"If you bring the coffee every day," I say. "Then it becomes mundane. It's not special."

"It's not special," he repeats.

"Right." I stay for a bit longer, and then as it reaches full darkness, I sit up. "I should go." Getting off this swing is going to be the death of me, and thankfully, Beckett gets up and holds it for me so I can without making a fool of myself.

"Thanks for the cookies," he says as he takes my hand and leads me toward a door that leads into the house. But it's not the house; it's the garage. "Stay here," he tells the dogs, and then he closes the door behind us so they can't follow.

A light flips on in the garage, and I don't imagine how slowly we walk toward my car. My lips are too dry to kiss him, and panic starts to build behind my ribs. I have no idea what I'll do if he tries to kiss me. My brain short-circuits. Do I want to kiss him in his garage? His driveway?

He opens my door and smiles. "I'll see you at work in the morning, sans coffee."

I step into him, and this time, I kiss his cheek. "And dinner? What time should I be ready?"

"The reservation is at seven-thirty," he says. "It's downtown Charleston, so...maybe six-forty-five?"

"Sure." I ease past him and glance back to him. "When's your birthday?"

He searches my face for a beat and then says, "March third."

I pull the door closed a little and give him a smile. "Mine's coming up," I say. "December eleventh."

"Noted." Beckett grins as I sink into my SUV. "'Bye, Claudia."

"You know," I say, looking up at him. "My friends and family call me Claude."

"If I was writing things down, maybe you'd notice I was using my left hand."

I shake my head, and Beckett closes my door with, "'Night, my midnight beauty."

Midnight beauty rings through my mind in that sultry voice of Beckett's all the way home.

———

I'M SITTING in my car again the next morning when my phone rings. Winslow's name sits there, and I swipe on the call. "Good morning, Mister Harvey."

"Claudia," he said. His gravelly voice reminds me of his age, that he's retiring in only a few short months. "Have you left for your office yet?"

"No, sir," I say.

"I'd love to meet with you this morning if you've got a moment."

I think of the things I have on my schedule this Tuesday morning. Nothing that can't wait, that's for sure.

"Of course," I say. "I can be to the City Center in about twenty minutes."

"I heard a rumor you had a proposal for the Christmas Festival."

I hesitate, because I have a lot of notes for the festival, sure. Mine...and Beckett's. "Yes, sir," I finally say. "We've been working on a few things."

"Bring what you have. I need to get this nailed down sooner rather than later, and there's no one I trust more than you."

Surprise darts through me. Yes, Winslow and I have always gotten along, but he doesn't dish out praise very often. "Th-thank you, sir. I'll see you soon."

"Thank you," he says, the last word getting cut off halfway through. Winslow doesn't mince words, that's for sure. He never has.

I glance over to the shiny green folder riding shotgun. Yes, I brought it home to review. No, I didn't spend more than thirty minutes on it. Even if I had, I don't have to defend myself.

"All right," I say. "Let's go see what Winslow wants to hear."

BECKETT

Nine o'clock comes, and Claudia doesn't. I read through my emails. A planned power outage later. I answer my IDMs. Yes, yes, I can be in a meeting tomorrow morning about the improvements to the parking lot here at this building.

Then nine-thirty arrives. Claudia still hasn't entered the building, and I focus on cleaning up my desk.

Ten strikes. I don't normally micromanage her day, but I check the department calendar, and I don't see any meetings on hers. When ten-thirty arrives, I finally get up and head out to Sybil's desk.

I'm not wearing a jacket today, and my shirt is a pale butter-yellow with a navy and silver tie. "Sybil?"

"Yes, Mister Fletcher?" She turns toward me, her perfectly sculpted eyebrows up.

"Do you know when Claudia will be in?" I hook my thumb toward her dark, empty office. "Did she call out today?"

Sybil gets to her feet, and I honestly don't know how those heels support her. She's mostly skin and bones, but those pinpoint heels seem impossible to walk on. Her hands go round and round one another. "Well, sir, she's..."

"She's what?"

"She's meeting with Winslow this morning." Sybil lifts her chin, her jaw jutting out.

My stomach sinks. I look toward the doorway that leads out of our department, almost expecting Claudia to walk through it and explain. I pull out my phone and check it, sure I'll have a text from her. She definitely sends longer messages than me, but maybe I missed a quick *Hey, I'm meeting with Winslow and I'll update you as soon as I get in.*

But I have nothing from her.

"Mister Fletcher?" Sybil asks.

"Thank you, Sybil," I say as diplomatically as I can, but my voice doesn't even sound like mine. I take my phone and turn back to my office. But I don't enter my office.

I enter Claudia's, because I need to see her and speak to her the very moment she arrives.

It takes another forty-two minutes and thirteen seconds before Claudia walks in. I hear her before I see her, and she sounds stressed and rushed. "...took so long. Can we postpone our afternoon meeting?"

Sybil says something, and Claudia enters her office. I'm sitting in her desk chair, and I steeple my fingers as I look at her.

"Beckett," she says with pure surprise in her voice. She's carrying a to-go cup of coffee that's not from Legacy Brew—her first crime—a bag over her shoulder, and that shiny, green, traitorous folder. Claudia stops only two steps into her office, hopefully from the sheer weight of my glare.

"You met with Winslow?" I ask. "This morning? Without me?"

"He called me on my way to work." She goes back into motion, coming all the way around her desk.

I stand, but I don't move out of the way to allow her access to her chair. "What did you two talk about?"

"Beckett."

"He just called you on the way to work?" I squint at her like I'll be able to extract her thoughts that way. "Were you driving?"

"No."

"So you couldn't send me a fast text?"

"I—didn't think of it, to be honest." She drops her bag and sighs as she pushes her hair off her shoulder. She smells like apples and blossoms, and I wish that didn't please me so much. "It was last-minute, and I was stressed, and I just...went."

"So tell me what you talked about."

She opens her mouth, but her phone rings. The one on her desk, not her cell. She glares at me and reaches for it. "Claudia Brown," she says. A pause while she listens. "Yes, that's right. My whole morning got blown up, so can you arrange with Sybil for another time?"

More pausing, wherein my annoyance sings through me.

"Thank you," she says, then she hangs up and steps back. Today, she's wearing a maxi dress in light blue, with dark blue flowers splashed all over it. Her hair is down, as usual, and I wonder if it's her shampoo or her lotion that tickles my nose and makes me want to lean in and kiss her.

No, I tell myself. I don't want to kiss her. She just had a solo meeting with Winslow two days early without telling me. There will be no kissing. I'm *upset* with her.

Even more so when she stands there glaring at me. "Well?" I prompt. "What did you and *Mister Harvey* talk about this morning in your *last-minute* meeting?"

"Jealousy is not a good look on you."

"Claudia," I say with plenty of exasperation in my voice.

"It was nothing," she says. "It was a good meeting, and he said—"

"Claudia," Sybil says from the doorway. "I need you to sign for this." Someone is with her, and Claudia walks away to sign for some package that Sybil takes back to her desk.

She faces me again, and it irritates me that she doesn't immediately say that she pitched the Christmas Festival as the ideas of *both* of us. I'm once again George Constanza in *Seinfeld*, in the episode where Jerry takes credit for George's idea for the sitcom they've been writing together.

We'll find something for you.

That's the line from the show, indicating that someone else is going to play the lead part, and I'll be sidelined.

I hate feeling sidelined. My father did it when he left me, my momma, and Liv. My mother did it when she met Malcolm, married him, and left South Carolina. I feel stagnant at work, and my life is stale and boring. I run with the dogs. I sit in this horrible trailer day after day. I go to Aunt Jill's and feed her cats and dog, help her, and then sit in my porch swing as the sun goes down.

The only thing I had to liven things up was Claudia, and now *she's* sidelining me. "I should've known you'd do this," I say. "You make this bogus bet with me just to get my ideas, and then you steal it all and present it as your own."

"No," Claudia says.

Her phone rings again, and I lunge toward it while she stays still. "Claudia can't come to the phone right now," I bark into the receiver. I set it back in its cradle, but I can see how someone would think I slammed it.

When I look up, Larry is coming into Claudia's office. "Hey, Claudia," he says, and he's carrying too many folders for this to be a quick chat.

My patience is completely gone, and I bellow into the office that isn't mine. I storm toward Claudia and Larry and grab her hand. "I need her for a minute," I say as I burst out of her office with her in tow.

"Beckett," she protests.

"I just—" Larry says, but I don't hear the rest of what he says. Sybil makes a bird-like squawking noise, but I just keep going. I leave our department and instead of going right toward the main door and the other departments, I go left. There's a back door this way, but no parking lot so no one uses it. There's a bathroom and a couple of conference rooms the groundskeeping department uses in the spring when they're prepping for their huge town clean-up.

I start for one of those doors, but it opens, and a couple of men come out of it. I make a hard left and go toward the back door.

"Beckett," Claudia protests again. "What—are—you—doing?"

I pull open the only door here and see a janitorial closet. This will do. No phones in here. No secretaries. No co-workers. "Come on." I enter, noting the scent of lemon and pine and antiseptic.

"Beckett, you're being crazy." But Claudia enters the closet with me. I release her hand and push the door closed. I turn to face her, my chest heaving. She's glaring at me from five feet away, near a utility sink and a rack of cleaners.

"I'm sick of getting interrupted," I say. "And I want to

know everything you said to Winslow, and everything he said back to you." I take a step toward her. "Right. Now."

"You need to calm down."

"I'm perfectly calm." I fold my arms. "It's time for you to deliver many sentences in a row. The whole story."

"Winslow called me while I was sitting in my car in the driveway at the Big House," she says. "He said he wanted to see me, because he heard I had ideas for the Christmas Festival."

"Yeah, sure, I bet you do." She had gone over her plans with me yesterday too, but I'm not the one who'd run straight to Winslow the very next day. The first chance she'd gotten.

"I had my folder," she says, ignoring me. "So I went straight there. He wanted to know everything, so I...gave him everything. After I baked the cookies yesterday, but before I came to your house, I started combining our plans into a single proposal."

She swallows, and I see the fire in her eyes. Part trepidation, part determination. "It wasn't done yet. I fully planned to go over it with you before Thursday. We were *certainly* going to have the meeting with him together. He just called this morning out of nowhere. What was I supposed to do?"

"You were supposed to call me," I say, because I'm not letting her off the hook, even if she was combining our proposals into one. She never told me she was doing that either.

"So I pitch it to him on the fly, Beckett. I did a pretty good job, but it would've been better if you were there, if we'd had more time to perfect it." She shakes her head. "I hate the bet. I was going to ask you about doing the single proposal, but I didn't have time." She looks at me with that desperation. "There was no time. I did what I thought was best."

"Let me get this straight." I reach up and stroke one hand down my beard, my mind working fast, trying to remember and re-hear all the things she's said in this janitorial closet. "You combined our ideas into one proposal."

"Yes."

"You pitched it as a single proposal to Winslow."

"Yes."

"You told him it was our idea?" I gesture between me and her. "Or your idea?"

"I told him we were working on it together."

"And?"

"And nothing."

"And nothing?" I scoff. "Try again, Claude."

She sighs and throws up her hands. "He said he loved our ideas. He's glad we're working together on it, because we're two of the brightest minds in Public Works. Those were his words, and he said he'd let me know soon."

"He's let *you* know."

"*Us*, Beckett." She takes a couple of quick steps to me and takes my hands in hers. "I pitched it as one proposal, that the two of us were working on together. I told him we were planning to come talk to him on Thursday, because we know proposals are due Friday."

She gazes up at me. "I did not throw you under the bus. I brought you along for the ride, and I was going to tell you the moment I walked in."

"You stopped and got coffee."

"Yeah, because I went straight to the City Center this morning."

"You have time to get coffee but not time to text me."

"I didn't know you were going to be in Beast Mode."

"You were two hours late for work."

"I have been working for hours," she throws back. She pulls her hands away too, sighs, and turns. But she's only facing the sink now, and she has to face me again. She starts playing with the end of a lock of hair, and I can admit I like this vulnerable side of her.

"You really told him we worked together on it?"

"Yes."

"Do we still have a meeting with him on Thursday?"

"He said he didn't need it. That I'd given him what he needed this morning."

I pause for a moment, taking in the unrest on her face. "It's killing you that you didn't have the perfect pitch, isn't it?"

"I was going to ask you if I could give it to you, so you could tell me if it was okay."

"I'm sure it was amazing," I say.

"It was rushed," she admits.

"You were put on the spot."

"I knew nothing about Mobile Adventures. I told him you'd have to fill him in on that—the cost, all of it—because we hadn't hammered out that part of the budget yet."

She really did tell him the ideas belonged to both of us. My stomach growls, and I wonder if Claudia will go to lunch with me, even if it's work-y.

"Can I still give you the pitch?" she asks. "I won't be able to do it verbatim, but it definitely pointed out some holes we need to fill."

"If we get it," I say. "They're taking proposals from the general public."

"Between you and me, I don't think they have very many," Claudia says. "I sensed that from talking to Winslow this morning."

"Do you want to pitch me over lunch?"

A tiny smile erases the discomfort in her expression. "Well, since I've canceled my afternoon meeting and you dragged me out of the office in front of Sybil, I think we should at least stop by the office and let her know you didn't bury me in the rail yard." She grins more fully, and the last of the irritation and weirdness between us dissipates.

"I'm sorry." I take her into my arms, glad when hers go around me too. I haven't hugged anyone except Aunt Jill in so long, and I really sink into Claudia's embrace. "I get a little...fly-off-the-handle sometimes. That's what Liv calls it."

"I should've texted you."

"I would've appreciated that." I pull back, but I don't go far. I hold her close, and if I dip my head down, I can kiss her. My eyes even drop to her mouth; my fantasies run wild; my brain screams at me that I'm standing in a smelly janitorial closet.

There's no way I'm kissing Claudia for the first time here.

"I'm sorry I didn't text."

"I'm sorry I assumed the worst about the meeting." I press my cheek to hers. "Can we go to The Corner Diner for lunch? They'll let us sit there as long as we want, and you can pitch me the way you pitched Harvey."

"I love the broccoli cheddar soup at The Corner Diner," she whispers.

I step back and drop my hand to hers. "Okay, let's go." I take the few steps to the door and push down the handle and pull. The door doesn't open.

I try again, my adrenaline shooting to my brain for the second time that day. "This door..." I pull again, and nothing.

"Beckett," Claudia says from behind me. "Open the door."

"I'm trying." I try again, and it's like the door handle isn't attached to anything. It takes almost nothing to push it down, and the door—the very solid tan-painted metal door—doesn't budge.

"Let me try."

"Oh, sure," I say as I step out of her way. "You're going to get it when I couldn't."

Claudia tries the door handle, and to my great relief, the door doesn't open. She turns back to me and says needlessly, "The door won't open."

CLAUDIA

"You locked us in the janitor—" I swat at Beckett's chest, and he mock flinches away from me.

"Closet."

Swat.

"In."

Swat.

"Our."

Swat.

"Building."

He takes a step back with every flap of my hand, and I take one toward him. "How was I supposed to know this door locked?" he asks. "None of the other ones in this dumpy trailer do."

I go to swat at him again, but he grabs my wrist. My pulse pounds with fear of being trapped in a small space that smells like a pine tree, a lemon, and a bottle of bleach had a little too much fun. I swear, I'm going to pass out at any moment.

Maybe that's from the racing heartbeat at the nearness of Beckett Fletcher. At this tiny room we're stuck in. At my crazy-insane morning in Winslow's office, doing a pitch I'm certain is a pile of dung the more I think about it.

I can't get a full breath, and that means I'm panting. Beckett is too, and his eyes drop to my mouth. "Nope," he says right out loud. "Nope, I'm not kissing you in the janitorial closet." He dodges by me and strides for the door. It only takes three steps, and I spin to watch him.

"You think you're going to kiss me?" I ask.

"I'd like to," he throws over his shoulder. "Just not here."

Before I can comprehend what he's said, he starts pounding on the door. "Hey!" he yells, and I press my eyes close at how loud he is. I've always thought he was loud, and it bothered me. Now, maybe it'll save us.

Bang! Bang! Bang!

"Hey, we're stuck in here! Help!"

"Maybe I can text Sybil," I say, and I reach for my pockets. But I don't have my phone. It's probably still in my briefcase bag, as Beckett intercepted me literally the moment I walked into my office. Then he towed me out of it without a moment's warning.

He turns toward me, but I shake my head, my annoyance singing like a choir now. "You dragged me out of my office," I say. "I don't have my phone."

"Of course you don't."

"Well, where's yours, Smarty-Pants?"

He pulls it from his pocket and says, "I have no service in here."

"Where did we go?" I cry as I tilt my head back and look at the ceiling. "Through a portal to another dimension?" I step next to him and slap the door with an open palm. "Sybil! Come open this door!"

Slap-bang, slap-bang, slap-bang!

Beckett and I yell for several more moments, and then I'm so winded, I have to stop. I swear I do more than just walk three dogs for an hour once a week, but I feel utterly exhausted, and as I turn in a full circle, I wonder if I'm going to have to sleep in this minuscule space, and if so, where I might end up.

Maybe curled in the corner here by the door. Then I spot a stain on the plywood, and I don't even want to imagine what that might be. I look away, trying and failing to contain a shudder. "Beckett," I whimper.

"It's fine, Claude," he says, and I'm not even sure he realizes he's used my nickname. "This is a janitorial closet. I'll just take the doorknob off."

"Do you know how to do that?" I watch as he steps over to the rack next to the sink.

"I just need a hammer or something."

"Or something?" I narrow my eyes at his back. "How handy are you?"

"I can use a screwdriver," he says over his shoulder like

I'm the dumbest woman on the planet. I sincerely hope he can, because I can't. Not really. I'm not mechanically inclined, let's just say that. I once tried to change an outlet cover and ended up shocking myself badly enough not to pick up another hand tool ever again.

"Screwdriver," he mutters, and since the space is so small, I hear him fine. "Screwdriver." He moves something on the rack, which causes a terrible metal-on-metal noise. Everything grates me wrong right now, and I take a slow breath in through my nose to try to prevent myself from committing homicide.

Is there a word for killing a co-worker? I can't think of one, and I manage to distract myself with thoughts about matricide and fratricide and wondering if there's one for throttling the man who works in the office next door to you.

Then Beckett spins, a grin on his face and that precious screwdriver in his hand. "Found one."

"I see that," I say acidly. I move out of the way as he comes back over to the door. "I still don't know if you can use that thing."

"Watch and see then, sweetheart," he says. He does give me a glare before he starts to work on the door handle. "And thanks for the vote of confidence."

"You're an accountant," I throw at him. "Mathy people aren't usually installing doorknobs."

"I put in my own camera doorbell," he says. "And wow, that's a horrible stereotype you just threw out there."

He gives me a smile and goes back to working on the door handle. It's not a knob, but a longer handle that he can push down and then it pops right back up.

My stomach growls, and it feels like I've been stuck in this closet for hours and hours. I pace away from him, take in the stained sink and turn back around. Three steps that way, then three the other. My heels click on the concrete with every move, and I'm sure it's annoying Beckett, because it's annoying me.

Then he emits a noise of pure triumph, and he says, "Got it!" only a moment before he drops the metal handle onto the concrete. I spin toward him, sure we're in space and about to run out of air. He yanks and fiddles with more metal pieces, and then he hooks a couple of fingers through the empty space where the handle was and pulls the door open.

"Toronto Blue," I sputter as I push past him. Out in the hallway, I pull in breath after breath and bend over my knees.

"Claudia." Beckett's hand lands on my back, and I steal strength from the warmth and pressure of it. "Hey, you're really freaking out."

"I didn't like that." I take another breath and straighten. My hair feels like it's been glued to my head, and I run my hands through it and start to settle. Another breath, and I can look at him. "I'm okay."

"What's Toronto Blue?" he asks.

I open my mouth to tell him about the perfect blue—

not too much gray, or green, or yellow—for the perfect beach cottage, but I hesitate. "Uh..."

"Sounds like a paint color," he says.

I stare at him, blinking rapidly. "It is," I say. "I, ahem, swear in paint colors. Usually just the indoor ones, because those are the ones I know best."

Beckett does the rapid blinking now, almost like what I've said isn't English. That, or I should've broken it down into bite-sized text messages so as to not overwhelm him.

"It's a really nice blue," I offer next. "Blue is such a hard color to put on walls, and people lose years of their life trying to choose one." I swallow, but Beckett doesn't jump in and save me from myself. "You'll see them with paint swatches taped to their walls, you know? Anyway, Toronto Blue doesn't have too much gray, which a lot of blues do. And it's not sickly with too much yellow. It's pretty much the most amazing color for any house within the vicinity of the beach."

By the time I'm done talking, Beckett's smile has started growing. "I love how much you talk," he says. "Once you get going, that is." He puts his hand on the small of my back and adds, "Let's go show Sybil you're still alive and get over to The Corner Diner."

I nod, my tongue somehow tied into a knot again. I do tend to spew mouthfuls of words at once or hold my tongue completely, and I'm not sure if I'm glad Beckett has picked up on that or not.

I feel a little clammy, and I'm not sure I'm fit to stay at

work. I do want to pitch Beckett, but I was already planning to leave a little early so I have more time to get ready for our date tonight.

I slide my hand into his. "It's been a weird day."

He tosses the janitorial closet a look. "That it has."

"Did you get any work done while I was out this morning?" I tease. "Or did you just stew in your office and then take over my office chair?"

"I did a few things," he says with a smile, and he's more good-natured than I thought. He takes a step to go back down the hall, but I don't go with him. Beckett turns back to me. "You okay?"

"I just need a minute." I turn the other way, dropping his hand and moving for the exit. There's nowhere to go out here, but there is a small landing, and I'll be able to breathe fresh air. I leave the building first, with Beckett right behind me.

"Let me just check and make sure this door doesn't lock behind us..." He catches the door and goes back inside. He lets it close and mimes for me to open it.

My adrenaline spikes again, and I have to force myself to reach for the door handle. If we got stuck out here, we could probably jump down to the ground and go around the front. But it's not exactly cool, and it's probably a bigger drop than I can make.

Thankfully, the door opens, and Beckett joins me outside. I move down the railing so there's room for him, and I take a big drag of air.

"Are you claustrophobic then?"

"I didn't think I was."

He nods and we survey the railroad behind us. "Broccoli cheddar soup, huh?"

"It's really good."

"Not much butter in that."

"I like other foods."

"Yeah? Tell me another one."

"Uh, let's see. Chicken parm. One of my favorite pasta dishes." I glance over to him. "You?"

"In the pasta category, I'm going to go with shrimp scampi."

"Sounds like you." I smile at him, and I'm not teasing or poking fun.

He puts his arm around me and asks, "It's Friday night. Do you like going out or staying in?"

"Depends on the week I've had. This week? Depending on how the rest of the days go, I'll probably want to stay in."

"And when you stay in, what do you do?"

I let only the breeze whisper between us for a moment. "I change into stretchy pants and a tank top, and I pop a big bowl of popcorn. There's TV involved, and depending on how bad things are, I'll watch something with my roommates or just put something on my tablet in my room."

"Plain popcorn?"

"What do you think?" I cuddle further into him. "Am I the plain-popcorn type of woman?"

"No, ma'am," he murmurs. "I imagine you to put on that cheddar cheese powder. Or caramel."

I smile, my gaze still on the big cranes they use to load and unload the train cars. "You're not wrong."

"I'm the plain-popcorn guy."

"Is that so?"

"I've been feeling like my life is pretty stale lately, yeah."

"Why's that?"

"It just feels...stagnant. I go running. I go to work. I go to my aunt's. On the weekends, I'm out in the yard like every other man on the street, trimming the grass. There's no...flavor."

"So you just need some cheese powder."

He chuckles, and I like the joyful sound of it. "Sometimes it's not so easy to do that in real life."

"Mm."

"There you go, humming again."

"That was an agreement hum," I say. "I wasn't judging you."

"I'll learn them all eventually."

I want to challenge him on that, because for him to learn all the minute differences in my hums implies that we're going to be together for a long time. Part of me yearns for that, and another part of me is scared of that.

"Do you want a family?" I ask. "Or would that just add to your staleness?"

"How would that add to the staleness?"

"Those other men on your street probably have families, and they're still out there, mowing the lawn on Saturday mornings."

He thinks about it for a few seconds, and then says, "I think a family would spice things up, yeah. Heck, just going out to dinner on a Tuesday night has spiced up my life considerably."

I try to look at him out of the corner of my eye so he won't notice. "You haven't dated much?"

"Not lately," he says coolly.

"No deflecting this time," I say. "I just had a mini-panic attack coming out of that closet. You can tell me about your dating history."

Beckett looks at me fully now, and I turn to meet his gaze. "Mini-panic attack? Are you sure you're okay?"

"I'm feeling better and better," I say. "I just get myself worked up sometimes."

He nods and his jaw jumps as he clenches and unclenches it. "I'm not great at dating. Inevitably, I say or do something that drives women away."

"Like what?"

"I don't know," he says. "I haven't had a serious girlfriend in a while. A few years."

"What happened to the last one?"

"We only dated for a couple of months, and then she

—" I clear my throat. "She said she couldn't be with a runner."

"A runner? Like, you running was a problem? What didn't she like? The muscles for miles?"

He scoffs, or maybe it's a half-laugh. "She said that people who run have issues they should be talking about, but instead, they're running from them."

"Wow," I say.

"So I got on Matchmaker. But I don't know. I just couldn't do it. I'm too old for it."

"Too old?" My heartbeat skips over itself. "How old are you?"

"Thirty-five."

I scoff. "Baby, you're not too old for Matchmaker."

"It felt like it. Everyone I got matched with was a decade younger than me." He sighs. "I don't know. It just wasn't my thing."

"Okay, fair enough." I take another breath, feeling back to myself. "We can go back in, but I just have one more question—and this one is a deal-breaker."

"Oh-ho, boy," he says. "Maybe we'll end before we even start."

"No, we've been out once," I say, looking over to him again. "We've started."

"Have we?" His eyes drop to my mouth again. "I haven't kissed you."

"Is that when things start for you?"

"It's when I think they might be something, yeah," he

says. Those aqualicious eyes—if I had to name them according to Sherwin Williams, I'd go with Palm Coast Teal—meet mine. "I'm not kissing you on the tiny landing at the back of our building, so stop looking at me like that."

I smile and duck my head. "You seem to have a lot of requirements for a first kiss."

"You can't tell me you've dreamed of being kissed in a janitorial closet." He scoffs and shakes his head. "No way. I may not have had a girlfriend for a while, but I know that much."

"Okay," I say. "My question is on condiments."

"Excuse me?"

"Condiments can make or break a meal," I say.

"I don't cook," he says. "Remember?"

"At all?"

He shakes his head. "At all."

I blink-stare at him. "Well, now my question is irrelevant."

He grins at me and tucks me into his side again. I lay my head against his chest and smile to the rail yard. "If I came to your house and made you an omelet, what would you put on it?"

"This is a trick question," he says with another scoff. "I'm not answering it."

"You're no fun."

"I'm an accountant," he says. "I thought you knew that came with the degree."

I laugh, and my stomach reminds me it's lunchtime.

I'm about to suggest we head inside now when Sybil chirps from behind me, "Claudia? Are you okay out here?"

Beckett and I turn toward her, and I casually step away from him like Sybil's my mother, and she's just caught me with the bad boy in my bedroom. The way Sybil's fingers flutter, she's more nervous than furious, but I still feel like I've been caught.

"Fine," I say. "We were just coming in."

Sybil nods, her eyes darting over to Beckett. "Mister Harvey called for you, Beckett. I didn't know where you were, and I said you'd call him back."

Beckett reaches over and grabs my hand, squeezing the life right out of it. "Great," he squeaks out. "Thanks, Sybil." Then he releases my hand and steps past her and into the building.

I stand there and watch him go, doing everything I can to prolong not looking at my secretary. That lasts about four seconds, and then I'm forced to meet her gaze. She folds her arms and demands, "What's going on?"

"Nothing," I say.

"Yeah, it sure looked like nothing."

"I had to tell him about this morning."

"While cuddling into him where no one can find you."

"I wasn't—" A smile fills my face. "Fine, I was cuddling with him."

Sybil gasps, her eyes widening and making her even more bird-like. "Claudia, *what* is going on?"

It's such a long story, and I've already had an eventful

day. Plus, I don't want to betray Beckett's confidence. So I simply lean into her and say, "I'll tell you after our date tonight."

I'm surprised I have any air left to breathe Sybil sucks in so hard. "You're going out with him?"

I nod, grinning widely, and indicate she should go back into the building too. "Later, okay, Sybil? I've had a busy morning."

She stumbles as she turns, and I follow her back inside. "You okay?"

"The world doesn't feel right," she says, her steps still a little sideways. "You're going out with *Beckett Fletcher*." She looks at me like perhaps I don't know who he is.

"Yes," I say as we round the corner and our department looms. "I am." And with a little luck, maybe tonight, Beckett's requirements for a first kiss location will be met, and we'll both get to see if there's really something real between us.

BECKETT

"You sure I can leave them overnight?" I look at my canine duo, both of them asleep on Aunt Jill's couch.

"Yes," she says. "Or stop by and get them after your date." She beams up at me. "I'm just so happy you're going out with someone again, Becks."

"I could crash and burn tonight." I untuck my shirt and proceed to tuck it in again. "Is this shirt really okay?" I've chosen a button-up in blue, orange, and white, because a wardrobe consultant once told me that blue makes my eyes look even more like the ocean. I wonder what paint color Claudia has assigned to them, and I'm a little embarrassed at how much I think about Claudia and all the things she's told me.

But I do think about her constantly, and the way she fits against my side, and how I need to find a way to kiss her tonight. I might go crazy if I don't.

"It's wonderful," Aunt Jill says. "You look great in bright colors."

I look up, alarm pulling through me. "Is this shirt bright?" I might still have time to run home and change into something black. I'm so sick of wearing dark colors, though, as it's all I dress in for work.

"It's not bright," Aunt Jill says. "Honestly, Becks, calm down. You look great. She's lucky to go out with you. Go. Have fun."

Calm down. I take a breath and find my center. "I'll come back and get the dogs," I say. "You're all set for tomorrow morning, and you don't need them tripping you up." Or crowding into her in bed, which they'll totally do. If my dogs can take an inch, they'll try for a mile.

"You hear that, you hounds? I'm coming back for you."

Duke looked up, his eyes filling with all the puppy-dog pleading in the world. Rocky yawns, and that about sums up the dogs. I step over to Aunt Jill and bend down to sweep a kiss across her cheek. "Wish me luck."

"Oh, pish-posh," she says. "You don't need luck. You're a fine young man."

I smile as I leave the house, checking my pockets for my keys and my phone and my wallet. *Check, check, check.* I drive to what Claudia calls the Big House, and it is big. It's got six bedrooms and four bathrooms, and according to Claudia, it's her favorite place she's ever lived. She's told me via text that she lives with former college roommates, and they all get along great.

I park in the wide lane in front of the house and sigh. "Here we go," I say. The sky has started to darken, and by the time we get to Flavor, I expect it to be full dark. Then there'll be lampposts and lights, and I hope everything will be bathed in magic.

I need tonight to go well, and I need to figure out another place to kiss Claudia. This porch...no, this porch won't do. The women here already know too much, and there's a security camera.

It's way too hot in my truck already, so I leave it on and make sure the AC is pumping hard before I get out and head for the front door. Since it's still early September, it's plenty warm in the evenings, and I've traded my slacks for a pair of dress shorts that reach almost all the way to my knee. They're silky like slacks, and they're a dark gray color that matches some of the lines in my shirt.

They're still shorts, and I wonder what Claudia will think of them. I'm wearing loafers instead of tennis shoes, so I'm definitely still dressed up for this soft grand opening, and I reach to ring the doorbell about the time I remember talking to Claudia about what she might wear tonight.

I groan and mutter, "I'm so underdressed." I turn away from the door, suddenly so nervous. The door opens, and I spin back to it. A blonde woman stands there, and she seems calm and kind. Two others had answered the door earlier this week, and neither of them was this person.

"Beckett, hello," she says.

"Hello," I say, and she obviously knows who I am and why I'm here. "I'm sorry. I don't know your name. Claudia said she's got a couple of blonde roommates, and I met Lizzie and..."

"I'm Tahlia," she supplies for me. "Emma's a bit blonde too, but she doesn't think so, so we don't say anything." She smiles at me, and she's relaxed enough for me to play off that. I return her smile and pocket my hands.

"Hey, there." Claudia crowds into the doorway too, and she's stunning upon a simple glance. She looks at Tahlia and says something to her, and then she steps out of the house in a bright blue dress that curves and swells in all the best places. She's wearing a black leather jacket, and it seems totally at odds with the dress but also completely perfect with it.

"Hey," I say as I reach for her naturally. She leans into me, and I press a kiss to her cheek as my eyes drift closed in bliss. "You smell great." I step back, the warmth of her perfume still in my nose. "You look like a million bucks."

"Thank you." We go down the steps to the sidewalk, and she casts me an out-of-the-corner-of-her-eye look. "Shorts?"

"They're dress shorts," I say quickly. "Men get married in these."

She scoffs. "They do not."

"I can assure you they do." I open her door and wait for her to climb in and settle her skirt where she wants it.

The bottom hem barely brushes her knees, and she really does light my red blood cells on fire. "I bought them from the same shop where I got my tux."

"I'm going to look this up."

I grin at her. "You do that." I close the door and round the hood. When I get behind the wheel, she's on her phone tapping and swiping.

I back out and get us moving toward Flavor. She's only on the phone for ten seconds before she says, "Fine. They're dress shorts."

I chuckle and glance over to her in time to see her shove her phone under her thigh. "I don't like wearing pants if I don't have to."

"Would you get married in them?"

"Sure," I say. "They're luxury shorts. With the right shoes and vest and tie...it would be amazing."

"A vest, huh?" She giggles—actually giggles—and pushes her hair over her shoulder. "I mean, you're thirty-five, but a vest?" She shakes her head. "Seems like something an eighty-five-year-old would wear."

"I've got the porch swing too," I say. "I'm just an old soul, I suppose."

"Nah," she says. "Your dogs are too big."

Our eyes meet, and as we start to laugh together, I reach over and take her hand in mine. This drive is so much better than our first date, and we talk about this, that, and nothing as I make the journey from Cider Cove and into the city.

"I'm glad I don't make this drive every day," I say as I pull into a nearby parking garage and find a spot.

"Right?" She unbuckles but doesn't get out. "Though you do go to Legacy Brew, and that's not in Cider Cove." Her eyebrows go up, and I quickly get out to help her down.

As she slips into my arms in the narrow channel between my truck and the car next to us, I wonder if I can kiss her here. But Claudia puts one palm against my chest and says, "I think the shorts are sexy."

My heartbeat responds to her words and her touch, and then she's moving away from me. I stare after her for a moment, then close her door and hurry to follow her. There are a lot of people crowded around Flavor, but Claudia and I make our way inside. It's noisy and dimly lit here at the hostess station, and I start to regret my decision to bring her here tonight.

"Beckett Fletcher," I tell the woman in a slinky black dress at the hostess station. "I have a reservation for two at seven-thirty."

She smiles and looks down at her tablet. "Yes, you do." She taps and looks up at me. "It should only be a few minutes until one of my runners comes back for you."

"Sure," I say, thinking of the *Seinfeld* episode where Jerry and his friends are waiting for a table at a Chinese restaurant. The host keeps telling them, "Five or ten minutes," but it's way longer than that.

I turn and tuck Claudia against my side. "A few

minutes," I manage to say to her. I dip my chin to get my mouth closer to her ear. "I didn't think it was going to be noisy like this."

"It's okay," she says. "There's a lot of energy here."

"I'll say." It's not super great for me, because I already carry a lot of energy inside myself. Sometimes I can feed off other energy and not let it affect me, but I'm already so nervous for some reason.

A woman carrying a couple of menus calls a name that's not mine. Another does the same thing. A third finally says, "Beckett."

I take Claudia's hand and go with the young woman. "Good evening," she says like the music and chatter around her doesn't exist. "How are you two tonight?"

"Great," I say.

"Celebrating anything?"

I glance over my shoulder to Claudia. "Uh, not killing each other?"

She grins, but the runner in front of me looks at me like I've lost my mind. I laugh and shake my head. "No, we're not celebrating anything."

Without asking us anything else, she leads us through a beautifully decorated restaurant to a table-for-two in front of the windows. "How's this?"

"Amazing," I say, my eyes locked on the quintessential rowhouses across the street. "Look at this view, Claude."

She comes to my side. "It's wonderful."

"Do you want this seat?"

"You can have it." She slips past me and onto the bench seat facing the restaurant, leaving me to take the chair with the view. We settle into the booth, and I take the menu from the runner. We bury ourselves there for a minute, and then I look over to her.

"See anything you like?" I ask.

"Definitely." She glances up, something mischievous in those dark eyes that intrigue me so.

"Oh, you've got something up your sleeve." I lay down my menu completely, my smile appearing almost instantly.

"I want to guess what you'd get." She then gestures to herself. "And you can guess for me."

I want to immediately reject the idea. I've known Claudia for years, but not on a personal level. I've never paid all that much attention to what she likes or doesn't like, though I've been trying for the past few days. "Is this like your bet?"

"No," she says, but none of her sparkle dulls. "Nothing at stake here. Just a getting-to-know-you thing. I'll pick what I think you'd order and tell you why, and if I'm right, then I know you better than you think. If I'm wrong, then you can tell me why I'm wrong, and I get to know you more." She picks up her menu again. "That's all."

"Okay," I say. "Let me look for a minute."

A waitress interrupts us and asks us for drinks and appetizers. Claudia only raises her eyebrows at me, and panic starts to stream through me. I haven't even looked at drinks yet, and I flip over the menu.

"We have a great line of beer," she says. "Wines, and some great mocktails."

I've never seen Claudia drink anything but coffee and water, but I refuse to look over to her.

"He's driving," Claudia says in a smooth, cool voice. Her cat-like, princess voice. "So I'm going to guess he wants a Diet Coke."

I nod along in agreement. "With lemon," I say. "If you've got it."

"No problem," the waitress says.

"I think she'll take the Sunrise Paloma." I look up then. "It's a mocktail. Look at it." I reach over and poke her menu near where the mocktails are. "It's got liquid smoke in it."

Her eyes widen, and she says, "Wow."

"And bring her some water too," I say. "And we want to try the Puckered Lemonade." I meet Claudia's eyes, and she gives me a slight nod. The feline princess approves.

"You got it. I'll give you a minute with the menu." The waitress leaves, and I keep my gaze on Claudia.

"How'd I do?"

"I love lemonade," she says. "I'm not so sure about the liquid smoke."

"It has a chili salt rim," I say. "It sounds really interesting."

She hums, and I laugh. Claudia's face starts to flush,

and she won't meet my eyes. "You're distracting me, so I can't find your perfect meal."

"Is that what I'm doing?" I ask while still chuckling. "You're the one who hums like that. And by the way, that one totally sounded judgey."

"I'm just not sure about the Paloma."

"If you don't like it, then you don't drink it. That's why I got you water and lemonade." I go back to the menu too, because I've only minorly won with the lemonade. "I can't wait to try it."

"Oh, you think we're going to share?"

I look up. "Are you not a food sharer?"

"We've been out to eat twice. Have we ever shared?"

My mind blanks, but the answer is still there. "No." I look over my shoulder. "I'll order my own."

Claudia trills out a laugh now. "It's fine, Beckett. We can share the drink."

"I'm never sure with you," I say. "Are you serious? Joking? It's very discombobulating."

"Discombobulating?" She sits back against the booth. "I've been called a lot of things, but not that."

"I'm still learning how to talk to you," I say, and that's probably too much information for tonight. "So...help me out with the menu."

"What would you get for me?" Claudia's not looking at her menu anymore, and I've abandoned mine too.

"Given your penchant for butter, I think—"

"Penchant? Are you taking a vocabulary class or something?" She grins at me, those eyes back to dark diamonds I'll see twinkling and blinking in my vision after I lie down to go to sleep tonight.

"Don't tell me you don't know what it means."

"I know what it means."

"All right, then. Why are you giving me grief over this?" I shoot her a glare and go back to the menu. "Given how much you like butter, but also knowing that we just indulged at Better Than Butter a couple of days ago—and the fact that you only ate a tiny bowl of soup for lunch—"

"I told you I wanted to be hungry for this."

"—I think I'd order the pasta carbonara for you." I look up to judge her reaction. "I think I should get points if I'm even in the right category."

"So points for pasta," she says.

"Yes."

"I can say I would be ordering pasta for myself tonight."

"But not the carbonara." I straighten my shoulders too and wait for her to deny me.

"I've been craving spaghetti and meatballs," she says. "I'm not sure why, but that's what I want tonight."

"Fair enough," I say, nodding over to her menu. "What about me?"

"Well, using similar logic, and knowing you have a whole chicken at your house, I decided to stay away from poultry."

"Smart."

"Because I know you like variety. You don't cook, but you eat out for every meal."

"I mean, is coffee and a scone a meal?"

"It's food you don't cook at home," she says. "And you're distracting me."

"Oh, you mean the way you did me? Interrupting every other word?" I grin at her, but she glares back at me. I'm learning more about her looks and glares, and this one has bright eyes, which means she's not really irritated with me. But she could be quickly, so I mime zipping my lips and gesture for her to go on.

"I'm thinking steak," she says. "But I don't know which one."

"What would the cook be?" I ask.

"Medium-rare?" she guesses. "Medium? Anything more than medium is a crime against beef."

"I'll go with medium." I smile at her. "Appetizers?"

"I want all of them," she says. "Did you see they have pork belly?" She meets my eyes. "Do you like pork belly?"

"It's okay," I say. "I was thinking of the duck confit."

"They have fried Brussels sprouts too," she says. "I love those."

The waitress returns with the mocktail and the lemonade, with a second man with her with our waters. "You two ready?" She glances over to Claudia, and she nods.

"We want one of each appetizer," I say.

"Oh," the waitress says at the same time Claudia says, "Beckett."

"And I'd love the ribeye, medium, with the loaded baked potato." I nod to Claudia. "That's me."

"Do you want any sauces or embellishments on the steak?" the waitress asks.

"Oh, yes," I say. "I want the blue cheese cream, and the chimichurri."

"Ribeye, medium, loaded, blue cheese, chimichurri." The waitress turns to Claudia without having written anything down. "For you?"

"I'd love the Al Pomodoro."

"That's not meatballs," I say.

"That's because you ordered every appetizer, and one of those is three giant meatballs in marinara." Claudia barely looks at me before she goes back to the waitress. "And I'd love a Caesar side salad with that."

"Yes, ma'am," she says. She repeats Claudia's order in quick, clipped, single words, and then she leaves.

I shake my head and ask, "Why can't they just write stuff down? I don't get why they do that. I guarantee she's going to mess something up."

"What?" Claudia asks. "What would she mess up?"

"My sides," I say. "My sauces. Your salad."

"It's a Caesar salad, Becks," she says with that beautiful smile.

I reach across the table and take her hand into mine. "I like that smile. It's gorgeous." I lift her hand to my lips.

Claudia nods her acceptance of the compliment at me. "You called me Midnight Beauty. What does that mean?"

"I did? When?"

"Last night," she says. "When I was leaving your house." Her eyes burn now, and I'm learning what all they can do too.

My mind races for a plausible story, and a loud voice in my head that sounds suspiciously like my sister says, *Tell her the truth.*

"Okay, here we go." I pull my hand back lest she doesn't like the story. "I have a hard time remembering names, right?"

"I didn't know that about you."

"Well, I do." I clear my throat. "I usually give everyone a nickname in my head, so I can remember who they are. The more I work with them or the more I get to know them, then I can eventually remember their name."

"So you named me Midnight Beauty." She's not asking, and I simply nod. "But you've never liked me."

"I've always liked you just fine," I say. "You're the one who's never appreciated my company."

"I have good reasons for that."

"I know," I say softly, my eyes suddenly bouncing all over the place. "It's not like I don't know who I am, Claudia."

"Hey, now." She's staring at me, but I can't make my gaze settle on hers. "Beckett."

My eyes dance past hers again, and she slides over and gets up. Surprised, I look up at her, and the next thing I know, I'm moving back as Claudia is clearly going to sit in my lap. She does exactly that, and my arms go around her and my hands find the exact-right spot to settle on her hip and waist.

She strokes one hand down my beard, and while I'm aware we're now sitting atop one another in a very public restaurant, I can't hear anything around me. No restaurant music. No chatter. No clinking of silverware on dishware.

There's only Claudia, and I can't think of a reason why I shouldn't kiss her right here, right now. George Constanza would.

"Claudia."

"I don't like it when you're self-depreciating."

"I'm not kissing you here."

"Did you see the dessert menu?"

It feels like we're having two different conversations, and my brow wrinkles. "No, I didn't."

"I did, and it didn't look like anything we'd like." She strokes her hand down the side of my face again, and she really needs to stop doing that, because I can't contain the shivers cascading through my shoulders, my jaw, and my entire chest. "Maybe we can go back to your place for coffee."

"Mm." I give her humming right back to her, because I don't even know if I have coffee at my place. I can text my neighbor and ask her to leave some on my porch, and she will. My mind is splintered a little, and then Claudia stands and returns to her place across the table from me.

"No more bashing on yourself."

I nod, but I do know the history Claudia and I have over the past seven years of working together. "I haven't always been the nicest," I say. "I'm sorry about that."

"Heaven knows I could've been nicer too." She nods like that's that, and then two men approach our table, and they're each carrying at least two dishes.

"Ah." I clap my hands together. "The appetizers are here."

———

A COUPLE OF HOURS LATER, I'm lazily walking with Claudia's hand in mine, my belly the happiest it's been in a while. She's told me she likes to walk a little after eating so much, and we bypassed the parking garage and have been wandering down the boardwalk along the beach for several minutes.

It's quiet here, with lights from various houses and businesses barely piercing the night sky that seems so black over the open ocean. The conversation has stalled after a great meal of back-and-forth, laughter, and great food.

"I love that place," Claudia finally says into the silence around us. "Tara and Alec are going to do well with it."

"I hope so," I say.

She slows even more, and we come to a stop next to some foliage and a palm tree. "We should head back now."

"I never texted my neighbor about the coffee," I say.

A frown twitches across her expression. "What?"

"I don't think I actually own coffee," I say.

"What about on the weekend?"

"I get in the truck and go to Legacy," I say.

"I don't drink coffee this late at night anyway," she says.

"Then why did you...?" My voice trails off, because Claudia's eyes are telling me so much right now.

"Do you kiss for the first time on the beach?" she whispers.

"Yes." I don't waste any more time, because I've just-now realized that Claudia has set us up for the perfect first kiss. I take her face in both of my hands and lean down, praying with a pounding heart that I remember how to kiss a woman.

My lips touch hers, and every cell in my body explodes with heat and desire and tension and absolute joy. Turns out, I do remember what to do, and I press into her further as she kisses me back and our kiss goes from simple and new to passionate and delicious in only a moment.

CLAUDIA

BECKETT KISSES LIKE A TOTAL PROFESSIONAL. HE pulls away far too soon and asks, "You don't even drink coffee this late at night?"

My heartbeat races through my ears, making his words somewhat muted. My face is still tilted up toward his, and I stretch up and kiss him again. The first time held pure passion, and it made me feel like a queen.

This time, he lets me set the pace, and I keep it a little slower than last time, really trying to commit him to memory. When I pull away, I breathe, "No, I don't." I open my eyes and look up at him.

"You just wanted to get me back to my place so you could kiss me." His eyes are dark in the dim light, and I find him so deliciously handsome.

"You said you wouldn't kiss me at the Big House."

He doesn't argue with me, and he doesn't kiss me

again. Beckett simply looks down at me, and I'm not sure I can walk in a straight line right now anyway. I didn't drink alcohol—and I didn't super love the mock Paloma, but Beckett drank the whole thing—but the Earth has shifted slightly from those kisses.

He holds me in his arms, his eyes drifting closed again, and then he brings me closer in a light, yet perfect, embrace. "I sure do like you, Claudia."

I swallow, because I can't just say nothing in return. Besides, I like Beckett too. Obviously. I don't go around kissing everyone. "I like you too, Becks."

"I like it when you call me Becks."

"I can't believe you don't have coffee at your house."

"I'll get some for next time." He pulls away and takes my hand again, leading me gently back the way we've come. "When can we go out again?"

I know what I want to say, but I don't know if I dare say it. "Whenever," I say. "What's your aunt's schedule like?"

"I'm meeting my sister and her husband for dinner tomorrow," he says. "We try to get together every couple of weeks, and tomorrow's dinner at her house."

"Oh, that's fun." I smile over to him, though I'd love to go to dinner with him again tomorrow. "Do you have your schedule memorized?"

"I try to have the next twenty-four hours mapped out," he says as if everyone does that. "Plus Liv has texted me fifteen hundred times today about this date." He glances over to me now, and I find him so intriguing.

"She has? What does she say?"

"Stuff like 'be cool, Becks. Don't talk too much, okay? Promise me you'll call me tonight, unless you get back after eleven, then call me in the morning.'" He grins, and it's obvious he loves his sister. And that she loves him.

"So you're going to tell her how it went?"

"Mm-hm, yeah. Yep. I tell her almost everything." He focuses now that we're in the parking garage, and we don't speak again until we're both in his truck, buckled, and backing out. "Does that bother you?"

"Depends on what you say," I tell him. "I mean, are you going to say it was the best kiss of your life? Then that's fine. If you're going to tell her you're going to have to end things with me, because there wasn't any spark, then I don't want to know."

"Claudia, sweetheart," he says, his voice almost a whisper. "There are infernos with you."

I smile to the side window, because that's exactly how I feel too. "So Thursday for dinner?"

"Sure," he says, glancing over to me. "Do you have a preference?"

"Yeah," I say. "I prefer you plan the perfect date and take me on it."

He chuckles and says, "Noted."

We settle into comfortable silence, and I'm still getting

used to that since nothing with Beckett has been comfortable until the past few days. "If you turn right here, and then take the next left, you can park behind the Big House," I say.

"Do you want me to do that?"

"The camera back there only goes to the edge of the porch."

"Ah, someone wants to kiss me again."

"If you don't want to—" I cut off as he makes the wild right turn, yelping as I reach up for the handle above the window. After we're back on all four wheels, I breathe and say, "All right then."

He makes the left, and I nod to the left. "We're the third one down on this side."

"These lots must be huge."

"They're five-acre parcels," I say. "Tahlia inherited the house from her aunt a few years ago. She can't afford to keep it up without roommates, so she started texting a few of us."

"Why'd you move in?"

I sigh and reach back into my memories. "Well, I was at a point in my life where I needed a change. I thought about buying a place of my own, but the market was really high at the time. And I don't super love yardwork. My lease was almost up, and I didn't care to renew where I was."

"Why's that?" He pulls down the lane to the back of the house, and there's not another single car back here, as we all usually park on the other side.

"My housemate was getting married," I say. "I didn't want to find someone else. And my closet had more spiders than clothes."

"Yikes."

"You own your place?"

"Yeah," he said. "I bought it when I first moved to Cider Cove."

"It's a nice place."

"I like it." He casts me a smile as the truck comes to a stop. "So, work tomorrow. I thought the pitch was great, Claude."

"We can go over the budget," I say. "I've got to get the October calendar finalized, and there's something broken on the website that's not allowing any registrations to go through for the rec center."

"And that's your problem?"

"I helped build the website when I first started here." I sigh and unbuckle. "Walk me up to the porch?"

He doesn't answer verbally, but he jumps out of the truck with plenty of energy, like a golden retriever eager to please me. This date has been practically perfect in every way, but when I get out of the truck, Beckett isn't there. I glance over the corner of the hood, and he's not coming.

"Becks?"

"I'm pretty sure I broke my ankle," he calls, and the pain in his voice isn't hard to hear though I can't see him.

"What?" I hurry around the truck, which isn't much of a hurry at all due to my shoes.

He's sitting on the gravel, leaning against the front tire of his truck, holding his right ankle. "There's a big rock there, and I landed right on it." He nods to the offending stone. "My ankle bent right in half."

I drop to my knees. "Beckett, I'm so sorry." I reach for him and push his hair off his forehead.

He looks up at me, and it takes a moment for my brain to compute that he's grinning, not about to burst into tears.

"You devil," I say, moving to swat at him the way I did in the janitorial closet.

He starts to laugh, and he pulls me into his chest. His kiss is sloppy this time, but it's still one of the better kisses of my life. I start to laugh against his lips too, and since kneeling on gravel isn't the most comfortable thing ever, I roll onto my hip and sit beside him instead.

Beckett takes my hand in his as we settle our laughter into silence. "Now we've both stumbled during drop-off."

"Yours was fake," I say, though I appreciate the sentiment.

"No, I really did twist my ankle," he says. "Do you think I'd get down on the ground in these shorts?"

"You and your clothes."

"You love my clothes."

I can't deny it, so I say nothing. I look up to the house, which has some cheery yellow light coming from one of the second-floor bedrooms, as well as the kitchen. "My room is on the third floor," I say. "I'm the only one up there now that Hillary moved to LA."

His head leans against the truck, but he flops it toward me. "You miss her."

"Yeah," I admit. "I've got my other roommates, and my brother—Iron Mountain."

"And there's the paint color swear," he teases. "What's that for and what color is it?"

I sigh, my thoughts already moving and shifting to try to make room for dinner on Thursday. "It's actually a great dark gray for bathrooms and bedrooms."

"Okay," he says, chuckling now. "What made you break out the cursing?"

"My brother, Luke, lives here. Remember I told you that?"

"Yeah, sure."

"We're going to this new psychological thriller he's obsessed with on Thursday. He's got a sitter and everything." I lean my head against the truck and look at Beckett. "I can try to change it."

"It's okay if you go with him," he says. "We can go out Friday."

"I've got nothing on Friday," I say. "At least, I'll check."

He smiles at me, and we move toward each other at the same time. He kisses me in a slow yet urgent way, and I cup my hand around his jaw as I kiss him back. Then he pulls away and gets to his feet with a groan. "All right, Midnight Beauty. Let's get you home."

I feel like a fairy-tale princess as he holds my hand all the way to the back door, and then he whispers, "I'm going to kiss you on camera," and then does exactly what the Prince in all movies do—they kiss their princess for anyone and everyone to see.

———

WEDNESDAY FADES INTO THURSDAY, and Beckett texts me about his dinner with his sister. I meet up with my brother for the movie he's excited about, and I text Beckett about how I love movie theater popcorn so stinking much.

Friday arrives, and we're both on-edge in our separate offices. About four o'clock, Beckett bellows from next door, a loud sound that startles me as it has several times in the past.

"What's going on?" I yell at him without getting up from my desk. We dress down on Fridays, but for me that means I'm wearing a pair of jeans that flow and move like slacks and a pull-over blouse without buttons down the front.

"It's four o'clock," Beckett yells. His footsteps sound throughout the trailer, I swear, and then he appears in my office doorway. "When are they going to email out who got the Christmas Festival bid?" He paces toward Sybil's desk, grabs one of the candies she keeps there, and comes back toward me.

Behind him, I see Sybil's look of distaste, but it only makes me smile now.

"I'm *dying*," he says.

"You're so impatient," I tell him, though there's a certain amount of unease rippling through me too.

He pops the strawberry candy in his mouth and immediately starts choking. I jump to my feet and hurry toward him at the same time my phone rings. The one on my desk. Only Sybil calls me on that phone, and only so she can put through calls that have come in through the department.

"Sybil?"

"Not me," she says, and then she's behind Beckett. She gives him a decently hard *slap-slap* on the back, and he coughs as the candy comes out of his windpipe.

Then we're all staring at the phone on my desk.

"Get it, Claudia," Beckett barks.

His voice launches me into motion, and I lunge for the receiver. "Claudia Brown," I say, my voice breathless.

"Claudia," a man says. "It's Winslow Harvey."

"Winslow, hello," I say. Before I can turn toward my co-workers, Beckett is at my side, pressing the speaker-phone button.

"Hello, sir," he says before I can say another word. Irritating, sure, but not nearly as much as it would've been a week ago. "It's Beckett Fletcher here. Sybil is here with us too." He gestures for her to come closer, and I stand there with the receiver at my ear needlessly.

"Oh, good," Winslow says while humiliation runs

through me and I have the good sense to lower the receiver. "You're all there."

"I hope you have good news for us, sir," Beckett says, his worried eyes meeting mine.

I want to add, "Yeah," but I don't want to be petty, and I've got nothing else.

Winslow chuckles. "It depends on what you consider good news, because we'd love your department to take on the Christmas Festival this year, and that's no small task."

I pull in a breath, because while this is what I wanted, I didn't actually think we'd get it. "Wow, thank you, sir," I say.

"Does that include Larry?" Beckett asks. "Because we haven't kept him up to speed on this project."

"You'll need the manpower," Winslow says. "We have some temporary employees we'll be sending your way too."

Beckett and I look at each other, and it's clear neither of us like this news. At the same time, it might take a whole committee to pull off the Christmas Festival. I suddenly feel like I can't stand up under the weight of this assignment, and I sink into one of my guest chairs.

"What do you guys think?" Winslow asks. "I'll need a final budget by the end of the month, and if you have more needs for personnel, you'll have to submit the proper forms."

"Of course," I say.

"We're excited to take this on," Beckett says, and he

actually sounds like he is. Of course. He's the golden retriever between us. I'm already thinking how I'd rather curl into bed and let someone else handle the massive Christmas Festival for Cider Cove, the way a diva-cat would.

Beckett says something else to Winslow, and then the call ends. He reaches over and taps the button to take it off speaker, and then he takes the receiver from me and resets it back in the cradle.

A moment of silence passes, and then he thrusts both fists high into the air, and bellows, "We got the Christmas Festival!"

His enthusiasm is contagious, and I start to come out of the stupor I've fallen into. I smile as Sybil says, "My word, Beckett, you're *so loud*." She rolls her eyes, glances at me, and then marches out of my office.

I get to my feet about the same time Beckett sweeps me into his arms. "Becks," I squeal, because while I sat on his lap a few nights ago, I'm far too heavy for him to swing around. Yet somehow he manages it, and when I stumble back to my feet, he's laughing.

As he sobers, his smile stays stitched in place. "We got it, Claude."

"Yeah," I say. "We got it."

"We got it," he whispers, and I match my smile to his and melt into his embrace—because we got the Christmas Festival...together, and somehow that feels way better than beating him.

RYANNE

I STRIDE DOWN THE AISLE, IGNORING SOMEONE AS they call my name. Yes, I hear them. No, I don't have the patience left to deal with someone who should know what aisle the paperclips are on.

Miguel is a nice guy, but he has the attention span of a gnat and a worse memory than Dory on that fish movie I can't remember the name of. Dory, though, I can remember.

The black plastic door signals relief, and if I can just make it there, I can disappear into my office for a few minutes, gather my sanity back together, and then figure out how to answer all the texts that have flooded my phone today.

Work texts. Roommate texts. And the worst of all, family texts.

My hand slaps the door just as someone else—not Miguel—says, "Ry?"

I roll my eyes and keep going. Elliott Hutson is my co-manager here at Paper Trail, and I can't blow him off as easily as our newest hire, but I still don't slow my steps. He'll follow me, and I won't be able to get into the office we share and lock the door.

It's fine. It's Elliott, I tell myself, and I glance over my shoulder as he comes through the swinging door and says, "Ryanne."

I don't know what he sees in my face, but he doesn't call after me again. I turn the corner and then make another sharp left into the office where we've got two desks. Mine is the furthest from the door, and we have a full-size fridge standing between our workstations. Across from them is a black leather sofa where I've been known to take an afternoon nap and covering that whole wall is our company goals and objectives, a white board with our employees on it, including their names, pictures, and hire date, and a corkboard with the next two weeks of the schedule.

I do all of that, and I spend a lot of time standing in front of that wall, so I deserve those afternoon naps sometimes.

I don't close the door and lock it like I'd planned, because I know Ell is right on my heels. Still, I move over to the fridge, a big sigh coming out of my mouth as I open the door and reach for a package of the not-for-sale-any-longer Strawberried Peanut Butter M&Ms.

I'm the easiest person on the planet to shop for—all you have to do is buy me M&Ms. I love them in all their flavors, though I will admit the crunchy espresso ones aren't my favorite. If someone really wants to win me over, they'll buy the biggest bag of peanut butter M&Ms they can find, though I like these strawberried ones too.

"Ry," Elliott says from the doorway, and I turn toward him with the bag of candy clearly visible. His eyes drop to it, and then so do mine as I rip open the top. You can't just rip straight across either. That's why the bags have those fringed ends. You have to go down into one of those and then across, a skill I mastered at the age of six.

"What?" I ask, and if the appearance of one of my most coveted candies hasn't tipped him off to my foul mood, my tone certainly has.

He enters the office and closes the door. It's got a window in it, and another big window overlooks his desk as well. They've got blinds, but we never close them. In fact, the office door is rarely closed, but everyone knows to knock if it is.

"What's going on?" he asks. "You haven't answered any of my texts for hours."

I reach into the bag and pluck out a couple of M&Ms. "I'm texter-whelmed," I say.

Elliott smiles at me, and it's no wonder he's always got someone on his arm. He's practically perfect in the looks department, what with his dark hair that curls on the ends. That full beard. Those dark, dreamy eyes, that symmetrical smile, and all those white teeth.

He once confessed to me that he can't stand feeling like his teeth are dirty, so he brushes after every single thing he eats. I gave him a multi-pack of toothbrushes and toothpaste in bulk a couple of months ago, and he laughed, hugged me, and said none of it would go to waste.

Sure, I've entertained a crush or two on him, but we work together, and he's literally always had a girlfriend. He flits from woman to woman like a dog after this ball—no that one, or oh! This one!—and I'm not super interested in someone like that.

I want a man I can settle down with, who'll do all the jobs around the house and yard I don't want to do, and who'll understand that I'm perfectly content with my management job at a mid-size paper company in small-town Cider Cove.

"Let me see your phone." He holds out his palm as he comes forward.

I don't even hesitate to give it to him. "You're going to be sorry." I turn away from his good-looks and sink into my desk chair. I get a new one every few months, because this is an office supply store, and I can literally walk out onto the sales floor and take one.

Elliott sits in his chair too, his eyes trained on my phone. I eat my PB&J M&Ms while he swipes, taps, and reads. He scoffs a couple of times, then he exhales, and then he goes, "Oh, boy."

"Which one are you on?" I glance over to him. "The one where my roommate says we have to do the yardwork ourselves this year, or the one where my mama *and* my daddy are asking if I have a boyfriend?"

Before he can answer, I go, "Wait. Or the one where you're asking me where the cardstock brights are?"

He looks up then, and he has the decency to look sheepish. He does have the puppy dog eyes down pat, and he gives them to me now, looking up at me through his long eyelashes—I swear, why do men always have the luxurious-eyelash gene when we women would literally sacrifice a goat or two for them?—and giving me a half-smile.

"I couldn't find it."

"I'm tired of being a tour guide in our own store." I pop another candy-coated chocolate into my mouth and wait for him to explain. When he doesn't, I ask, "Did you find it?"

"Yes," he says curtly, his version of being upset.

"And where was it?"

He glares at me and extends the phone toward me. But we're too far apart for me to simply reach out and take it from him, so I don't even move. He sighs like I've caused him to climb Mount Everest to give the phone back, and he gets up and puts it on my desk near my elbow.

"I'd do a yardwork trade with you," he says nonchalantly.

But I inhale sharply and nearly choke to death on one of my favorite candies. I start to wheeze and cough, because those Strawberried Peanut Butter M&Ms are just the right size to fill a windpipe without going down it.

"Oh, my word." Elliott wears his eyeroll in his tone and gives me a couple of smacks on the back. Just enough to get the candy out of my lungs, and as I quiet, he hands me a water bottle from the fridge, the cap already twisted off.

No wonder women like him so much. I can't figure out why he ends things with them, but he does when he claims "things get too serious." But he doesn't like being alone, so he'll have someone new within a couple of weeks.

"You'll come do the yardwork at the Big House?" I ask. "That's huge, Ell. You can't just say that and expect me not to react."

"It's a trade," he says pointedly as he retakes his chair. "That means you have to come help me with mine."

"Oh." Well, that changes everything, and I don't want to do more yardwork than I have to. But if he comes and helps, the leaves at the Big House will get cleaned up faster. None of us will have to do as much. Claudia has said her brother can come help, and Emma said she thought she could get Aaron from the hardware store to come too.

Another male would be handy, and I can't really tell

him no now that the offer's been extended. "Okay," I say. "Tahlia wants us to get things cleaned up this weekend." I glance over to the corkboard. "You're working until two."

"I can be there by two-thirty. You guys won't be done by then, will you?"

"Who knows?" I roll my shoulders slightly. "We don't like getting up too early on the weekend, and we have five acres and big trees..."

"I can be there by two-thirty," he says again. "And if I'm only there for a couple of hours, then you can come help me for a couple of hours." He backs into his seat, and it further slides away from me as he falls into it.

"Fine," I say. "I'll tell everyone." I twist and pick up my phone to text on my Big House thread. "What should I tell my parents about the...boy-friend-iss-hue?"

Elliott chuckles, and while my thumbs fly across the screen, I still see him shaking his head in my field of vision. "I don't know on that one, Ry. Why do they care so much?"

"Because, Ell, most people in their thirties are looking for a life partner. You know, someone to settle down with, get married, that kind of thing."

"Yeah, but is that what *you* want?"

I finish telling everyone Elliott can come help with the yardwork this weekend and look at him. Surprise moves through me at his somewhat judgmental and somewhat distasteful expression. "I...yeah, Ell. Most people want that. Just because you're a total player doesn't—"

"I am not a total player." He turns away from me and toward his desk. "Just because I don't want to get married doesn't mean I'm out with different women all the time. I have one girlfriend at a time." He throws me a murderous look, but I've seen and withstood it before. "The way normal men do. I'm not doing anything wrong because I don't want anything serious."

"Why don't you?" I ask. My phone starts to buzz all over again, and I glance at it. "Everyone is excited you'll be coming. Oh, wow." I grin at Lizzie's text.

"What?" Elliott asks.

I flip my phone over, my own fantasies now running wild. "Nothing." But Lizzie now has me thinking of my co-manager shirtless.

"I know that look, Ry," Elliott says.

I turn away from him too, because I actually have a corner desk, and I can put my back to him and the door and look like I'm working. "I don't have a look."

"Oh, but you do." His chair rolls against the tile floor, and I'm not surprised when he hovers over my shoulder only a moment later. "Let me see."

"It's just Lizzie," I say. "She'd like to see you rake leaves in only shorts."

"In only...shorts?" He starts to laugh, but it's all I can think about now. Which makes no sense. I haven't been crushing on Elliott for a while now.

"Or use a power tool," I say as nonchalantly as possible.

"Yeah?" He finishes chuckling. "Like a topless lumber-jack? Chopping wood?"

"I think it would need to be a chainsaw," I say as I look up to him, a smile touching my mouth. There for only a moment, and then gone. I look back at the desk calendar, trying to remember what I need to do before I can go home for the day. "And men aren't 'topless.' They're 'shirtless.'"

"It's still objectification," he says.

"Absolutely it is," I say.

"What would you say if I texted that you had to rake leaves shirtless?"

I face him again, noting the sourness twisting his lips. "I didn't text that."

"But you were all smiley about it."

"Well, you're not bad-looking, Ell. It's a compliment." He rolls his eyes, and I quickly say, "I'm sorry on her behalf. Okay? Because you're right. It's not fair to objectify you."

He nods and says, "Thank you," as he sits at his desk.

"I'll tell her you're going out with Millie. Then she won't be all flirty this weekend."

"I broke up with Millie."

I pull in a breath. "You what? When? Didn't you just take her to the Harvest Festival?"

"Yeah," he says. "But she asked me if I'd ever thought about having kids, so..."

"Deal-breaker," I say, because that's Elliott. I know he didn't have the best childhood, but he hasn't told me everything about it. His parents divorced young, and according to him, he was used as a pawn by both his mother and his father. In fact, he only started talking to them again in the past couple of years. Maybe three or four.

"Who are you going out with now?" I ask him.

"No one," he says. "Contrary to your belief, I don't have women waiting in the wings, so when things end with one, I don't go out with the next the very next day."

"Hey." I spin toward him, a pinch in my chest. "I don't think that."

Elliott throws me another glare, and this one is serious. He's not kidding, and he's not giving me any mock attitude. He's legit upset.

I don't want that. "I really don't."

"I know you do," he says quietly. "Everyone does." He gets up and reaches for the doorknob, twists it, and walks out while I say, "Elliott," in my best *don't-go* voice.

"Ell!"

He still goes, and that's just the cherry on top of my no-good day. And I still don't have an answer for my parents about when I might have a boyfriend to bring home.

"Wait, wait, wait, wait-wait-wait-wait."

I sigh so Liv knows she's being overly dramatic. "I'm waiting," I say.

"So you're working on the Christmas Festival together."

"Yes," I say though my sister hasn't asked me a question.

She gazes at me from across the table, her London Fog rapidly cooling in front of her. "You've been out with her several times now."

I smile, because Liv gets texts—and sometimes calls—after every date. "Yes."

"Things are going well."

"I think so."

"And now, you want to invade her dog-walking weekends."

I roll my eyes. "I'm not invading her weekends. I suggested we walk her dogs together this weekend." I reach for my post-dinner cup of coffee—a regular dark roast with plenty of sugar—and take a sip. "And she said yes."

"But she needs her alone-time," Liz protests. "Listen, Becks, I know you don't get this, because you're an extrovert. You're some, some, some overeager beaver. You don't need personal space. But Claudia? I mean, I've never met her—" She points at me violently. "Which I'm still mad about, by the way, but from what you've said, she likes her personal space."

"I have never uttered those words." I set my coffee cup back on its saucer. "And we've been dating for what? Two weeks? Maybe two and a half now." I think of that Tuesday-night kiss, and yes, it was two weeks and two days ago. "That's way too early for me to introduce her to a family member."

Liv scoffs and tosses her dark hair over her shoulder. "That's ridiculous."

"Well, not all of us fall in love on the first date and get engaged within thirty days." I raise my eyebrows at her, but my sister's eyes narrow at me.

"You're not going to distract me with my own love story." She lowers her pointed finger but now folds her arms. "And you know what? Matt and I are still together, and we love each other, and we have a great marriage."

I nod, sobering. "I know."

"I think you should reconsider the dog-walking."

"Maybe just on Sunday," I muse, because I generally trust Liv when it comes to her advice on my love life. "Things went fine last weekend with the yard work at the Big House."

Liv rolls her eyes. "That's different, Becks."

"How?" I challenge. "I saw her on the weekend then—and with her roommates." I glance up as the waiter arrives with the chocolate tuxedo cake we ordered to share. He sets it down, along with two forks, and nods his way off to his next task.

I reach for a fork, because this is one of my favorite desserts in the world. I don't eat a ton of sweet stuff, but when I do, I want it to be chocolate cake, chocolate mousse, vanilla custard, chocolate frosting, and chocolate chips.

"Surely going walking with her in the morning won't be that big of a deal."

"It is if it smothers her."

"Believe it or not, Liv, she seems to like me." I fork off a bite of cake while Liv picks up a utensil.

"Becks, just think for two seconds." She pauses with a bite of perfectly layered cake on her fork. "You see her all day at work. Then you go out together at night, every night."

"Not tonight," I say, but Liv forges on anyway.

"Her hour on Saturday and Sunday mornings might be all the time she gets to be alone," Liv says. "She lives with other women. You were over there last weekend to help with yard work for both weekend days." She slides her cake into her mouth. "I'm just saying."

I grin and half-laugh. "Yeah, I know what you're saying. This cake is the bomb." I take another bite too, but now I'm all worried about crowding into Claudia's space when she doesn't want me there.

After I swallow, I say, "And for the record, I don't see Claudia all day, every day. We still have plenty of separate things we're working on."

"You know what I mean, Becks."

"Claudia is a grown woman," I say. "If she doesn't want to see me, she'll tell me." At least she's never held back in the past, on anything.

"Do you go to lunch every day together?"

"Not every day," I say. "Sometimes Sybil orders in. Sometimes we run out. It's...casual."

"Oh, Becks." Liv shakes her head. "Does she know that nothing with you is casual?"

"No." I point my fork at her. "Which is why I haven't introduced her to you yet, thank you very much."

Liv scoffs. "Please. I'm the easiest person to introduce to a woman."

"But you talk too much," I mutter.

"Family trait," she shoots back at me. Our eyes meet, and as one, we both burst out laughing. She sobers faster than me, and when I look at her again, she's wearing only earnestness in her eyes. They're wide and quite a bit darker than mine. "Seriously, Becks. I know how much you like this woman, and I don't want you to go too fast."

"I'm not," I say. "We're walking around Riverside Park with five dogs. That's like, the definition of not-serious."

"But you *want* to be serious with her," Liv said, frowning. "Right?"

"Of course," I say. "I'm just saying, you're making this dog-walking thing into something when it's nothing." I wave my fork like it's a magic wand, and whatever I say next will automatically become true. "It's literally a walk in the park."

"Ha ha." Liv rolls her eyes and finally lifts her now-cold London Fog to her lips. She moans and makes a scowly face and practically spits the tea back into her cup. Okay, she doesn't do that, but I can tell it takes great effort for her to swallow it. "That's cold."

"That's because you've been lecturing me for too long," I say as she starts glancing around for our waiter. She'll demand a hot London Fog, and then the conversation will finally turn to something besides my love life, and I grin at my sister.

Now I'm a little worried about "invading" Claudia's alone-time on Saturday morning, so I determine I'll simply ask her about it tomorrow.

———

I FORGET to ask Claudia about going dog-walking together, and so when I wake on Saturday morning, it's with anxiety and anticipation swimming in my blood. "Shoot," I say, rolling over to reach my phone. I sit up while one of my dogs yawns, and I swipe and tap and tap again to call her.

Her phone rings once, then twice, then three times, and that's when I realize how early my alarm goes off, no matter the day of the week. Swearing under my breath, I pull the phone away from my ear to hang up about the time Claudia answers with, "Your house better be on fire," in the sexiest, throatiest voice I've heard her use.

"I forgot," I blurt out as I bring the phone back to my ear. "It's so early. I'm sorry."

"You forgot what?"

"What time I get up."

"Why are you calling me?"

"I wanted to make sure it's...okay—uh, okay for me to —invade." I press my eyes closed and take a deep breath. "I just wondered if we're still okay for dog-walking this morning."

"Yes." She yawns. "But I swear, if you call me before eight a.m. on a Saturday morning ever again, that'll be it for us."

I laugh, but Claudia, in all her black cat aloofness, does not. "Okay, go back to bed, Midnight *Sleeping* Beauty." I hang up before she can growl or yowl or otherwise protest. I'm up now, and I don't nap or fall back asleep unless I'm sick, so I head into the bathroom to get ready and brush my teeth. I don't normally get ready before my run on the weekends, but I'm not running today.

Claudia made that very, very clear. *Today is a walking day, Becks. I don't run.*

Since I just want to see her in those Spandex pants again, I don't care how fast we go.

I get dressed in my shorts and tee too, leash up the dogs, and say, "Let's go, guys." I can get in a few miles before Claudia shows up at the park, and I might even have time to run, get coffee, and then meet her at Riverside. No matter what, she didn't cancel at my dawn wake-up call, so Liv might not be the dating expert I've been led to believe she is.

We arrive at the park and I take a moment to stretch my calves, though I really should go through a full-body warm-up. I tell myself I'm going to go slow, and I do. At least in the beginning. It always takes me a half-mile or so for my thoughts to truly settle onto what they need to work through, and today, it's the Christmas Festival when I anticipated it being Claudia.

She's been rotating through my mind for the past few weekends now, but this morning, there's a checklist of what needs to be accomplished this next week so we can stay on track for the Christmas Festival to begin on December fourth.

I'd brought up the idea of a Living Bethlehem, and Claudia's whole face had lit up like the downtown

Christmas trees we contracted to have decorated by Thanksgiving. The town of Cider Cove just concluded their Harvest Festival, and thankfully, neither Claudia nor I had much to do with that.

I also have a half-dozen phone calls to make this next week to my benefactors. I also got the job of finding sponsors for the festival, and that hasn't proven to be too difficult. Our small town businesses want their names in programs and on banners, and the hardest ones will be the bigger places that can afford to pay more.

We're gonna need it to fund the catered breakfast and subsidize the couples' movie night.

I let that thought sit there and ruminate while I round the bend, Rocky and Duke right in step with me. I love running, because everything goes soft in my life, and the important things come to the front.

Today, I only have lists in my head instead of questions, and I don't realize how long I've been going or how far, because my phone rings. It vibrates against my bicep, and I slow with realization.

"Claude," I pant into the phone. "You here?"

"Yep, just arrived," she said. "You just ran past me without even seeing me."

I reach to pop out my earbuds and turn at the same time, and sure enough, about a hundred yards back the way I've come is an entrance to the walking path in Riverside Park.

It's Saturday morning, so plenty of people have come

this morning, but I start walking back that way. "I don't see you."

"I'm headed your way. See you in a sec." She hangs up on me—legit ends the call without even telling me—and I try to get my pulse to calm down a little.

I'm on the wrong side of the path, so I dodge a woman and her tiny dog to get back where I belong now that I'm going the other way. Only a few steps later, I spot Claudia and her three canines.

She's pulled her hair back, and she's wearing a rainbow striped tank top with a pair of black leggings that have sparkles down the sides. She steals my breath, and she hasn't even looked my way yet.

"Claude," I say, and she looks over to me. She smiles, and I do a wide arc to go to her side and get walking the same direction as her.

"Morning," I say.

"Yep," she says. "It's morning." She's walking a big black schnauzer, a teeny little beige poodle, and a more apricotty goldendoodle. They don't seem to mind Rocky or Duke at all, and all five of the dogs trot or walk along without issue.

"Bad night?" I ask.

She looks over to me out of the corner of her eye. "Lizzie had some chemist friends over for a dinner party."

"Sounds...*reactive*."

She scoffs, but I've got more where that came from.

"Did they *ionically* bond?"

"Becks, stop it." But she sounds only a moment away from laughing.

"Oh, you're upset because the conversation was so *elementary*. Hopefully she only does these types of parties *periodically*."

She laughs then, and I feel like I'm king of the world. I grin into the sunshine, but my calves and thighs have popping muscles since I was running full-out and then stopped so suddenly.

"How do you come up with this stuff?" she asks through her giggles. "Especially when you hate puns."

"Hey, you gave me the material by mentioning chemists." I glance over to her. "Does Lizzie work at ChemTech?"

"Yeah," she says. "Yep. She says chemists are boring."

"Sounds stereotypical."

"You only say that because there are a lot of accountant jokes." She gives me one of those sideways grins I like so much.

"We're not all dry as toast," I say. "It is possible to like math *and* have a personality."

"If you say so."

I grin and put my arm around her. I lean down and press a kiss to her forehead. "I'm not invading your space, am I?"

"Invading my space?"

"Yeah." The whole story with Liv pours out, and we've gone at least a quarter-mile while I've been jabbering. I finally tell myself to stop, and I succeed. We walk in silence now, the activity around us grating on my nerves.

"So?" I prompt.

"Beckett." Claudia nudges me to the right, which means I have to step off the path. I do, the grass softer under my sneakers, and while I prefer the hard surface, I'm more keen to hear what Claudia has to say.

We take the dogs to the edge of the grass before it slopes down to the river, after which the park is named, and Claudia stands there.

"Do you, uh, get paid to do dog-standing?"

She shakes her head and faces me. "Beckett," she says. "If I don't want you to come walking with me, I'd just tell you that."

"Okay."

"You sound like you don't believe me."

I shrug slightly. "I dated a woman once who told me over and over she didn't play games. Pretty much what you just said. That she'd just tell me what she wanted, but...she didn't."

"Do you think I'd play games with you?"

"I...honestly, Claude? I don't know. We've been dating for a few weeks now is all."

"We've worked together for seven years."

"We've disliked each other for seven years," I say softly.

She leans her head against my bicep, and the moment

is quiet and sweet, despite the busyness of the water in front of us and the park behind.

After several moments, wherein my heartbeat finally slows enough from the running I'd been doing, she says, "You're right. They don't pay me to dog-stand. Let's get going again." She turns away from the river and starts back toward the path.

I follow her, because I'm like one of her leashed canines. I want to be where she is, and I want to trot along at her side and ask her questions, get to know her, share myself with her, all to find out if a woman like her could ever fall in love with a guy like me.

CLAUDIA

I've about got the November calendar finalized and the email with all the bullet points ready to send off to Public Relations when a commotion outside my office door has me looking away from my computer screen.

It's not Beckett, because he'd be far louder than that. His voice deeper. The noise angrier.

This noise is cheerful and shrill, and I get to my feet to see who's come in. I've barely gained the door when I realize it's Tabby, Beckett's secretary. She's back from her maternity leave.

Or she should be in another week or so. Today, she's brought in her baby, and I'm drawn to the infant in a way I can't describe. Smiling, I leave my office and head toward the couple of desks where Sybil and Tabby usually sit.

Tabby's baby is sitting in her carrier on the desk, and

as I arrive, Tabby lifts the infant out. "We named her Penny," she says, grinning at her baby.

"She's the cutest thing alive," I say.

"She really is," Sybil says. "Can I have her?" She takes the little girl, who's decked out from head to toe in pink, from her bow to her booties. "Oh, Tabby, she's simply amazing." She coos at the little girl while I step into Tabby.

"Hey." I give her a hug and pull back. "We are *dying* here without you."

"I know I am," Beckett says from behind me, and Tabby straightens. She tugs on the hem of her shirt, and she looks like she's been stunned by a taser when Beckett laughs and engulfs her in a hug too.

"Mister Fletcher," she says, her voice marked with scandal.

"Don't worry," Sybil says in her baby-coo voice. "He and Claudia are dating."

"You're *what?*" Tabby pulls away from Beckett like he's the source of the taser electricity. She looks at me with clear shock, her eyes blinking and blinking like she has to do it manually. "You're dating him? You don't even—"

I don't have a baby to distract me, but I shoot Sybil a glare I wish had knives coming out of it. "Like Sybil hasn't been texting you for the past few weeks."

"Am I really that different?" Beckett asks, and that brings all of our attention back to him. He looks from me, to Sybil—who cowardly uses the baby to avoid eye contact

—to Tabby. He folds his arms, making himself look bigger, and glares. "Well?"

"Oh, there you are, Mister Fletcher." Tabby grins, and I manage to crack a smile for half a second. Beckett sees it, though, and he is not amused.

"You're...a little..." I look to Sybil for help, but she's curled up in her desk chair, that adorable pink-dressed human consuming her whole attention.

"Barky?" Tabby supplies.

"I mean, you *used* to be," I say to Beckett as I move a little closer to him. I've never been one for overt displays of affection with any of my boyfriends, and Beckett is no different. Certainly not here in the office.

"And so arrogant," Tabby says.

"Okay," I tell her. Usually, I don't mind how she stands up to Beckett, but the way his face falls is obvious, and she doesn't seem to see it. She meets my eye, and she seems to understand that I'm telling her not to make such a big deal out of this.

Her face blooms red, and she scurries to her desk. "Should I call for lunch?"

"You're not working today," Beckett says. "You don't need to do that." With that, he turns and re-enters his office. He doesn't look at me before he departs, and my heart jumps up into the back of my throat. I don't want him to feel bad, and that's my first inclination that so much has changed in the last month or so.

Only three weeks, my mind whispers at me. I can't

believe it's only been three weeks since I kissed Beckett on the boardwalk by the beach.

"How long can you stay?" I ask Tabby while eyeing Beckett's open doorway. He's not so much of a beast that he's slammed it, as that would go against all of his anti-door-closing policies.

"An hour or so," Tabby says with a smile that falters quickly. "I'm not going to get fired, am I? He's just so different." Her green eyes search mine, and she's clearly nervous.

"Oh, honey, he's just being Beckett," I say. "I'll talk to him."

"I've forgotten how to work with other people." Tabby's gaze drops to the ground as shame pours off her. "I didn't mean to upset him. I'll go talk to him."

"No—"

But she turns and marches after Beckett and into his office. "Mister Fletcher," she says right before she closes the door. Oh, she's got less than four minutes before he blows his top, and I find I actually want to see that.

So I stay out in the lobby of our department, and Sybil lets me hold baby Penny. "She's like a squishy bag of flour," I say, grinning at her. "She's so stinking cute." I take a breath of baby, and it's powdery and soft and sweet and amazing.

Beckett's door opens, and both he and Tabby come back out into the lobby. "Mister Fletcher says we can go to lunch today, if everyone has an hour." She looks so hopeful, and she cuts a look over to Sybil that stays for a little too long.

I take the time to study Beckett, as he's paused just outside his doorway, and his eyes haven't left mine. I have no idea what he sees, but he's doing quite a bit of blinking, and his shoulders rise and fall like he's just climbed a couple flights of stairs.

"Did you meet Penny?" I ask. I'm sitting in Tabby's desk chair, the baby cuddled into my arms. I smile down at her and then add, "Come see, Becks."

I ignore the exchanged glance between Sybil and Tabby, and Beckett blinks himself out of whatever trance he's fallen into. He takes the few steps to me and lets his gaze drip down past me to the baby. "She's beautiful," he says.

Penny is beautiful, but I have a feeling Beckett is talking about me. I give him a smile as I wonder what nickname he's making up for this baby, because there's no way he'll remember it. "You said we could go to lunch?"

"Can you?" he asks. "I know you wanted to get that calendar off to Phyllis."

"Her name is Rhonda," I say, my voice full of teasing.

"But she looks like Phyllis from *The Office*."

I stand up and slip the baby into Beckett's arms. He freezes completely as I say, "I need ten minutes to finish up. If you guys want to go ahead without me, I can catch up." I take a couple of steps away from him, and then turn and look over my shoulder.

He's standing there with that baby in his arms, and while she's blonde, and he's not really, and I'm definitely not, I can't help but wonder if Beckett and I would have a beautiful baby like Penny.

Someday.

I go back into my office and settle behind my desk, but my thoughts are all jumbled up now. Tangled with ideas of marriage and family and babies...and I've been dating Beckett for three weeks.

It's too fast to bring up marriage and family and babies, and I vow to myself that I won't do it. I even lift my chin a little higher and get my fingers tappety-tapping on the keyboard. When Beckett comes into my office about five minutes later and collapses into the chair opposite my desk, I can't help but look over to him.

He's babyless now, and he lifts one hand as if to say, *Take your time. I'm just gonna hang here until you're ready.*

We've done this charade before, and I return my attention to my computer. I put the finishing touches on the email, attach the calendar, and hit send. "What did Tabby say?" I ask as nonchalantly as I can.

"You heard her."

"You're not arrogant," I say as I pretend to keep working.

"I am."

"It's tempered when a person knows you better." I finally look over to him.

"Explain."

"For example, when I found out you take care of your aunt every evening, it made you more human. When I saw you running with your dogs, I realized you have a life outside of this office. When I've gone to your house and sat on your old-man swing, you show some vulnerability."

"Okay," he says quietly.

"I'm just saying that we're all a little bit compartmentalized." I lean forward and plant my palms on the desktop. "You have a certain way you act at work, and until any of us see you without the pristine ties and the form-fitting shirts, this version of you is all we know."

I desperately want him to understand. "Don't you think? I mean, you didn't know me outside of work until recently. It took your dogs knocking me down for you to even *see me*." My chest heaves for how much I've spoken, and it's usually the other way around between us. Beckett blabbering while I wait for him to stop.

He appraises me, and he doesn't look as happy as I wish he did. "I saw you."

I scoff and shake my head. "No, you didn't." I get to my feet. "I don't want to talk about this." I open my bottom desk drawer and pull out my purse. "Let's go to lunch." I round my desk while Beckett watches me.

Just as I'm about to pass him, he jumps to his feet and blocks me. I come to a complete standstill, my chest practically touching his. "What?"

"I saw you."

"Beckett." I shake my head, but I don't drop my eyes. I look right into his. "You didn't even recognize me until Landon said my name. It's fine. I don't need you to say you saw me."

"If I didn't see you, why is your nickname Midnight Beauty?"

"Because you're terrible with names." I put one hand on his chest. "I don't want to talk about this right now. Tabby doesn't have much time. Can we go to lunch?"

"Yes," he says huskily. "Let's go to lunch."

I nod, and he turns, taking my hand into his. He squeezes once, because while we haven't talked about it, he also doesn't want to parade our relationship around the office. So, by the time he leads me out toward the secretary desks, his hand is long gone and mine is cold.

As I realize how far I've fallen for Beckett, the only things I can think are paint colors with the word *Midnight* in them.

Midnight Prince.

That's what Beckett is, and I'm still a little surprised that a man like him—yes, smart and confident at work, but also helpful, vulnerable, patient, funny, happy, positive, and the world's fastest texter—likes a woman like me.

I'm pretty quiet on the ride over to Edna's, which is one of my favorite restaurants and Beckett suggested it because of that. I'm a little lost inside my head, because I'm imagining a place where the Midnight Prince and his Midnight Beauty build their life together.

And it's such a great life. One built of trust and love and sunshine the color of Golden Nugget paint.

———

"I'M JUST SAYING," I say as I sit cross-legged on my bed. I adjust my computer so it's not looking up my nose. On the other side of the country, Hillary has a bowl of popcorn too. I reach for mine and continue. "I'm falling too fast for him."

"How long has it been?" she asks.

"Almost a month now," I say. "I told him I couldn't go out with him tonight, because we had a call scheduled." I shake my head and throw back a handful of popcorn. "He knows about the anniversary thing. He says he has something amazing planned for tomorrow night."

"Well, don't sound so happy about it," Hillary says with a smile.

I try to give her a smile. "Hill." I don't have to say much more for her to get it. She's still at work, but she eats some popcorn as she considers me. I take a deep breath. "You're lucky you moved before the fall clean-up. Luke came and helped, though I swear Dylan spread out more leaves than Luke raked up." I smile at Hillary, as she knows my rambunctious nephew. "Ry's co-manager came. Even Aaron came, and hoo-boy, you should've seen the way he kept making eyes at Emma."

"We're coming back to this."

"Of course we are," I say.

"Emma and Aaron?"

"I mean, I didn't ask her about him or anything. Apparently he helps her with things around the flower shop, since it's right next door to the hardware store, and I don't know. She said she mentioned the clean-up, and he volunteered."

"He does take care of Liam's place," Hillary says. "I think he's going to move in there."

"Then they'll be next door at work and at home." I pop more popcorn into my mouth. "Sounds intriguing."

"Yeah, like you being worried about falling too fast for your nemesis."

"He's so much more than I thought he was." I sigh and glance over to the spread on my desk. "I should be devoting more attention to my portfolio, but..." I had been working on it before this call, since Hillary is three hours behind me, and I had to wait for a decent hour for us to chat.

"I don't know," I say. "It's more fun to go to new restaurants with Becks."

"Yeah, I'm sure it is." Hillary grins at me. "You've always liked dating, Claude. The dinners. The dressing up. The magic of the street lamps while you stroll along." She grins at me fondly, and I wish she was here in the room with me.

"I miss you," I whisper.

"The talking, the picking up, the kissing..." She raises

her eyebrows.

"I do love kissing him," I say. "But don't you dare repeat that to anyone."

She giggles and shakes her head. "I would never."

"You'll tell Liam."

"Well, Liam is different," she says.

"Got a diamond yet?"

She shakes her head and eats more popcorn. "We've looked at a couple of shops is all. I don't want a long engagement. Oh!" She leans forward and picks up something off-camera. "Speaking of Aaron and Emma... They sent the map of the wedding. Since we're getting married in Liam's orchards, we had him map it and then Emma went over where the flowers and altar can go."

She holds up a single sheet of paper, but I can't really see what's on it. "And because I don't have to pay for a venue, and Em's letting us have the flowers at cost, I'm going to book the lanterns."

She lowers the paper, and Hillary's face is lit with joy. I grin back at her, her happiness so effusive. "That's amazing," I say. "So an evening wedding?"

"Yes," she says. "A Sunday evening. In the orchards." She shifts at her desk. "My parents have agreed to pay for the dress and the catering." She clears her throat, which is her tell that she's acting happy about what she's said. If I asked her, she'd tell me my tell is silence, because I can't mask my voice as well as she can. "So we splurged on the lanterns."

"You guys can afford the lanterns, even if your mama wasn't paying for the catering." I want Hillary to have more confidence when it comes to her parents and her wedding, but I get why she doesn't. "Is your daddy walking you down the aisle?"

"Yep."

"At least you have that." I duck my head, because I didn't mean to make this about me. "Ahem. Beckett's daddy isn't around here either. He really just has his sister in Columbia and his aunt."

"So," she says, pushing her popcorn bowl off-screen. "Who would walk you down the aisle to Beckett?"

I shake my head, but my grin paints across my face. "Nope," I say. "We're not going there. Talk to me about your dress. Are you going with a traditional white? Like Blinding White or Gardenia? Or maybe something with a touch of gray in it? Silver Satin? Something cream? Lemon Chiffon? I sent you all those paint samples."

Hillary laughs, but I don't get the joke. "You can't pick a wedding dress from paint samples."

"You absolutely can," I say, immediately defensive. "They have dresses in a multitude of white tones these days, Hill. You've got to go in prepared. There might even be some with blue hues." I groan and roll my neck. "I can't believe I didn't send you a blue swatch. There's one called Barely Blue that would be amazing in a shiny fabric for a wedding dress."

"Claude, they don't make blue wedding dresses."

"Of course they do, and you're in *LA*, Hill. You can get anything you want there." I straighten my shoulders and push my hair over them. "I'm going to send you some blues. When are you going dress shopping?"

"Probably not for another month," she says. "The documentary is crazy right now."

I quickly grab a paper and pen from my desk next to the bed. I scrawl out *Icing on the Cake* while saying, "Yes, tell me how the documentary is going." Then I won't forget to pull that pale, pale blue sample for her too.

Once we get off the call, I'll have to go back to my portfolio application. I haven't asked Beckett about his, and he hasn't asked me, but I start toying with the idea. We don't have a bet anymore, but I can't help wondering what will happen to us once the position of City Planner is announced.

If I get it, will he be upset? If he gets it, will I?

Of course you will be, I think as Hillary starts outlining how amazing it is to work with real Hollywood producers. I nod, ask questions, and listen with interest, because Hillary's out there doing what I want to do: she's living her career dreams.

She didn't have to give that up to be with Liam, and I hope I won't lose Beckett if I get the City Planner job over him.

I hope, I hope, I hope...

BECKETT

I look up as someone leans in my doorway. I pull away from my work and relax back into my desk chair. "Hey, beautiful."

"Do I need to dress up tonight?"

"It's our one-month anniversary. What do you think I have planned?"

"I'm guessing something I need to dress up for."

"I'd wear some good shoes and be hungry," I say.

Her eyebrows go up. "Good shoes? Like, hiking shoes?" Her nose wrinkles cutely in disgust.

"No, baby." I get up, laughing. "Dancing. *Dancing* shoes."

"Like *Footloose* dancing?" She grins at me as I take her into my arms. "Or like this?" She sways with me right there in the doorway, and as I look past her, I see both secretary desks empty. Tabby comes back to work next week, but Sybil is clearly off somewhere else at the moment.

"Like this," I whisper as I slow-dance her further into my office. I want to kiss her, something I've never done in my office, but I don't want anyone to see should they happen to come around the corner and into our department.

I dip my head, but Claudia pulls away. "Becks, no."

"No?"

"We work here," she whispers. Then she takes my hand and leads me out of my office.

"Where are we going then?"

"Just come on." She drops my hand as she goes around the corner, and she turns toward the conference rooms. I don't believe it, but she then goes left, looks over her shoulders as if checking for spies, and pushes down the door handle for the janitorial closet we got stuck in weeks ago.

I did call maintenance and let them know about the faulty handle which I'd dismantled, and they came and fixed it. Now, I slink into the closet with her, and she tests the door from the hallway before joining me. Satisfied it'll open again, Claudia ducks into the closet with me. Then the door closes, and she presses her back against it.

My heart is beating so fast, but she brought me here. I step into her, take her into my arms, and lean down to kiss her. Apparently, this is okay, because she kisses me back among the mops and cleaning supplies, the rags and buckets, the racks and metal door and utility sink.

She breathes in sharply through her nose and breaks the kiss. "Where are we going tonight?"

I take a breath, trying to calm my own racing pulse. "You brought me in here to pump me for information."

She doesn't deny it, but she shakes her head. "No, I just didn't want you to kiss me in your office."

"It feels kind of forbidden, though, doesn't it?" I murmur the words against her ear, the orangey-flower scent of her hair making me drunk with a single breath.

"It's more forbidden in here," she whispers back.

"But it smells like bleach and pine." I grin at her and push my fingers through her hair. "We're going to Purple tonight. They're kicking off October with live music this week."

Claudia pulls back a couple more inches and searches my face. "Purple? Becks, that's too expensive."

"It's our one-month anniversary," I say. "It's barely enough."

She sighs and the softest, most beautiful smile touches her face. I've never seen this one before, and I thought hearing her laugh or seeing her face light up with a smile because of me was the best thing ever.

I was wrong.

This small, hidden, soft smile is better than both of those. Her true emotions show on her face, and she lets them linger long enough for me to see them, identify them, and seal them into my mind and heart.

Love. Adoration.

Claudia Brown is falling in love with me. She *likes* me.

Good thing I like her too. Good thing I'm falling in love with her too. "Are you mad about Purple?"

She starts to shake her head.

"I can take you somewhere else," I offer.

"No."

"I mean, we can go to Subway any night of the week. No reservations required."

Claudia fists her hands around my jacket lapels and giggles against my chest, and I move my hands to hold her tightly in place there. "No, Becks. Stop doing your fast-texting-short-sentences in person."

I chuckle with her, and as we quiet, I look at the brick wall across from me. "I keep thinking of you holding that baby," I say. My throat suddenly feels like I've swallowed white glue, but I press through it. "Do you want kids, Claude?"

"Yes," she whispers as she tilts her head back to look at me. "Do you?"

"I...think so," I say. "If I found the right woman, I think yes, I'd like to have kids with her." I haven't told Claudia a ton about my own childhood, or where my dad is. She knows my parents are divorced; hers are too. She knows my dad doesn't live around here; hers doesn't either.

"How will you know when you've found the right woman?"

"I don't know," I admit. "My sister says it's something you just know." I dip down and kiss her again, and as we breathe in and out together, I sure enjoy the kiss, enjoy this woman in my arms, enjoy the way I'm falling in love with her.

————

I KNOT my tie in front of the mirror in my bedroom, both dogs up on the bed and giving me the worst puppy dog eyes on the planet. I take a breath that almost pops the buttons of my dress shirt, and I smile as I think of Claudia saying I get them tailored to my body. I don't, but I happen to be a perfect size large for this brand.

"You guys." I turn toward the dogs. "You look so pathetic." I move toward them, intending to give them a good scrub and a good lecture.

Duke looks up at me with only his eyes as I near, and Rocky sighs. "Yeah, I'm going out," I say. "But I got Bobby to come sit with you tonight. He's going to bring a couple of friends, and they're going to throw you a ball in the backyard, and let you sit out front while they play basketball, and I even left my leftovers from lunch today for your dinner."

I stroke my hands down each one of their sides, and both of them roll so I have better access. They're such cuddlers, and they're each so greedy with the rub-downs they want. "So no puppy dog eyes. No barking when Bobby gets here. Duke, don't you dare run away when they take you out front."

I give them my sternest look, one that usually makes my secretary wither and nod and do whatever I've asked for. My dogs? They don't care at all. They simply look up at me, and Rocky actually yawns.

"All right." I straighten. "I have to go, or I'll be late, and I can't be late." I head for the door, hearing both dogs jump to the floor behind me. "Bobby will be here in like, twenty minutes. Do you want to wait for him outside?" I've given the sixteen-year-old from down the street the code to my garage. So he'll be able to get into the house and yard that way, and I'm literally paying him fifty bucks to play with my two canines for three hours. It's honestly ridiculous.

But I've left Duke and Rocky with Aunt Jill several times now, and I went by her place on the way home so she's okay until tomorrow. She's doing a lot better, but she still needs a bit of help, and I don't mind doing it. I like it, in fact, because she's someone to talk to, and she always has my best interest at heart.

I check the doggy door to make sure it's not locked, that the dogs can come and go as they please, and then I say, "Be good tonight. I'll know if you're not." Like they care, but at least it makes me feel better.

On the way to Claudia's, I keep the radio off in the truck. I think about work for a minute, then my mind jumps to one of my favorite *Seinfeld* episodes, where Jerry takes care of a stranger's dog. I smile though my stomach quakes with nerves.

"It's fine," I mutter to myself as I make the turn and the Big House comes into view down the lane. I've been to this house plenty of times in the past month. I've met all of Claudia's roommates; I helped with the Raking of the Leaves Event; I even kiss her for the cameras now.

But something about tonight feels big, and I'm not sure what it is. I pull up to the house, get out, and I'm only climbing the steps when the front door opens.

Tahlia leans into the doorway, a smile on her face. "Wow, Beckett," she says, scanning me down to my shiniest shoes. "You are male perfection."

I glow and beam like a star at her. "That's kind of you to say." I reach her and swipe a kiss across her cheek. "How's things here?"

"Good," she says with a slight up-pitch to her voice. "Things are good."

"The yard looks good."

"Yes, Aaron's taken over the mowing for Liam." Tahlia scans the yard, her blue eyes coming back to me. "Thanks for coming to help with the leaves. They're a nightmare on the best of days."

"Happy to do it," I say. "Plus, you already thanked me." I give her a smile, because Claudia told me Tahlia thanks and thanks and thanks people. She just wants to make sure everyone knows how much she appreciates them.

"I know." Tahlia sighs and smiles. "Claudia is almost ready. Come in." She leads the way into the Big House, and I go with her. "If I were you, I'd gush over the earrings, okay?" Tahlia whispers out of the side of her mouth while keeping her eyes trained through the living room to where the stairs come down. "They're important to her."

"Yes, ma'am." I watch the stairs too, and Tahlia walks away and into the kitchen, leaving me alone in the foyer. Someone comes downstairs, but it's not Claudia. "Hey, Ryanne." I lift my hand in a wave, and the other woman stops completely.

She presses one hand against her heart. "My goodness, Beckett, you are just—wow." Her gaze slides down my slacks to my shoes and back to my eyes. She comes toward me. "Can I ask you something real quick?"

"Sure," I say, my pulse a bit erratic for a moment. I have no idea what she'll ask, and I sort of wish I was wearing a suit coat so I could pull it closed like a shield.

She stops a healthy, appropriate distance from me, her dark gaze appraising me. "If you liked a man—I mean, someone—and they didn't know it, but you wanted to sort of push them in the right direction, what would you do?"

I cock my head at her, trying to see the root of this question. "Uh, I don't know." I blink a couple of times. "You like this person? Or you have someone doing things— or sending messages—to you and you're not sure of the meaning behind them?"

"It's—"

"Hey, there." Claudia's voice sounds behind Ryanne, and I look away from her. She disappears completely at the sight of Claudia in a beautiful, bright crimson dress. Her bare shoulders call to me, and across the bust is a bow. It goes under her left arm, but over her right, creating an asymmetrical illusion to the bow.

I want to untie her immediately, and my gaze slinks down her curves, past the swell in her hips to where the dress falls to her ankle in the front and brushes the ground in the back. She's wearing black heels with more of a point than I see in the office, and her hair is all swept up off her face and neck. It swirls and curls around, with a gem glinting on the side where it's holding everything in place.

"Those earrings," I say, because I can't comment on how her body makes me hotter than the sun. Big teardrops hang from her earlobes, and they're studded with diamonds along every surface. "Where did you get those?"

She smiles at me as she passes Ryanne. "They're my grandmother's. I hardly ever wear them." She leans into me, and I press a kiss to the hollow of her throat right there in front of her roommate. My hands land on her waist and hip naturally, and oh my word, this dress...

I'm never going to get it out of my head. Ever, ever, ever.

"Special occasions," she says, looking up at me through her eyelashes. Then she turns back to Ryanne. "Sorry, Ry. Did I interrupt?"

Ryanne shakes her head vigorously, her eyes locked on mine. "Nope," she says. "Not at all. No. We were talking about *nothing*." Her gaze shoots lasers at me for a long moment, and then she whips around and walks away.

"Well, that wasn't nothing," Claudia murmurs, still watching her roommate.

"Let's go," I whisper. "We can't be late at Purple."

"No, sir." She turns toward me, the concern for her friend melting from her face. "I'm assuming you have a jacket in the car?"

I look at her again, and I count myself the luckiest man in the world to be standing next to her. "Yeah, I sure do," I say. "But first..."

I don't care that we're standing in the foyer of the Big House. I don't care if all of her roommates crowd into the doorway that leads into the kitchen and watch. I don't care if I pour too much of how I feel into this about-to-happen kiss.

I just want to kiss my gorgeous girlfriend when I'm feeling so many things, so I gather Claudia close and do exactly that.

CLAUDIA

KISSING BECKETT ON OUR ONE-MONTH ANNIVERSARY feels unlike anything I've ever experienced. He smells like fresh cotton, cool water, and the Perfect Male. My vision swims with *Caliente*, then *Golden Nugget*, then *holy Lilac Haze* as he strokes his mouth against mine again and again.

He doesn't go too far, and as he pulls away, he breathes in and then sighs it all out. "Claudia, sweetheart," he whispers, his head still very close to mine. My eyes stay closed, because I want to experience Beckett without my eyes. The feel of him so close to me, the scent of him, the sound of his voice, the brush of his lips against my earlobe.

My skin prickles with desire as he says, "I'm falling in love with you. Don't freak out."

I do stiffen, but I work hard not to jerk away. I succeed, and as the seconds tick by, I relax into his arms again. "I—it's fast."

He takes a small breath. "I'm not saying I'm there yet."

He sways with me. "I'm just feeling it, and Liv says I should say what I feel."

He kneads me closer, and I smile to myself at his rapid-fire sentences that feel like the multiple texts he sends me. That he's always sent me. "So don't freak out."

"I'm not freaking out," I say.

"What are you feeling?" he asks.

"I didn't know I'd have to answer hard questions on our one-month anniversary." I do shift my feet finally, and my eyes flutter open. Beckett pulls back enough for our gazes to meet. He's sober, though his eyes still twinkle and shine like the sun off a deep ocean.

"It's okay." He ducks his head, his smile slowly curving up that mouth I can't seem to get enough of. "I can see it in your eyes."

My pulse skips and hops and frogs around in my chest, but Beckett settles me by taking my hand and stepping toward the door. We definitely don't want to be late to Purple, so I flow with him. I let him guard me, guide me, and graciously get us where we need to be.

At the restaurant, he shrugs into his suit coat before he comes to help me out of his truck. And in this dress, I need all the help I can get. I've rented it from a formal shop that caters to women for special occasions, and just the expression on Beckett's face when he saw me in it was worth the price tag.

"Have I mentioned how gorgeous you are?" he asks,

his hand sliding along my low waist. "This dress...those heels...the earrings..." Beckett takes a breath of *me*, and that makes so much...love run through me. He makes me feel strong and sexy and supremely female, and I love that. I love that he cherishes me for who I am right now.

"But it's not about all the frills and things," he says as he walks me slowly toward the entrance to Purple. He darts a look over to me, then quickly away again. He swallows, and both of those are tells of his anxiety.

I want him to relax, to enjoy this night as much as I am already. "It's about who you're with," I say, because I know that's what he's about to say.

He looks fully at me now. "Yeah," he says. "That's what I was going to say."

"So I could've worn my ratty pajama pants and a tank top, and you'd still be falling in love with me?" I raise my eyebrows, expecting a beat of hesitation. A lag in his response. After all, Beckett only sees me at my best. At work, I'm put together from head to toe. On our dates, I am too, even more so than at work.

"Yes," he says instantly as he brings us to a stop. "Yes, Claudia. Absolutely. In fact, I'd *love* to see the ratty pj pants and tank top." A dangerous, naughty little glint enters his eyes. "When can we make that happen?"

I swat playfully at his chest. "I save those for at least the three-month anniversary," I tease. "My mama always taught me to hide my flaws, you know."

He grins at me, his expression softening as he slides his

hand up my bare arm to cradle my face in his hand. "I like your flaws." He kisses me again, and I swear every pore on my body raises in awareness.

"I like kissing you," I whisper against his lips.

He chuckles and tucks me into his side again, and we enter the restaurant. Purple lights hang from the ceiling, creating the mood against the dark wood walls and the dark brick floor. I let Beckett take the lead, and he checks us in, and we're seated immediately. My skin tingles where he holds my hand, and I smile at him as he pulls out my chair before I sit at the table against the windows.

A pale purple candle stands in the middle of the table, with lilac flowers surrounding it. I don't know the name of them, but I reach out to touch the petals to find out if they're real. They are, and I glance over to Beckett as he sits down. He's wearing a purple plaid tie, and literally every piece of him is amazing.

How did I overlook him for seven years? I've always known he knows how to put every detail in place, but his perfection used to annoy me. Now, it draws me closer to him.

"Good evening," a man says, and I look up to our waiter who's dressed in black from head to toe. "I'm just checking with you, because you're in our seven-thirty group, and that means you can dance with our six o'clock diners or wait until after the meal." He has a great smile, and it shines down on us.

I look over to Beckett, my eyebrows up.

He pushes back from the table and stands. "We'll dance," he says, extending his hand toward me. I can't help smiling, because I want this experience with him. I want to be held by him, and have his strong arms encircling me, and that clean, woodsy scent billowing between us.

"Something I can bring you to drink for when you get back?" the waiter asks.

"I'll take pink champagne," I say, and Beckett lifts my hand to his lips. After pressing a tiny kiss there, he looks at the waiter.

"I'd love a virgin mojito," he says.

"You've got it." The music swells up over the last word the waiter says, and more couples start to rise from their tables.

Beckett leads me onto the dance floor, but we don't go too far from our table. He is effortless in his movement, in the way he provides shelter for me, and the private bubble he creates between us.

I close my eyes as I move into his chest and settle my head against his collarbone. I breathe in the scent of his skin along his throat, and I relax into his comfortable embrace. While I completely believe what I've told him— that it's not about the flowers, the chocolate-dipped strawberries, the purple candles, or the pink champagne—I also love all of those things.

They *do* create an experience I won't soon forget, and I'm glad I'm experiencing them with Beckett Fletcher...

who I'm steadily falling in love with too, whether I've said it or not.

I'm not like him, and I don't say everything that pops into my head. I like to think through my feelings first, and when I'm ready, I'll say them out loud. I just hope I can keep Beckett's attention until that time comes.

He says he can see it anyway, I tell myself, and I hope I can keep showing him how I feel until I can say it out loud.

———

"HM." I move down the table we've set up out by the secretary desks, where both Beckett and I have spread our portfolios.

"Oh, boy," he says in a dry tone. "I know that hum."

I glance over to him, unaware that I even hummed. "I didn't hum."

"Yes, you did."

I straighten. "I didn't."

"Did."

"I really don't think I did." I put my hand on my hip and cock it out.

"Sybil?" Beckett looks over his shoulder to where Sybil is sitting at her desk.

"Hummed," she says.

I frown in her direction, but I don't argue back. I return my attention to the pages of Beckett's most recent project, which he's laid out fairly well. He joins me, maybe pressing in a little close at my side, but I don't look at him.

"I like how you've laid this out with 'before' and 'after,'" I say, pointing to the awful before-pictures of the riverbank he's cleared. It's not frilly and cutesy like mine, and I'm having serious doubts about whether I should scrap my whole portfolio and start over.

I have about a month before applications are due, and I can do it. I really can.

But I don't want to very badly, and I tell myself, *I don't have to be Beckett.*

He's got charts of his budget and where his money went. That's important for his job, because he works with private donors and businesses, and it's required that every penny that comes through his office is accounted for.

I point to one of his pictures. "This one is sort of dark. Do you have a way to brighten it up?" I do glance over to him, but don't make eye contact for long. "And most of the others I've noticed for businesses along the Riverwalk have their owners out front. This one doesn't."

"I couldn't get her to pose," he says. "She's this little old lady, and she didn't even want people to know she owns the land there."

I straighten again and grin at him. "A little old lady? Becks, you'd get the job for sure with this." I spread my hands wide like I'm making a banner. "Beckett Fletcher Gives Female Senior Citizens the Keys to their Dreams."

He grins too, and we laugh together. For me, it's either

laugh or cry, because Beckett's portfolio is good. Really good. Great, even. Phenomenal, and I feel my confidence in my own application for City Planner waning and waning and waning.

"I think you need to pad some of your credentials," he says as he moves down the table to where I've laid out my portfolio. I wasn't going to let him see mine, but he's asked about it a couple of times.

I just want another set of eyes on mine, Claude, he'd said. *And I trust your eyes.*

I trust him too. I do. I just wish my pulse wasn't made of butterfly wings as I move to look at the page he's talking about.

"You just skim over your degree, number one," he says. "You surely have internships to talk about."

"Yeah," I say, but I didn't particularly enjoy my internship with the town of Huntington, South Carolina. "I didn't ask for a letter of recommendation from them."

"Why not?" Beckett turns those inquisitive eyes on me, and I swallow and try to cover over my emotions before I look up at him.

"I, uh, didn't have the best time there."

"No? What happened?" He looks back at my portfolio. "I think it would round it out. And you've only been here for seven years. You surely started somewhere else."

"Surely?" I bump him with my hip. "I'm only thirty, Becks. I worked for a year at the library over in Sugar Creek, as their director and events planner."

"So you've had a title with the word 'planner' in it," he quips without missing a beat. "It's not listed here." He leans closer. "Unless I just can't see it..." He's teasing me now, and irritation sings through me.

"I didn't put it," I say. "It was a dumb job. I was there for ten months before I moved over here." I'm mumbling by the time I finish, and Beckett trains those laser eyes on me again.

"Why wouldn't you put all of your community service work? I don't get it."

I sigh and move further into him, expecting him to move down the table to my next page. I mean, he found flaws on page one, paragraph two. Surely there's more he can comment on. "I don't know," I say quietly.

"Oh, I've heard that voice before," he murmurs. "And you know dang well, Claude."

I sigh, hoping he'll get the hint that I hate this topic of conversation. But Beckett makes me say things I don't like, and he doesn't give up easily on the things he wants to know. "Remember how I told you a little about my daddy?"

He straightens, everything in him turning tight. "On our one-month anniversary? That teeny-tiny little bit about how he cheated on your mom and left your family?"

"Yeah," I say. "And that wasn't a teeny-tiny little bit. It was everything he did."

"In like, ten words."

I want to count them out and argue with him, but I

don't. I sigh again instead to tell him how insufferable he is. "The guy I worked for in my internship was a lot like my dad. He wasn't...honest. He wasn't loyal to his employees. He talked trash about all of them behind their backs, so I'm sure he's been doing the same to me all this time. We didn't exactly get along."

"Weird," he says in a total deadpan tone.

I bump him again, and he puts his arm around me, his hand warm and comforting on my hip. "You value honesty and loyalty above almost anything."

"Yes," I murmur. "I do."

"So you don't want to ask him for help."

"No, I don't."

"And the library job?"

"It feels trivial."

"Did you see that I literally put that I worked in the mail room for the town of Beaufort for two months?" He chuckles. "And that's generous. I think I was there for six weeks before I came up here."

"But *Beaufort*," I say.

He laughs outright now, the sound rumbly and sexy as I hear it in his mouth, his throat, and his chest.

"What?" I feign surprise. "Beaufort is really ritzy, Becks. I'd put anything I did in Beaufort on my work history."

"Well, I think you should put on the library job," he says. "Number one, it's another suburban town here in the Charleston area, which shows that you know small-town government and culture. And two, it's not even close to what you do now, which means you know multiple limbs of a city system."

"Fine," I say like his advice is bad. "I'll add it." I reach into my pocket and extract a pad of pink Post-It notes. I scrawl out "library job" and stick it to the first page. "What else do you see?"

"I don't know," he says. "I'm being blinded by the sexiest woman in the world right now."

I glance left and right and even over to Sybil. "Have you told Sybil how you feel?"

He rolls his eyes and grins, and I giggle into his chest. These moments feel semi-stolen. We're not exactly standing a professional distance apart, but we're not putting on a show either.

"All right," I say. "Let's go to lunch. You promised me the story about *your* parents 'soon,' and it's been another week since our one-month thing."

"If you're going to call it 'our one-month thing' I'm not going to try so hard next time."

"Oh, please." I press into his chest with my shoulder until he takes a step back. "You know it was flawless." I meet his eyes, mine searching his. "I told you like, fifteen times how perfect it was."

"Your Discovery Park pages are flawless," he says.

I roll my eyes and move away from him. "I'm starving, and I want Cayenne's today." I stop at Sybil's desk. "Can I interest you in some spicy chicken fingers, Syb?"

"Yes, ma'am," she says, her fingers still flying across her keyboard. "I almost have that transcript of the Library Board meeting done for you."

"Perfect," I say. I've been spying on all the meetings around town in the past several weeks, since the City Planner position was announced. Either I or Sybil attends the meetings, records them, and then she types them up so I can pull out the most important things that our current town councils are talking about, or that citizens are saying over and over.

"I'll take the honey chipotle sauce," she says. "I want them dunked, of course, and if they have their half-and-half sweet tea and lemonade, I'll literally drink a gallon of it."

"A gallon of half-and-half," I say with a smile. "Becks?" I turn and look at him. He's still standing at the table, in front of my spread-out portfolio, and when he twists to look at me, he doesn't look happy. "Cayenne's? I'm going to actually drive over there. Get out of here for a minute."

His expression clears, and he says, "I'll come with you. I still can't figure out why Grayson Fullmer won't call me back, and I need to run some ideas by you."

"Sure," I say as he goes by me and Sybil and into his office.

Tabby looks away from her computer and over to me and Sybil. "I know I've only been back in the office for like seven working days, but he really is so different."

Sybil takes a break from her typing and leans back in

her chair. She's so tiny, it looks like it might swallow her up and burp out feathers. "If you could only use one word to describe him now, what would you say?"

Tabby looks toward his open office door, her eyes narrowed and her hand swooping through her curly hair. "Considerate? Calm? He's like, not so grumpy. Not so intense." She glances over to me. "No offense, Claudia."

"I'm not offended that Beckett has some intensity," I say. "I think when it's properly reined in, that's actually a really good quality to have."

Beckett comes out of his office while he's pulling on his jacket. Not a suit coat kind, but a windbreaker kind in the type of blue that makes his eyes shine like Ocean Water. Blue and maybe green if you look long enough, and definitely something deeper underneath. It's actually a really great color for front doors and shutters, but you have to have the right configuration of windows and the right paint color on your house to really make it work.

"All right," he says as he comes to a standstill. "What are you guys saying about me now?"

"Nothing," Tabby says, immediately burying her head behind her computer.

"Sybil?"

"How amazing your new haircut is," she chirps like a baby bird. She too dives back into her transcribing, leaving me to deal with Beckett the Beast.

He puts one hand in his jacket pocket. "What color is running through your head?"

"Ocean Blue," I say.

"Boring." He fake-yawns. "That's the best you've got?"

"It could be Baltimore Sky or Madison Avenue."

"I really don't understand paint colors," he says a he starts moving again. "Tabby, what are you getting from Cayenne's?"

"Barbecue wings," she says. "Boneless."

"I'll check with Larry." I head down the short hall from the foyer to his office, but he's not there. "Where's Larry?"

"Called out sick," Sybil says.

Great. Now we don't have to get him anything. "All right," I say. "I'm ready to brainstorm why Grayson has ghosted you."

"He hasn't *ghosted* me," Beckett says as he leads the way out of the department. "He just won't email me back."

"Or answer any of your calls."

Beckett doesn't say anything, but he strides ahead of me with long steps. When I unlock my car, Beckett gets in and I join him. "Why are you mad at me?"

"Because you're talking about me behind my back with the secretaries." He buckles his seatbelt and won't look at me.

I want to argue back with him, tell him that of course I'm not talking about him behind his back.

"You want unconditional loyalty," he says. "But you don't give it."

"I..." I grip the steering wheel with both hands, my

knuckles clenching and my stomach cramping. "It's nothing bad." I glance over to him. "You call your sister after every interaction we have."

"I do not."

"When did you stop then?"

He faces his passenger window. "A couple of weeks ago."

"What about Aunt Jill? You still go over there every day after work, and I don't believe for a second that Blabbering Beckett goes away after work." I look at him again while I come to a stop at a four-way stop. "You still send me sixty-four texts when it could be three. So."

"Sixty-four?" He scoffs. "I don't think I've been over fifty for a while now."

"Every evening, Becks," I say. "And we spend most of them together."

He says nothing, and my gut continues to churn at me. "Fine, you want to know what we were talking about?"

"No," he barks. "I don't."

"Beckett."

"I know you said you didn't like Halloween, but I now have both Tahlia *and* Emma texting me about the party they're putting together, wanting to know if we're going to be there."

He's irritated with me, but that doesn't mean we won't keep seeing each other...right?

BECKETT

"Have you seen me dress up for Halloween even once in the seven years we've worked together?" Claudia asks.

"I can't believe I got in this car," I mutter.

Claudia either doesn't hear me or chooses to ignore me. The silence in the car ripples across my shoulders. I do need her help with Grayson, but I don't want to ask for it now. I don't want to explain anything to her.

"I guess I can't skip out on my own Halloween party," she grumbles. "It'll be at my house. What? I'm supposed to sit up on the third floor alone?" She shakes her head, and she reminds me of the old Claudia, the one who's annoyed about everything, especially me.

A pinch of guilt rolls through my stomach and chest. I shouldn't have said anything about her, Sybil, and Tabby talking about me, but Claudia has literally just finished telling me about a former boss who talked trash about everyone.

And five minutes later, she's talking trash about *me*, her boyfriend.

"My parents got divorced about a decade ago," I say. "I was an adult, as was Liv." I don't care that I'm speaking in short, clipped sentences. Claudia's teased me about my "micro-texts" since we started dating, but I just don't know how to link together more than one sentence.

"It was still hard," I say. "Because it changed how I view my momma and daddy. Who I thought they were, they suddenly weren't."

"Hm." She makes that maddening humming sound, but this time, it's just her saying, *Okay, Becks. I'm sorry. Keep going.*

"My mother started dating before the divorce was even final. My daddy left town and moved up to Jersey, where he'd been working for the past decade."

"Was he seeing someone up there?"

"Not that I ever found out." I sigh. "But I felt abandoned. Liv certainly did, as Dad didn't even come to her college graduation."

"I'm sorry." Claudia doesn't always say everything on her mind or swirling in her heart, and I remind myself of that. Still, I think she needs to 1) apologize to me for talking about me behind my back, and 2) stop talking about me behind my back.

"Mom was more interested in—and I quote—finally living her own life than me or Liv. So she dated around for a few years, and then she met and married Malcolm, who lives in Corona, California. She gave up her entire life here to move there and be with him."

"So she abandoned you too."

"Felt like it," I say. "I know it shouldn't bother me so much, but I was just left here. I have Aunt Jill, and the dogs, and my job." I finally look over to her. "And since we started getting along, I've really felt like my life might actually have some meaning."

"Becks." She looks over to me, though she's entered Charleston now and really should be paying attention to the lunchtime traffic.

I shake my head. "I'm fine." I look out the window again, knowing I'm not fine. Just because I run a lot, and do a good job at work, and feel confident inside my skin and clothes most of the time doesn't mean I don't have feelings.

As Jerry Seinfeld says once in one of his funny monologues when a supermodel is breaking up with him, "Are we not human? Do we not bleed?"

I feel like I'm bleeding right now, but I don't know how to say it. Where's Blabbering Beckett when I need him?

Claudia's fingers slide through mine, and I sigh into her touch. "Beckett, I'm really sorry."

I turn and look at her. "About what?"

She's stopped at a red light, and she bravely gazes right back at me. "For talking about you with Sybil and Tabby. I think your secretary is just having a hard time reconciling who you are now with who you were when she went out on maternity leave."

"Am I really that different?"

"I'm not sure," she says slowly. The light turns green, and Claudia pulls her hand away. "I'm on this journey with you, Becks, so I don't know."

"Is that what we're doing? Going on a journey?"

She glances over to me, and then starts searching for a parking spot since we're close to Cayenne's. "Yes," she says. "I think dating is an adventure. Life can be an adventure."

"Sure," I murmur, because she's not wrong.

She pulls into a spot about half a block down the street from Cayenne's, one of the best Southern fried chicken spots in the city. In the state. My mouth waters, because it's a long time from coffee and a single scone to lunchtime, especially with the miles I put in with the dogs before work.

"You're right, you know," she says, and it sounds like it takes her a lot of effort to get those four words out.

"About what?"

"I do value honesty and loyalty highly, and I should be honest and loyal with you. To you." She swallows. "I'm sorry. I won't engage in any more conversations about you while you're not there." She places one fist over her heart. "I promise."

I lean over her console and take her face in my hands. "Thank you." I kiss her, wanting to go fast and show passion, but in this tender moment where she's actually apologized to me, I go slow and truly experience her.

I only kiss her a couple of times, and then I pull back. "Now, about Halloween..."

She sighs like I'm the worst person in the world, and she wishes I'd never gotten into her car. Before we started dating, I took that sigh literally. Maybe she meant it literally, I don't know.

But now, I know she's just pretending.

"They're *your* friends," I say softly. "I guess they're inviting co-workers and anyone else who might want to come to a fun party."

"Not anyone else," she says. "Co-workers. Friends. Significant others."

I thread my fingers through hers. "If we don't go to the party, can I hang out in your bedroom with you?"

She bursts out laughing, and a new smile comes to my face too. "No, you scoundrel." She pushes against my chest and turns to open her door. "Let's go get lunch."

I get out of her car too and call across the top of it, "I'm going to text Tahlia and tell her we'll be there."

"Fine," she says. "But I don't have a costume."

"If I get you one, will you wear it?"

She pauses at the corner of her hood and cocks that sexy hip. "Are you one of those guys who wants to wear matchy-matchy costumes? Because that might be a deal-breaker for me."

"A Halloween costume is a deal-breaker?" I chuckle as she joins me on the sidewalk. I take her hand. "Honey, I think you need new definitions for deal-breakers."

"I don't like Halloween."

"It's candy and caramel popcorn," I say. "I promise I'll get you a costume you'll be able to abide."

"Be able to *abide*? Holy College Dorm, Becks, you're not Merriam-Webster."

"What color is College Dorm?" I grin, because she thinks I speak with strange vocabulary sometimes, and she's the one who spouts off paint colors like we all know what they are.

Some I can figure out, obviously. Ocean Blue? Not that hard. But College Dorm or Salmon? She has to explain those to me.

"It's this really ugly shade of green that's all the rage right now," she says. "I actually think it would look good in a kitchen, with some framed fruited art."

"Oh, wow." I laugh and laugh as we walk down the half-block to the fried chicken restaurant. "Since you haven't objected to the Halloween costume, I'm going to assume I have the go-ahead."

"Please, nothing that requires face makeup."

"Oh, you don't want to be a clown?"

"If you get me a clown costume, we're done." She glares at me like I have the big red shoes in my truck right now.

"Claude, I know what to get for you." I reach for the door handle and pause. "Do you trust me or not?"

A moment passes while the whole world pauses. Then she says, "Of course I do."

"Then you already know there will be no clown costume." I pull open the door and let her enter first, like the Southern gentleman I am.

She called me a scoundrel, but I'm totally not one. I can't help my desire for her, but I respect her so much that I'd never do anything she doesn't want me to do. Now, I have to make it through Halloween without striking out, and then we'll be moving into the holidays.

And with that, comes the possibility of me asking Claudia to come meet Aunt Jill and then Liv. The thought of taking her home to meet anyone makes my mouth dry, because if Claudia doesn't know my faults by then, my aunt and my sister certainly won't hold back.

HALLOWEEN ARRIVES, and I have a bounce in my step as I enter the Public Works trailer, despite the rain outside. Probably because I'm wearing an enormous wizard hat and the drops didn't make it to my neck or face.

I grin and grin though there's no one to see it, and

when I walk into my department, I see Claudia standing with Sybil at her desk, setting something on it. "Shazam!" I yell as I lift both my arms, and Sybil, as fragile and frail as she is, yelps and stumbles backward.

Claudia looks up from the folder she's holding, her eyes wide. She makes not a move, and she really is just like a black cat. "You have got to be kidding me," she says, her eyes dropping down to my boots and back. "You're a wizard."

"Thus, the incantation," I say as I lower my arms.

Claudia grins as her face relaxes and her expression returns to normal. "So what? Are we frozen now? You put a spell on us?"

"Yeah," I say with a grin. "That's right. I put a spell on you." I move past her and into my office. I don't expect her to follow me, and she doesn't. We've been fairly normal since our mini-fight on the way to Cayenne's. I haven't invited her to Thanksgiving dinner at Liv's, though my sister has been bugging me about it for at least a week now.

My portfolio-application sits on the corner of my desk, and as I settle my wizardly self at my desk, I ignore the files in my briefcase bag and reach for it. Claudia went over it with me, and she had some good ideas.

I've been trying to implement them, but some of the pieces she suggested I get, I can't actually get. I know she'll work on hers until four-fifty-nine on November fourteenth, but I honestly feel ready to turn mine in.

It'll sit on Winslow Harvey's desk until November seventeenth, but it'll be off mine. I have a meeting over at City Hall early next week, and I'd really rather not show up to turn in my Very Serious Job Application in a wizard costume.

So I flip through the pages, peeling off Claudia's pink sticky notes with her loopy handwriting. It makes me smile, and I reach for my phone. It buzz-bleeps as I pick it up, which is the sound for Liv when she texts.

I ignore her and navigate to my email, where I set the confirmation message for the dress pick-up I've secured for Claudia for tonight's party at her house. The Halloween haunting isn't actually at the Big House, but I've been sworn to secrecy. If I break it, I know I'll never regain the respect of her roommates, especially the one I haven't met yet.

Claudia and Hillary shared the third floor before Hillary moved to LA, and I know they still talk all the time. I have to stay on all of the female good sides at the Big House, I know that, so I haven't breathed a word of the real location of tonight's party.

"Mister Fletcher." Tabby comes over the intercom on my phone. "I have Grayson Fullsom on line two for you."

"You're joking," I say, already reaching for my desk phone.

"I'm not. He says he has four minutes, and I told him—"

"I've got it," I say, already pushing the button to connect my phone to line two. "Grayson." I know I'm practically bellowing, and in The Before, Claudia would've appeared in my office door with a grumpy-cat-scowl and her arms folded. That, or she'd bang on the wall between our offices and yell something about how I need to be quiet.

But Grayson Fullsom is practically deaf, and I know he hates talking on the phone. So I got his attention by sending the box of whiskey truffles, which I can fully admit was my girlfriend's idea. She'd come up with it after we'd learned that it's illegal to mail alcohol through the United States Postal Service.

We could've used a courier, but only if we have a license to ship alcohol. Since I don't, we'd opted for the whiskey truffles, which I'd ordered from a company that has all the proper licenses in place.

"Did you get the truffles, Mister Fullsom?" I yell.

"Yes," he yells back. "Thank you, my boy. I don't know if there's anything better than chocolate and whiskey!"

I laugh like he's the funniest man on the planet. "I only need you for one minute to set up a meeting."

Thankfully, Tabby appears in my doorway, and she's holding a spiral notebook that opens flat. It's actually her calendar for me, and I motion her forward as Grayson yells, "Yes, I can come to you next week."

"Next week," I say as Tabby lays the planner-slash-calendar in front of me. "That should work just fine. Tuesday?"

"Monday is great! I can be there as early as eight!"

"Whoa, whoa." I chuckle. "Let's say ten, okay?" I look at Tabby and try to communicate telepathically with her. "Ten! Ten, Mister Fullsom!"

"Yes, yes," he says. "Monday at ten."

"Monday at ten." I nod to Tabby, and she takes the schedule and starts to write in it. "I'll have everything ready for you."

"See you then," he yells. "Thank you for the candy!" The line goes dead before I can bellow a good-bye, and I replace the receiver in relief.

"He called me back."

"I'll bring earplugs for everyone on Monday," Tabby says as she exits my office. I feel like a child on his birthday, all hopped up on soda pop and birthday cake. I hear the secretaries talking in normal voices out at their desks, and I fight the urge to go see if Claudia has joined them.

I've done that a couple of times over the past couple of weeks, and the once or twice she's been there, the conversations have been purely about work. I don't need her to prove herself over and over, so I stay at my desk. I pull out the papers I need to get done today, and about half-way through the morning, I get up and say, "Tabby, did we get that paperwork filed with Mobile Adventures? The permits with the county?"

"Yes, sir," she says as she swivels away from her

computer. "We got approval from the county already. I forwarded you that certificate a couple of days ago. You have a conference call with Claudia and Margie from Mobile Adventures this afternoon." Her eyebrows go up. "Did you not see the calendar invite?"

"I'm sure I have it," I say as I back into my office. I've only been going over the Christmas Festival checklist I've made for myself, so I quickly get on the computer. I have a dozen IDMs, and over two hundred emails.

I let my chin sag to my chest for a moment, and then I take a deep breath, pick myself up, and dive in. I'm still sifting through email when Claudia enters my office in a pair of straight, long, black pants that brush the tops of her heels and a long-sleeved black blouse that has sheer arms.

"You're in all black," I say. "One could consider that festive."

She smiles at me and sets a foot-long sandwich on my desk. "We need to go over the festival, and we have a call at two. Can we have a working lunch?"

"Yes, we can." I don't even reach for my food. "Can I have two minutes of personal time?"

Claudia perches on the edge of the chair across from my desk, her dark eyes glittering with delight and desire. "It'll take two minutes just to get down to the janitorial closet."

I get up and keep my eyes stuck to hers as I walk past her to my door. I close it, and turn back to her. "Then maybe we can just stay here."

She swallows and says, "Your office will be sweltering in less than five minutes."

"I only asked for two," I whisper as I lean down and touch my lips to hers. Seeing as how she doesn't push me away or keep the kiss all that chaste, I can only assume she wanted to take these two minutes in my office—behind a closed door—for personal things too.

CLAUDIA

"You're not dressing up?" Lizzie demands as I step down into the living room.

I pause and stare at her. "You're Maleficent." Complete with the horned headpiece and bright red lipstick. I would never, ever, *ever* wear that, but Lizzie looks like a million bucks. "You look hot."

She grins wickedly with those crimson lips. "Well, I invited Stewart, and he's coming." She waggles her eyebrows. "I'm hoping this will make an impression."

"I definitely think it's going to do that." I grin at her. "What will Stewart be dressed as?"

"He didn't say."

"You guys don't dress up at ChemTech?"

"Against company policy," Lizzie says. "Just one more reason why chemists are boring-as." She pushes out one hip. "But tonight's party should be fun." Her phone *brrrrrings*, and she adds, "See you over there," as she swipes it on.

Lizzie heads for the front door, already chit-chatting on her phone, but I'm stuck standing still. "See me over... where?" It's then that I notice that the Big House is not decorated for any kind of party, let alone a Halloween party.

There's nary a fake cotton web. No big spiders with electric-red eyes. No music piping through the house. Not even a bowl of nuts, let alone a bright orange pumpkin-faced bowl brimming with candy.

"Tahlia?" I ask.

The doorbell rings, though Lizzie just left through the front door, and no one calls that they got it. It seems like I'm the only one still at home. Confused but determined to figure out what's going on, I answer the door.

Beckett stands there in all his wizard glory, and he's wearing a very unwizardly grin. He holds up a black bag and looks at it. "Your costume."

I eye it again, realizing it's a clear plastic bag with a black dress inside it. I reach for it and say, "What is this?"

He hands me a pointed hat with a wide brim with wire in it.

I take it, a bit dumbfounded. Everything then clicks together. "You want me to be a witch." I fold my arms around the hat and dress. "And you're a wizard."

"This was the simplest thing I could come up with for you," he says. "I've had my costume chosen for a month, so it's just...coincidence." He leans into the doorjamb and grins like a wolf. "You won't break up with me over a coincidence, will you?"

"You practiced that 'coincidence' speech all the way from your aunt's house, didn't you?"

Beckett only smiles wider, and I turn away from him. "Fine. I'll go change." I leave him standing in the foyer as I head into Tahlia's room. Sure enough, she's not there, and she won't care if I step into a dress and pull on a hat in her bedroom.

I do just that, noting how well this dress fits. I grab my tank top and shorts and head back out to the foyer. "I need —" I cut off as Beckett holds up a knee-high pair of black, leather boots. "Shoes."

"Fits good," he says. "You didn't put on the hat."

"I needed shoes." I move into the living room and put them on, noting that they're the exact right size. I stand, pick up the hat, and put it on. I face him and throw my arms out wide. "Shazam!" I yell.

Beckett tips his head back and laughs and laughs. I join him, because while I dislike Halloween, I really like him. I move over to him and link my arm through his. "So, tell me where this party is."

He grins at me. "Next door. Come on, we're already a minute or two late."

"Next door?" I follow him outside and look left, where our only neighbor lives now. But the street is dark that way. To my right, where Liam used to live, the house glows with orange lights.

"At Liam's?" I look up to Beckett. "I didn't think Aaron had moved in yet."

"I don't know about that," he says. "But I know Tahlia said to bring you to that house." We walk down the road, because he's already parked at the Big House. Spooky music comes from the porch, and Beckett doesn't knock or ring the doorbell before walking right inside.

Music comes from inside the house, and there are all the usual things I expected to find at the Big House. Fake spiderwebs drip from the raw wood rafters. Bowls of chips, pretzels, candy, and more line the bar in the kitchen. Everyone I see is wearing some ridiculous costume, but since we're all doing it, it feels somewhat normal.

"She's here," someone says, and I turn just as my four remaining roommates come together to make a wall.

I take in Lizzie as Maleficent, Tahlia as a blonde surfer girl, Emma as the woman from the *Progressive* commercials, and Ry as Dwight from *The Office*.

"What is going on?" My eyes land on Ry, who's the most likely to crack and tell me. No one says anything, but they all wear clownishly huge smiles. "Ryyyy?" I draw out her name dangerously.

She says nothing. As if she and the others have practiced, they part down the middle, with Lizzie and Emma moving to the right and Tahlia and Ry going left. Through the middle of them comes none other than Hillary.

My pulse spikes; my tears come immediately; I rush toward her. "You're here," I say needlessly as I wrap her in a tight hug. One I never want to release.

Hillary giggles and says, "You're squeezing me so tight."

I step back and wipe my eyes. "You're not dressed up."

"We flew in literally an hour ago," she says. "I wasn't going to wear some clown costume on an airplane."

I grin and hug her again. "Oh, I've missed you so much."

"I miss you too, Claude." Hillary hugs me hard back, and then she whispers, "Introduce me to your hottie wizard."

I step back and turn toward Beckett. "Becks," I say. "This is Hillary, one of my best friends. Hill, this is Beckett Fletcher, my boyfriend."

Liam moves to his side and says, "I'm Liam, Hillary's boyfriend."

"Oh, hey, man." Beckett shakes his hand, no man-fist-bumping in sight, which I'm happy about. "I thought you two were getting married?"

"We are." Liam smiles at Beckett and then me. "Hey, Claude."

I rush into his arms too. "You brought her home."

"For a couple of days," he says into my ear. When he pulls back he look at me fiercely. "You know we're going to come back here eventually, right?"

"When?" I ask, reaching to wipe my eyes.

He glances over to Hillary, who's greeting and chatting with Beckett. "When she's done living her dreams."

"Costume contest!" someone calls, and everyone's attention gets diverted to a man dressed in a white chemist jacket, thick black glasses frames, and black slacks. I haven't met the man Lizzie's been crushing on at work, but the way she steps to his side with her supervillain staff and looks at those of us gathered in the kitchen says plenty.

"Stewart has ballots for the costume contest," she says. "Everyone needs to come into the living room for just a single pass." She looks around at the kitchen-dwellers. "Then you can come back in here for pizza, apple cider, and doughnuts."

"There are doughnuts here?" I ask, turning, but Hillary twists me right back around.

"Costume contest first, Claude. Doughnuts and pizza after."

"And all of your news from Hollywood," I tell her.

She nudges me with a knowing look, her red hair making her expression spicier than most I know. "And you'll tell me all about Beckett."

I smile, because of course I will. Of course I have already. I glance over to him, remembering my promise not to talk about him behind his back. But that was just with the secretaries at work. He knows I've been telling my roommates things about us, just like he's spilled the tea to his sister and his aunt.

"She dressed up?" a man asks, and I know that voice.

"I don't believe it. How did—?" Luke enters the kitchen, and he's wearing a cow onesie. I wish I was joking. A bright white onesie with bovine hooves and a pale pink nose poking nearly straight up off the hood. With moo-spots all over his chest and udders on his belly.

Udders.

This is udderly unbelievable.

I simply stare at my brother while he stares at me.

"You're a witch," he says.

A number gets called behind him, and others chatter around us. But I move over to Luke and hug him. "I didn't know you were coming." Now my stomach is all twittery because I need to introduce him to Beckett.

"You invited me."

"You never said if you could get a babysitter." I pull back and cock my eyebrows at him.

"Well, here I am." He grins at me. "Now, which one is Beckett?" He starts surveying the others still loitering in the kitchen, and Beckett has somehow integrated himself seamlessly into a conversation with Ry, her co-manager Elliott, Hillary, and Liam.

"He's the wizard." I point to him, and he somehow knows I'm talking about him, because he swings his attention my way. When he sees me looking at him, he puts down his clear plastic cup of cider and comes around the island.

"Becks," I say, easing myself into his side and turning to face Luke. "This is my brother, Luke. Lucas, this is my boyfriend, Beckett, and I'd very much like to keep seeing him." I give Luke a sharp look I hope says everything it needs to say for my brother to be on his best behavior.

"Oh, hey, man." Luke grabs onto Beckett's hand, and they shake. "Claude talks about you all the time."

"In a good way," I hasten to say, my eyes throwing desperation at Beckett. "It's always good, Becks."

He gives me a toothy smile as another number gets called. "She's told me about you too," he says to Luke. Then he nods to the number pinned on Luke's bicep. "You want to strut around in the costume contest?"

"Me?" I ask.

"Yeah, you." Beckett chuckles. "I'm gonna do it, but you don't have to." He looks back over to Luke. "I'm just glad I got her to dress up."

"Yeah," Luke says, his eyes locked on mine and refusing to let go. "That's a Southern miracle to be sure."

"Luke," I warn.

Another number gets called, and it's his. "My turn," he says. "I'll be right back." He ducks back into the living room, and I take Beckett's hand and go with him. I have to see what this costume contest parade is all about.

The other party-goers have gathered around the sides of the room, as well as a few in the middle, leaving a clear oblong track for the person whose number has been called to walk. Luke struts forward with sure steps, and when he reaches the corner behind a long couch, he pauses, puts one hand on his hip, cocks it out, and turns back the way he's come.

People laugh and hoot, and then he goes past the couch, walks in front of it, and comes back toward the kitchen. I laugh at him, but he doesn't so much as crack a smile. He's like those British guards who stand out in front of Buckingham Palace, their eyes trained forward and their focus singular.

"Number six," Stewart calls, and Tahlia says, "Excuse me, Claude. I'm number six."

She hulas past me, and a couple of the men hoot and catcall as she dances her way around the room, her smile so sincere and so bright. She's brought a few of her teacher co-workers with her tonight, and they all give her a high-five as she jigs by.

She's giggling when she makes it back to me, and Stewart calls another number. Beckett returns to my side, and he holds out a slip of paper about the size of the sticky notes I love around the office. It has a thirteen on it, and nothing could ever be more unlucky to me.

"You're joking," I say.

He hands the number to Ry and says, "I tried." Then he pins a fourteen to his wizard cape over his right bicep. "You hungry, baby? They've got pizza and salad and stuff in the kitchen."

"Can I vote in the costume contest?" I ask.

"You didn't see them all," he says.

Lizzie hands me a five-by-seven card and says,

"They'll all go around again once at the end. Plus, we're keeping voting open until ten, and then we'll announce winners at ten-thirty."

She must think we're still in college, when we started getting ready to leave the house at ten-thirty. Now, I'm headed to bed by that hour, and the only good thing about this Halloween is that it's on a Friday night. No work tomorrow.

I start making notes on my card about Aaron as he walks by as number seven. He's all smiles, and when he's done making the rounds, he grins and grins as he joins Liam and Hillary—and Emma. She smooths down the front of his plaid shirt—he swaggered around as a cowboy —and if she's not flirting with him, I'll give up my annual salary.

I nudge Ry and nod over to Emma and Aaron. "What's going on there?"

"Major crush," Ry says. "And Lizzie's currently got two here."

"Two?"

She chin-nods over to Elliott and, and then we both look to where Lizzie is passing out voting cards to Tahlia and her teacher friends.

"Ell doesn't have a girlfriend?"

Ry shakes her head, her expression one of amusement and joy. "Been single for over a month now, actually."

"Mm, surprising," I murmur. Ry's entertained a

couple of crushes on Elliott in the past, but I haven't heard her say anything about him for a while.

"Your witch dress is amazing," Ry says. "Where did you get that?"

"Beckett got it for me."

"I love how it's ripped along the bottom." The music changes to the Chipmunks singing Monster Mash, and it blasts through the house. Several people groan and complain, and Liam rushes to turn down the music.

"Wow, that song came out loud," Stewart says. "We're still looking at number nine, guys. Number nine!" He has more personality and spunk than any chemist Lizzie has described, and she doesn't get too far from him, despite her supposed crush on Elliott.

I stay through the end of the costume contest, get caught up on the five or six I missed, and mark my card with my top three votes.

Then I retreat to the kitchen, where the music is quieter and there's more food and more people I actually know. I could branch out and get to know my roommate's friends and co-workers, but I'm still getting used to the fact that I'm dressed as a witch, so I stick close to Beckett and Hillary, who stays close to Liam and Aaron. And he brings along Emma. All of them are fine with me, and I'm actually enjoying this Halloween party.

And it gets really interesting when I head to the bathroom and as I round the corner, I see Lizzie with her hand in Stewart's. She giggles as they slip out the back door. I pause, part of me wanting to find the nearest window that overlooks the backyard, as we've spied on others that way at the Big House.

The other part of me really needs to use the bathroom, and Lizzie deserves some privacy with Stewart the chemist—who dressed as a chemist for Halloween. She hasn't had a boyfriend in a while, and I'm not going to ruin anything for her.

So I head into the bathroom, and I'll ask her about Stewart tomorrow.

When I come out of the restroom, someone yells, "Monster Mash!" and when I meet Beckett's eye in the kitchen, I can tell he really wants to get out of the kitchen.

So I indicate the living room, where everyone is dancing in disco-ball light like Frankensteins. We join them, and I jerk around like I have nuts and bolts in my joints and the apple cider I drank made me all rusty.

Beckett laughs and laughs, and he's plenty handsy with me as we "monster mash." I don't mind at all, because we're not being inappropriate, and it's okay for my boyfriend to dance with me.

We seem to be meshing our opposites decently well, and I grab onto his shoulders as we go round in a circle and say, "I'm falling in love with you, Becks."

That gets him to sober right up, though he's not had a single beer to drink tonight. He opens his mouth to say something, then closes it and swallows. The song changes to one of croaking frogs, and I recognize it from the *Harry Potter* movies.

Still, Beckett holds me while the party continues around us, and when he lowers his head to kiss me, I try to make my actions match my words.

BECKETT

"Will that work, Tabby?" I can't quite make myself look across the desk to her, but I somehow catch her nod.

"Of course, Mister Fletcher. I'll start prepping the folders."

"Blue, green, and yellow," I say.

"Yes, sir." She stands. "I'll do them in our shared drive as well, so anything we have digitally, we can drop in there."

"Thank you," I murmur. She leaves, and I'm left to work on the letter I've put off for the past couple of days. My portfolio application is ready to turn in. It's not due for another week and a half, but I just want it off my desk.

Claudia says she's going to hold onto hers and "obsess" over it until the last day, but I can't do that. I just have to finish up this last thing, and then I'm planning on stopping by City Hall on my way to Aunt Jill's.

With my fingers in proper homerow position on the keyboard, I re-read what I've already got. My chest hitches with every sentence, but I've already decided to do this, and I'm not backing out now.

I start typing, and within a few minutes, I finish the letter. After sending it to the printer, I jump from my desk and stride out into the main part of the department to pick it up before anyone else can see it.

In fact, the ancient printer the city has gifted us out here in the drab Public Works trailer is still humming when I arrive. So I stand there and wait, and I pluck the paper from the printer while it's still warm.

"Beckett," Claudia says, and I press the paper to my thigh as I turn toward her. She still sees it, of course, and me picking up something I've printed certainly isn't abnormal behavior. My heart pounds like it is, though.

"Hey, baby." I smile at her.

"We're still doing the map for the festival today, right?" She glances back at her phone, a tiny frown appearing on her eyebrows.

"Yes, ma'am. I believe Sybil ordered the crepe bar to keep us going all afternoon."

"Okay," Claudia says, obviously distracted by something on her device. That used to irritate me a little, but right now, with this letter in my hand, I simply let her drift away from me and back into her office.

I do the same, tucking the letter deep inside my portfolio where no one will see it until I'm ready to show it to them. I make a couple of phone calls, update a document with my projects, and then move over to and open my filing cabinet.

A keen sense of complete overwhelm descends on me, but this thing has to be gone through. I keep meticulous files, and it shouldn't be terrible. It's just time-consuming to go through old things and make sure we have the things I'm legally required to keep and that we shred the things that we don't need any longer.

Tabby helps with this project every year, and she'll get everything organized, and then it'll go fast. Still, I pull out a folder and flip it open. A smile touches my face, because this shows a beachfront property that private money cleaned up and got open for the citizens of Cider Cove.

I sure have loved working here, and I slide the folder back into place and pick out another one.

"Beckett," Tabby says, and I twist away from the improved roadway that was done around the fairgrounds a couple of years ago. "Lunch is here. We're starting in Claudia's office."

"Yep." I replace the folder, ignore the one that contains my application for the City Planner job on my desk as I walk by, and go from doorway to doorway to enter Claudia's office.

She has two six-foot tables set up against the wall we share, and she's covered them with four giant-sized sticky pads. *Her and her sticky notes*, I think, but it makes a joyful smile fill my face.

That, and the brightly colored pens and markers she's laid out. Oh, and the scent of buttery crepes and whipped cream. Sybil has put the crepe bar on a smaller four-foot table against the other wall, and with another chair in here so the four of us can work, Claudia's office feels ten times smaller than usual.

Or maybe that's because of the way she glances over to me with that desire-filled expression on her face. That soft smile that says she wants to take me down the hall and around the corner to the janitorial closet.

I join her in front of the two tables. "Giant sticky pads."

She picks up one of the four-color pens. "I got this for you." She smiles and taps the end of it against the knot of my tie. "I think we should do colors for different booths, so we can see where we've over-committed and what we still need to book."

"Smart," I murmur.

"Sybil is printing a small version, but I want to *see* it." Claudia backs up a step, and I let her. She is a very visual person, and that's not a bad thing. She's walked the square four times, three of those with a measuring tape and one of those devices painters and general contractors use to measure distance.

Larry planned the Living Bethlehem, which will constitute nightly performances for the week, as well as a

Christmas market with pointed white tents. We've ordered those, and he and Claudia have gone over and over how many will fit around the sidewalk in the square.

The ice skating rink will go in the middle, around the statue already there, and everything is set with Mobile Adventures for that. With the Christmas Festival only about a month away now, I suddenly understand why Claudia needs this map done.

Then she'll be able to *see* what's done, and what still needs to be completed. It's a different picture than we get with a checklist, and her way isn't better or worse than mine. It's just different.

"Okay," she says as she blows out her breath. "I think we're ready to start. Everyone sit first, and the crepes are here, so we can eat whenever."

I take a chair and give Claudia my attention, because her attention to detail supersedes mine, and there's no reason not to let her lead this. It's her baby, after all.

"Let me get a crepe," Tabby says, and as she bustles over to the other table to do that, my phone buzzes.

It's Liv, and she's asked,

> Have you invited Claudia to Thanksgiving yet?
>
> Is she going to come?
>
> I know it's a few weeks out, but I'm prepping the food assignments.
>
> I need to finalize the guest list.

I realize as I read my sister's four separate texts that she messages just like me. I smile and look up. Claudia hasn't taken a seat, but she's standing at her desk looking at the contents of an open folder.

Sybil and Tabby chatter at the crepe table while they load up with fruits and creams. I have a narrow window here, but I decide to take it.

"Claude?" I get to my feet and join her at the desk. We stand across from one another, and she lifts her gorgeous eyes to meet mine. "What do you think about coming to Thanksgiving dinner at my sister's house in Columbia?"

Claudia blinks like her contact lens got put in wrong. "I—"

I don't jump in and tell her I've met all of her room-mates. Her brother. Literally everyone important to her except her mama, who doesn't live around here and Claudia herself hasn't seen since last Christmas.

"Are you doing something with your family?" I ask her. "Your friends?"

Her blinking normalizes, and she shakes her head. "Who'll be there?"

"Liv and Daniel," I say. "Their kids—they've got two. Aunt Jill. Me. She sometimes invites a few friends in the area who don't have family around."

"So your whole family."

"I mean." I shrug. "Kind of."

She shoots a look over to Tabby and Sybil. When her gaze comes back to mine, it's blazing hot with those white diamonds among all the dark fire. "I'd love to go to Thanksgiving at your sister's."

I grin at her and reach over to squeeze her hand quickly. "Great." I pull my hand away at the same time I turn toward the crepe table. "All right." I take a deep breath, because this invite feels like a huge accomplishment for me.

She said yes.

That's the real miracle.

"What have we got over here?" I go to get a plate of food, and when Claudia joins me, I glance at her. "When are you turning in your application?" I focus on the blueberries, taking them one by one so I won't have to look at her.

"Oh, you know." She sputters out a quick laugh. "I'm sure it'll be the last day. I'm going to make everyone at the Big House go over it with me this weekend."

"You probably won't change a thing."

"You're probably going to turn yours in today."

Wow, sliced bananas are slippery little things. "Guilty," I finally say.

She pulls in a breath and looks at me. The side of my face can take the brunt of her stare better than my eyes, so I keep loading my poor crepe with fruit. It's probably going to rip into shreds when I try to eat it.

"Becks," she says quietly. "Really?"

"It's ready." I spoon in a copious amount of whipped cream. "So yeah." I finally look at her. "I'm not going to go over it again. It is what it is." I give her what I hope is a dazzling smile and turn to take my crepe over to my chair. Sybil's taken it, so I drop into the one closest to the table—and Claudia.

More words teem on the tip of my tongue, but I stuff my mouth with berries, ripped crepe, and sweet cream. I'm not ready to tell Claudia about the job boards I've been looking at, because I don't want to have that conversation with her yet.

She loves a competition, and if I don't apply for the City Planner job, when she gets it, it won't feel like a victory. I want her to have that victory, but that means I have to find something else for my own career.

Something soon, but I give her a toothy smile as she settles behind her desk with her own overloaded crepe. I'll tell her about the job hunt soon, because I want her advice. I'm going to have to go through rounds of interviews, and that's *after* I find something I even want to apply for.

Soon, I tell myself. *I'll talk to Claudia about it really soon.*

CLAUDIA

I CLUTCH MY BINDER, FEELING A LITTLE RIDICULOUS my application to be a City Planner had to be expanded from a folder to a binder. I hover in the doorway of Beckett's office, but he's squinting at something on his monitor, and he doesn't look at me.

"I'm going to head over to City Hall," I tell him.

Another beat, and then he leans back in his chair, his attention diverting to me. It takes another moment before his smile graces his face. "Today's the day, huh?" He's already holding a pen, and he scratches something out on a notepad next to him. "It's not even the fourteenth."

It's the eleventh, and I just don't see why I shouldn't take it over to Winslow and his team. I spent the weekend going over every single letter with every single roommate. If there's a typo or missing picture, fact, or figure in this thing, it's because someone snuck into my office or bedroom and tampered with my binder.

Beckett gets to his feet and comes toward me. "Go on, then. Just go get it over with."

"I'm not going to come back to the office," I tell him as he draws me and the binder into his arms. It hovers between us, my arms crossed around it. "Lizzie's finally going to tell us what happened on Halloween."

"Oh, boy." Beckett grins down at me, his face so handsome and everything about him warm and welcome and comfortable. "She's really been torturing you guys."

"She has." I push my binder against his chest. "She disappeared, and I saw her go outside with Stewart. They never came back to the party." I've been worried about Lizzie, that's for sure. I finally told everyone else that I saw her and Stewart slip out the back door, and no one knows when she returned to the Big House.

After I'd texted that I'd seen her and Stewart leave the party together, she'd responded once with, *I'm never dating again.*

So something happened, but she's gone into classic Lizzie-protection mode, which for her is silence. None of us, not even Tahlia, has been able to get her to say another word about it. Then, this morning, she texted to say she was taking the day off from ChemTech to do a modeling gig, and she'd be done in the early afternoon.

So I'll get dinner for everyone. It's time to talk.

And that means she's going to talk. Tahlia will probably get out the pink sparkly microphone and make us all tell a bit of news, so I want to have something more than, "It's going great with Beckett."

I already texted everyone that he invited me to his sister's house for Thanksgiving. That text got sent while he loaded up his plate with crepes and fruit last week. I've been plagued with thoughts about a road trip, meeting his important people, and what drink I should take, as Liv texted me and asked me to bring them for everyone.

> Just whatever you like, Claudia.

In another text—

> Anything, really.

A third text:

> We're not picky.

Then,

> Can't wait to meet you!

Four texts to ask me to bring some drinks and say she was happy to see me. It's like a sickness in the Fletcher family. Beckett and I laughed about it at brunch on Sunday, and I lean into him now as I press my lips to his.

"Wish me luck."

"You don't need it," he says. "Go. Turn that thing in. Lighten your load." Beckett heads back to his desk, calling over his shoulder, "Say hi to everyone tonight."

"Yeah," I call after him. Then I force myself to turn away from where I'm comfortable—standing in Beckett's office, in his presence, in his embrace—and go to turn in my application for the City Planner.

"This is my dream job," I whisper to myself. And it is. I want it. I've been working for this for years, and I've put my whole soul and all my energy into this portfolio. My stomach rages at me as I make the drive away from the rail yard and over to City Hall.

My heels click on the tile as I walk toward the elevator. My heartbeat throbs as I wait. I want to flee as I ride up to the fourth floor, where Winslow's office is. I don't expect to see him; I just need to drop off my binder with his secretary.

So surprise only adds to my nerves when I walk in and find Winslow standing at his secretary's desk. He's got a clipboard, and he looks at me as I walk in. My steps slow even as Janice's smile widens. "And there she is."

Here I am, I want to say, but I can't get my voice to work.

Winslow takes a step toward me, his face brightening too. "We were just talking about who we expected to apply for the City Planner job and hadn't yet." He lifts the clipboard. "Your name was on the list."

I hold out my binder. "Here's my portfolio and application."

It could be my imagination, but Winslow sure seems to gaze at my binder with a little too much wonder on his face for a little too long. Then he nods me over to Janice with the words, "She'll take it."

"Thank you." I quickly mince my way over to her and give her the binder. She smiles at me encouragingly and gets out a cover sheet. She fills it out with today's date and slides it into the front cover.

"You're all set," she says.

For some reason, I thought this would be harder. "Thanks," I say, and then I smile-nod to Winslow on my way out.

"That didn't take so long," I mutter to myself, and back at the Big House, I'm home earlier than everyone except Lizzie, but when I walk in, she's nowhere to be found.

"Lizzie?" I call. No answer, and I open the fridge just because I can. I'm not exactly hungry, but there's so much on my mind. I finally close the fridge and go change out of my work clothes. Since I don't have anything else to obsess over, I text Beckett.

> Binder dropped off, and I'm home alone. Sort of. Lizzie's car was out front, but I haven't seen her.

> Maybe she brought a man home.

> She's not dating anymore, remember?

> Maybe that's just something she says.

> Maybe she's been having a secret relationship with Stewart.

> Maybe that's the real confession tonight.

> Too many maybe's.

"You are home," Lizzie says as she opens my door.

I toss my phone onto the bed in front of me. "Yeah," I say. "I called out for you, but..."

She enters my room, and she's got her hair dye on. "I was finishing up with the dye." She sinks onto my bed and sighs. "I don't know why I keep dying my hair."

I want to reach out and draw her into a hug, but I don't want all that dye on my clothes, even if they're my rattier ones. "Then why do you?"

"Everyone at work takes me more seriously if I'm not so blonde." She shrugs one shoulder. "Even my modeling agency likes that I'm not yellow-blonde." She sighs again. "Of course, they also told me not to cut my hair without checking with them, so."

I don't need to be the one to tell her that she hates being dictated to, whether that's her dying her hair to be taken more seriously as a chemist, or her modeling agency controlling what her hair looks like. Lizzie really hates being told what to do, or what she can and can't do, and everyone in the Big House knows it already.

"How was the shoot today?" I ask.

"Good." She turns toward the door and gets to her feet. "Sounds like Tahlia is home."

I follow her, and we both go downstairs to greet her. She's wearing the cutest fit-and-flare dress, but she's tossed her bag on the table. That's not good. Out of all of us, Tahlia is the neatest. It is her aunt's house, and her bedroom is on the bottom floor. So she doesn't pile things up in the living room or on the stairs to put away later, when she finally goes up to her room the way the rest of us do.

And that's only my first clue. The second is the bag of Byrd's cookies she's already eaten half of.

"Uh oh." I look at her and then the cookies, my eyebrows flowing upward. "Byrd's cookies?"

"Backpack on the table." Lizzie actually picks it up as if Tahlia doesn't know it's there.

"What happened?"

"When's dinner going to be here?" Tahlia pops another cookie into her mouth. They're the ginger snaps, which are her favorite.

Lizzie checks her phone. "Forty minutes." She meets Tahlia's eyes. "Are we doing the mic thing?"

"Yes." Tahlia walks out of the kitchen, taking her cookies with her. "I'm going to go shower, and I'll tell everyone tonight."

There's not much more either of us can do, so neither Lizzie nor I say anything.

———

AN HOUR LATER, we're all gathered in the living room, with the kitchen counter laden with creamy broccoli salad, dilly potato salad, a six-foot sub sandwich, and more potato chips than I've seen outside of a grocery store aisle.

Tahlia has declared it too hot and she opened the front windows to let in some of the breeze. We're in this weird phase where we need the furnace on at night, but not during the day, and I'm not sorry we've got a bit of cool air coming in.

We've been chatting and eating for several minutes, and I'm wondering when Tahlia is going to get things started. Or maybe Lizzie will do it. I've noticed all of us glancing over to her and then away, as she's the one who set up this mid-week confessional dinner.

"Is anyone going to get the sparkly mic?" Hillary asks from the TV where we've got her connected to the party.

"I'll get it," Tahlia says, and she gets up with a groan to collect the paper towel tube that's been painted a bright, sparkly pink. It has a tennis ball atop it, and someone's sprayed more pink paint over the green fuzzies since last time we used it.

"I'll go first," she says. "I've done the Spring art contest several times, right? Well, this year, they don't have funding for it at school, so we're not doing it."

Ah, and there's the reason she ate a whole bag of cookies before dinner.

"Oh, no," Ry says. "That's too bad."

"No way," Emma said.

"That's awful," I say, my mind already churning. "Maybe we can get some donors to get it going again."

Tahlia shakes her head. "No, it's not worth it." She hands the mic to Emma, who stares at it for a moment.

"I've got nothing." She looks up to Hillary, who shakes her head.

Ry takes it and says, "I'm fighting another crush on stupid Elliott." She sounds miserable, and she looks it too. She gives the mic to Lizzie as she says, "That's all I'm saying about it."

Lizzie takes the fake mic, but she looks at me. "Do you have something, Claude?"

"I turned in my application for City Planner today." I nod. "That's all. Nothing more to say about it."

So Lizzie keeps the mic, and she says, "I know you guys want the whole story, and that's fine. But bottom line, Stewart is a good chemist, and a good kisser, but a very bad boyfriend." She cocks the mic away from her mouth and then brings it back, as if she's really speaking into it. "Or rather, he only wants to be a casual boyfriend, and that doesn't really work for me."

I'm not sure which part to address first, and the rest of

the girls are quiet too. Then Ry goes, "A good kisser? Keep talking."

And the rest of us laugh and agree to that.

Lizzie tells us that "Stew" literally chatted her up the week before Halloween, got his invite to the party, took her into the backyard to kiss her, and then acted like he didn't know who she was on Monday morning at work.

We all gasp and gripe in the right places, and then Ry says, "We need more information about Beckett, Claude. Is he still nasty-wasty at work?"

"Nasty-wasty?" I shake my head, sure I've never used those words to describe Beckett, even in our worst times. "I think Tabby had a hard time adjusting to his new persona when she came back to work, but I think we've all settled in now."

"Remember when you thought he'd bugged your office?" Tahlia asks. "I just can't believe you're dating him."

"He used to pound on the wall between your offices," Emma says.

"Well, we—"

"And you thought he'd spiked your coffee that one day, remember?"

"Yeah, I know." I send a glare over to Hillary, who said the last comment and who should also know about dating and falling in love with a Grumpy Gus next door. "So he's been at the bottom of my list for a while. He's difficult to work with, and yeah, I've loved to hate him."

I glare around at all of my roommates, something building in my chest. Something I haven't even admitted out loud to myself yet, and I'm pretty sure I don't want to tell the ladies at the Big House that I'm in love with Beckett before I tell him.

"But—"

"I can hear you, you know."

I suck in a breath, because that was a man's voice. A very familiar man's voice. "Beckett?"

I look over to the window, but the blinds aren't open. I look around the room. Then all five of us there in person jump to our feet and rush toward the front door.

"Caliente," I say as Ry gets to the door first and flings it open.

BECKETT

THE SNICKERDOODLES IN MY HANDS FEEL LIKE LEAD weights, and they prevent me from moving as fast as I'd like. Which is stupid-stupid-stupid, because I'm a runner, and I run.

And yet, I can't seem to get off the porch at the Big House fast enough. My legs don't work. The snickerdoodles—which I'd stopped to get for Claudia—are like bricks.

I hadn't planned to stay for long. Just to drop off the cookies and tell her congratulations for turning in her application. I had no grand illusions that she'd invite me in; I really wasn't trying to crash her roommate party.

But the windows are open, and I'd heard them talking as I'd gone up the steps. Then I'd recognized Claudia's voice. And the ridiculous smile that had been playing with my lips had vanished at the things she'd said.

*He's been at the bottom of my list for a while. He's diffi-
cult to work with, and yeah, I've loved to hate him.*

"Beckett," she calls.

I turn around and face her, because while I'm a
runner, I don't usually run from hard conversations. And
never have I shied away from confronting Claudia. Heck,
we've spent seven years having conversations just like
this.

My pulse has never been this rapid before, though,
because I've never stood outside her house—a place where
I've kissed her several times—to have a conversation like
this.

She moves around her roommates, who have all gathered on the top step of the porch. Claudia comes down
them quickly, and I wait for her to get over to me. I want to
march toward her, but I think she'll appreciate it if the
conversation is kept at least semi-private, and her roommates haven't gone anywhere.

My nerves feel like someone put them in an air fryer
and forgot about them, and I grip the snickerdoodles like
my life depends on having the cookies in my hand.

"Beckett," she says again, somewhat breathless this
time. "What are you doing here?"

I shove the cookies into her hand. "I brought you these
as a little...thing for turning in your application today." I
glare at her and lean closer. "You agreed not to talk about
me behind my back."

"Becks."

"I wasn't planning to stay long," I say as I turn and start away from her. "Aunt Jill needs me."

"Beckett, come on."

"See you in the office tomorrow." My feet act like stumps, and I can barely feel them as I walk away from her. She doesn't call after me again, and our eyes meet for a long moment once I'm behind the wheel and have my truck started.

Then I peel out, pretty sure I'm shooting gravel from my tires as I drive away from the Big House. I scoff. "The Big House. Don't they know that's what prisons are called?"

Fury boils inside me, and the drive to Aunt Jill's takes no time at all. I pull up to her house, and in that moment, I realize I didn't stop by home and get the dogs first. Frustrated, this time at myself, I back out and head home first.

Duke and Rocky bark before I'm even inside, and I'm not surprised at all to have both of them put their front paws up on me, Duke whining and yipping like he hasn't seen me in forty years, not just a few hours.

He would never say anything bad about me, especially after I asked him not to. Especially after *he* claimed that loyalty and honesty is just *so important* to him. I scoff again, and I say, "Come on, fellas. Let's get over to Auntie Jill's."

I don't want to be home anyway, because Claudia knows where I live, and I don't want her showing up here with cookies and apologies and that sexy self of hers. No, thank you. I get to be mad, and it's okay that I'm mad. Heaven knows Claudia's been upset with me a time or two.

"In fact," I say. "She loves to hate you." I open the fridge and take out a white Monster, add, "Let's go, guys," and open the garage door again to let the dogs out. They scatter out onto the front driveway, and if I don't bark at Duke, he'll run off.

"Duke," I bellow. "Load up." I open the back door, and Rocky does what he needs to. "Duke!"

The lab comes back, his face so alive, and he barks at me once as he jumps up into the back seat of the truck.

"Yeah, you're back," I say. The weather has been really nice during the day, but it cools off quickly at night. "I'll let you into the yard at Jill's, okay?" I get back over there for the second time that night, and I grab the cookies I bought for her before opening the back door for the dogs.

"Hey, sorry I'm late," I call as I enter her house.

"In the kitchen," she says, and I bypass the couches in the living room, my aunt already smiling at me as I do. "You brought cookies."

"Yeah," I say, wondering if, before I'd overheard Claudia bagging on me at the Big House, if I'd have smiled and half-laughed, then told Aunt Jill I'd stopped to get them for Claudia and figured she'd like some too.

Now, I just slide the plastic clamshell onto her counter and give her my fake *don't-ask-me-any-questions* smile. "I'm gonna let the dogs in the backyard, okay?"

"Of course," she says as she goes back to the dishes in the sink.

I move over to the door and open it for the dogs. With her chihuahua and the cats, I'm surprised she doesn't have a doggy door. But she doesn't. With them outside, Duke barking like a fool, I turn back to my aunt.

"You're doing dishes." I lean against the wall and watch her.

She smiles at me in a way she hasn't in a while. "Look at me, right?"

"Look at you." My smile feels genuine for the first time since I turned in my application. "Listen, I wanted to talk to you about something."

"Oh? Is it Claudia? Liv told me she's coming to Thanksgiving, but I wouldn't say no to you bringing her over for biscuits and gravy before that."

I chuckle, but that invitation so isn't happening. Especially now. I didn't exactly break-up with Claudia, but we certainly aren't on good terms. She hasn't even tried to call or text me since I left her house thirty minutes ago.

"It's not Claudia," I say, and I'm suddenly uncomfortable. "Listen, I'm...I'm looking for another job."

Aunt Jill slides the last already-clean plate into the dishwasher. She's still moving a bit slow with her knee and whatnot, especially twisting. "Why? What's wrong with the one you have?" She straightens and lifts the door to the dishwasher up too. "I thought you were applying for a promotion."

"I did," I say. "I am." I sigh, because there's so many roads in my head, all of them diverging from one another. "I'm not going to get that job, and then I'll be working for my girlfriend, and that requires all kinds of paperwork and forms and disclosure with the city of Cider Cove."

"Why won't you get that job?" Aunt Jill demands. "You're a smart man, with loads of experience."

"Yeah, yeah," I say. "I know. Listen, Aunt Jill, I don't want the job." I did, but now I don't, and I don't know how to put that in words. "Something came up in Beaufort, and I'm going to apply down there to be their City Controller."

"Beaufort?"

"It's only thirty-five minutes from here," I say. "I don't have to live there to be their Controller. If I'm okay commuting, I won't have to move at all."

Aunt Jill leans into the counter and folds her arms, a move so classically My-Mama that I miss her powerfully. "You won't commute. You hate commuting and leaving those dogs home alone longer than you have to."

"Yeah," I say, because she's right, and I don't want to argue with her. With anyone. I'm tired, and I just want someone to feed me and let me be.

I move away from the back door and toward the living room. "I just wanted to let you know. I don't know how long it'll take me to find another job."

"So you think Claudia will get the promotion here in town."

I think of the letter I turned in with my application.

"Yes," I say. "I think Claudia will get the promotion." I groan as I sink onto my aunt's couch. "Can we not talk about it anymore tonight? I'm tired, and I just want Chinese food and movies from my childhood."

Aunt Jill laughs, and she says, "How long are you going to keep this a secret from Liv?"

I have a whole lot to tell Liv—and Claudia—and that overwhelms and exhausts me too. "If you keep your mouth shut," I say with a half-smile and the remote control in my hand. "I bet I can make it to Thanksgiving."

Aunt Jill trills out another laugh and says, "Good luck, Becks."

"Yeah," I say. *I'm gonna need it.*

CLAUDIA

I PACE BEHIND THE COUCH WHILE MY ROOMMATES squabble around me. My phone goes flip, flip, flip in my hand, and I can't decide if I escape to the third floor and call Beckett or if I give him a few minutes to calm down.

"He's never needed a cool-down period before," I mutter to myself.

"She's talking to herself," Hillary says from the TV, and I give her a cursory look as I turn and go back toward the kitchen.

"Just call him," Tahlia says. "He's reasonable." She cuts a glance over to Lizzie. "I mean, you've said he's been more reasonable lately."

"He has been," I say. Why did he have to show up in the very moment when I was talking about him? I hadn't even said anything bad. I'm too keyed up to even enjoy the snickerdoodles he brought.

"I'm going to text him." I round the couch and sink back into my previous spot on the end. I tap to get to our message string, and I read up a few texts. For Beckett, that's four or five short sentences, and last we were talking it was about a quick question he had about the Christmas Festival after I'd left work early today.

My brain blanks as my thumbs hover over the screen. "Salsa Dancing," I swear. I look over to Ry, who's wearing a frown between her eyebrows and studying me. "Why can't I think of the right things to say?"

Ry shakes her head and goes back to her own phone.

"What?" I ask.

"The only words out of your thumbs right now should be 'I'm sorry, *Becks*.'" Ry really sneers out his nickname, and alarm pulls through me.

"Ry," Lizzie says with plenty of chastisement in her voice. "She's distressed. You've got to say it nicer when she's upset." She switches her gaze to me. "But she's right."

"I didn't say anything bad," I protest.

"Doesn't matter," Lizzie says with a toss of her hair over her shoulder. "*He* thinks you did, and you told him you wouldn't."

"Just tell him you're sorry," Hillary says. "And you'd love to come enjoy the cookies with him."

I meet her eye on the screen. "But tonight is roommate night."

"Yeah, and Hill used to sneak up to the roof during

roommate night to snog her boyfriend." Emma delivers the line without a single emotion in her voice.

"I did not," Hillary protests vehemently. "One, he wasn't my boyfriend then, and two, I didn't kiss him that night."

"Text him," Tahlia says as Emma, Lizzie, and Hillary start talking semantics, and how the roof definitely was her and Liam's special place.

I look at my phone, wondering if Becks and I have a "special place." Instantly, the janitorial closet comes to mind, followed closely by his old-man swing in his back-yard. I can't have tomorrow at the office be the next time I talk to him, and I start typing.

> I'm really sorry, Becks.

Send.

> I wasn't saying anything bad about you, I promise.

Send.

> I appreciate the cookies.

Send.

> The only thing that would make them better was if you'd stayed to eat them with me.

Send.

> Maybe I can come over and we can sit in the backyard with the dogs?

Send.

Some of those are a little long by Beckett-Standards, but I can't unsend them.

> I'm not home,

> It's fine, Claudia. We'll talk about it later.

> I'm not in the mood tonight, and we're already at Aunt Jill's.

> She ordered dinner.

> I'll see you tomorrow.

He matches my five short texts, but his are even shorter. I hear them in his clipped, irritated tone, and my heart quivers in my chest. I hand my phone to Ry. "He's mad at me."

She scans the short texts and looks back up. "Sounds like it."

Emma takes the phone and reads the texts. "He says it's fine."

"That means it's not fine," I say. I draw in a deep breath quickly, then release it slowly as I lean back into the couch and close my eyes. I let my roommates talk about me around me, say things about what Beckett's messages might mean, and then Emma moves the conversation to something about her shop.

She's always so good to try to find the positive in everything. She doesn't like gossip, and she's almost always the one to move us, wide-eyed, to something else.

"Your phone, Claude." Ry's voice causes me to open my eyes.

I blink and take my phone, tucking it under my thigh a moment later. "Thanks," I murmur, wishing my apology would've been enough for Beckett. I wonder what will be, and a plan forms in my mind. If words aren't enough, maybe coffee and scones and IDMs will be.

———

THE FOLLOWING MORNING, I pull up to the curb down the street from Legacy Brew. I've not been here in a long time, and either I've forgotten about their popularity, or they've gotten more popular. There are cars and people everywhere, and the line is out the door.

"Let's get this over with," I say to me, myself, and I, because I don't normally wait in long lines like this. I join it as the last person to be able to fit in the shop, and to my surprise, the line moves really fast.

Before I know it, I'm up to the tablets, and a blonde woman grins at me. "Welcome to Legacy Brew. Do you have a loyalty number?"

Thinking quickly, I say, "Not mine. Can I put it on my boyfriend's?"

"Sure." Her fingers wait, poised over the tablet. I fumble my phone for a moment, then manage to get Beckett's number to pull up. I give it to her, and her nose wrinkles. "Your boyfriend is Beckett Fletcher?"

"Yes," I say.

The woman studies me now, and I don't like it. She says nothing, and I glance to the next person in line behind me. "Uh..."

"Mace," someone says, and she turns toward a tall, handsome, bearded man. He slides his hand along her waist and adds, "That cappuccino machine is on the fritz again."

"She's Beckett's girlfriend." Mace nods to me, and now I've got both of them staring at me.

"Is he not allowed to date?" I ask casually. "Or maybe he brings another woman for coffee here."

"Beckett isn't a cheater," Mace says. "I'll go fix the machine." She gives me another appraising look in only a single moment, and then she leaves.

"How do you know Beckett?" I ask the man. He's not wearing a name tag like the other employees, so I don't know his name.

"He's a regular," the man says. "Oh, you've given his number." He takes in the tablet screen for a long moment. "Did you want his regulars?"

"Yes," I say. "Times two, please." I dig in my bag to get

out my money, and thankfully this guy doesn't say anything else about me and Beckett being together. As my card processes, I add, "And if you could keep this between us if he comes in this morning, I'd appreciate it. I'm aiming to surprise him." I flash him a smile; he nods; I go to wait for the coffee and scones.

When I walk around the corner and the two secretary desks span before me, I expect to see Beckett in his form-fitting shirt in Sunlit Coral standing at Tabby's desk. Him and his pale pink dress shirt are not there.

She's not there either, and neither is Sybil. I'm the first to arrive, and while this isn't the only time this has happened, I haven't intended it for today. I need everyone here to act as a buffer between me and Beckett.

The coffee and pastry bag in my hand suddenly weighs way too much, and I get myself moving toward his office again. I go around the desk to set down the coffee and scones, noticing his computer screen saver is swirling across the monitor.

His machine beeps, and that sound is so ingrained in my soul, I'll probably hear it after I die. Beckett has just gotten an IDM. Interdepartmental Message. I get them all day long, from anyone working for the city, and I'm willing to bet Beckett does too.

I bump the mouse as I set down the to-go carrier of two coffee cups, and the computer wakes. He's got three separate IDM chat windows open, and the message that just came in is from Winslow Harvey.

Interview next Monday at 1:30 PM? *I know you and Claudia are working feverishly on the Christmas Festival, so let me know if another time would work better.*

Our afternoons have been dedicated to the Christmas Festival, with our mornings dedicated to our individual work. I wonder what Beckett will tell him—and me—and I step back from the computer, my heartbeat suddenly on overdrive. Maybe *I* have an IDM for my initial interview too.

Before I can leave—surely Becks will know the coffee and scones are from me—another message pops up below Winslow's first message. *And we need to talk about that letter you included in your portfolio.*

"Letter?" I peer at the screen again. "What letter?"

A voice penetrates my eardrums, and I look toward the doorway. I suck in a breath, because that was Beckett. I do *not* want him to catch me in his office, reading his IDMs. There's no way I can get his computer to go back to sleep, and I slide my fingers along the bottom of the monitor to turn it off.

My heart pounds, and I keep glancing from the monitor to the door. Monitor. Door. Monitor. Door. It's not turning off, and I'm going to get caught. Beckett's voice comes closer, and I drop to the floor, completely unsure as to why. I brought in two cups of coffee and two scones. He's going to know I was in his office.

Dead Salmon, I think as his voice gets closer. I am so bad at lying. He's going to know I was snooping through his IDMs, and I'd only come in here to make a peace offering. I press my eyes closed, praying for a miracle but none comes.

Beckett only comes closer. And closer.

Then he says, "Claudia?"

I look over my shoulder to find him carrying his briefcase bag and a look of complete disgust on his face. "What are you doing?"

"I, uh." My hand goes to my ear. "I dropped an earring."

"In my office?"

I tilt my head and pretend to put in my earring, and then I stand up. My eyes meet his, and he cocks his right eyebrow at me. "Are you serious?"

"Fine." I huff and drop my hands. "I brought you your 'regular' coffee and scones from Legacy Brew, and your computer started making noises. I accidentally woke it, and—" I swallow. "I saw your IDMs." I take a couple of quick steps to my left, away from him. "I'm just going to go."

Beckett watches me as I go around him, and he turns in a full circle to do that until I leave his office. Purely humiliated, I slink into my office and sit down at my desk before I remember I was going to take one of the cups of coffee I got at Legacy. Not only that, but Beckett had his coffee in his hand, and he surely doesn't need three cups.

But there's no way I'm going back over there now. I wake my computer, deciding today will simply be coffee-less. I've done it before, and I can do it again. I don't have any IDMs, which irritates me that Beckett has gotten an interview before me, but I reason that he turned in his application a week before I did. Winslow's probably had time to review it and he just got mine yesterday.

As I'm trying to organize my thoughts and my plans for today, an IDM comes in. Perfect. I can make anything work for an interview on Monday.

But it's not Winslow.

It's Beckett. From next door.

> Janitorial closet? Ten minutes.

My breath trembles in my lungs the same way my hands do. I simply type, *Okay*, and then I spend the next nine and a half minutes freaking out over what might happen in the janitorial closet.

I leave my office and go between Tabby's and Sybil's desks, where only Tabby has arrived. "I'm just going to..." I don't know how to finish, and I don't have to make an accounting to Tabby about where I am or what I'm doing. So I simply leave the department, look both ways like I might get caught somewhere I shouldn't be, and then head over to the janitorial closet.

I twist the knob, half-hoping this is one of those things where I show up on the ninth green for a snipe hunt, and really the sprinklers come on while I'm wearing my best dress. I enter the closet, and it's empty.

The door closes, and I smooth my hands down the front of my blazer. It's bright pink, and it covers my Polar Bear White blouse—which is honestly a version of pale, pale, pale gray—and goes well with the pair of navy slacks Lizzie got from her plus-size modeling agency.

"It's fine," I say. "Beckett always kisses you in the janitorial closet." I turn away from the industrial sink to find the door opening again. Beckett slips inside, and he's not wearing his suit coat anymore. His dress shirt isn't the pale pinky-orange of Sunset Coral, but it's still festive and Thanksgiving-themed as it's more of a Whispering Peach color.

His slacks are dark gray, and I swear everything on him is hand-stitched to his exact dimensions. He looks at me, his expression hooded and hard to read.

"I'm sorry," I blurt out. "It was a total accident that I saw your IDMs. It's totally fine if you want to do the interview in the afternoon next week. Totally fine. I can work around whatever." I take a breath and wring my hands around each other.

"I wasn't saying anything bad about you last night," I say. "I was just telling my roommates about how much you've changed. About how adorably sweet you are, and how, no, you weren't on my list of potential dates, but things change. People change, you know?"

He tucks his hands into his pockets. "You said I was difficult to work with."

"*Was*," I say. "*Was*, Beckett, and you have to be able to admit that."

"You love to hate me."

"It was past-tense," I say. "I *used* to love to hate you. I was saying good things, Becks. I really was." He has to believe me. "Please. And the coffee thing. I stopped by Legacy Brew this morning, and I have to say, they seemed surprised that I was your girlfriend. Almost like we shouldn't be together? Or like you had a different girlfriend? Or, or, something."

"Breathe, Claude."

"I *am* breathing," I snap at him. "And I really did just happen to bump the mouse when I set down the coffee, and I wanted one of those cups for me, and then I was so flustered, I left it."

"I'll bring it to you."

I fold my arms. "Yeah, sure. Like you couldn't even walk next door and ask me to meet you here? Or text me? We haven't IDM'ed in ages. You text me, Becks." I don't like how my voice pitches up, but I also can't stop it. "You *text* me."

My chest hitches and pitches, and holy Baby Fern, I'm *not* breathing.

"If you want to break up with me, just say it."

"I don't want to break up with you," he says. He sighs like I'm a difficult child, and he even drops his head slightly. "Did you get an interview with Winslow?"

"Just like that?" I ask.

"What?"

"You wouldn't talk to me last night. Act like I'm a nuisance this morning, but hey, I don't want to break up with you?"

"Would you like me to break up with you?"

"No," I whisper.

Beckett takes my hands in his. "Good. I don't want to break up with you either." He pulls me into his arms, and it's everything and everywhere I've ever wanted to be. "Maybe I over-reacted."

"I wasn't saying anything bad," I say. "I would've said the same things in front of you."

He backs up enough to look at me, and I gaze up at him. "I will never talk about you again."

"That's irrational," he says. "I know you and your roommates have an open-door policy. Tell each other everything and all that."

"I mean, sometimes," I say. "I don't tell them everything. I don't kiss and gossip."

"No?" His gaze drops to my mouth.

I shake my head. "I want to know what letter Winslow was talking about in the IDM."

"Mm, I bet you do." He leans down and touches his mouth to mine, and I suppose I can give him a pass on the letter. For now.

"It's just a Friendsgiving," I say to Elliott. "I want you to come, because if you don't, then I'll have no one." I pour all the pleading I have into my voice and look at Ell with puppy dog eyes.

He's pushing the mop back and forth, and I'm not usually here this close to closing time. He's not usually the one cleaning up on aisle five, but tonight, he is. Elliott glances over to me.

"You haven't started dating anyone, right?" I ask.

"No," he clips out.

"Then you won't have to make any excuses or awkward explanations about how I'm your nerdy, needy friend from work." I grin at him, hoping he'll just stop being so grumpy and say yes. He came to the Halloween party, and he's met all my roommates before.

Just because I have feelings for him again doesn't

mean anything. It's not like Elliott knows how I'm crushing on him again. It's not like he even sees me as a female worth dating.

"You're not nerdy," he says when I wish he'd say yes.

"Elliott."

"I'll come," he says. "What should I bring?"

"If you bring something, Tahlia will kick you out." I grin at him, giddy that he'll be coming to the Big House this Sunday. It's early, because Tahlia is going to her parents' house down in Tampa, and Claudia is going to Beckett's sister's house in Columbia, and Lizzie is going on a cruise with her family. It'll just be Hillary, me, Emma at the Big House, and two of us have to work on Black Friday.

Maybe, I think. *If you're lucky, you can get Elliott to come hang out on the holiday too.*

"What are you doing on actual Thanksgiving?" I ask next, following him down the aisle.

"I don't know," he mumbles.

"You don't know?" He's been acting weird for a couple of weeks now. Ever since the Halloween party, really. He's never hesitated to answer my questions before, even all the personal ones about his love life, his family, anything.

He heaves a massive sigh and straightens. Leaning against the mop handle, he glares at me. I smile and tuck my hair—my only flirting moves, which are admittedly lame—and take another step closer to him.

I slip on the wet floor and scramble for a handhold on

something. A shelf. Anything. There's nothing, and I fall flat on my butt. A *crack!* echoes through my whole soul, and I swear my head hits the hard tile floor on aisle five.

Or was it aisle six?

Seven?

"Ry!" someone yells, but their voice moves further and further away from me. My gaze is stuck up on a metal vent way up on the ceiling, and I think someone calls my name again.

It's Elliott, and he's so dreamy and so delectable and so unavailable it hurts. It all hurts.

"Ryanne." His face fills my vision. "Are you okay? Talk to me."

"You're *soooo* good-looking," I slur at him.

He only looks concerned as he comes back into focus. "Did you hit your head?"

"I'm sure I did."

"I'm calling an ambulance."

That gets me to wake up, and my mind buzzes at me that I've said something wrong. Or weird. "No," I say now. "No, I'm not going to the hospital."

"I think you maybe hit your head."

"I'm fine." I hold up my hand. "Help me up." I feel like a beached whale as Elliott puts his hand in mine and pulls me up. I don't have the strongest abs on the planet, that's for dang sure, and a horrifying groan comes out of my mouth.

"Is the world spinning? How many fingers am I

holding up?" Elliott isn't holding up any fingers, and I simply scoff at him. "I really think we—"

"I am *not* going to the hospital," I say with plenty of force. My head throbs for a moment, but I take a breath and everything centers again. My eyes meet Elliott's, and he wears pure concern in his expression. "I just need to sit down for a minute."

"Ry, you are sitting."

"Not in the middle of the store." I glare at him. "Help me into the office, and then you can finish mopping."

"Right. I'm going to leave you concussed in the office so I can mop." He rolls his eyes and gets to his feet. He pulls on my hand, and I use the nearby shelving to help myself get to my feet too. The world swims for only a moment, but when Elliott asks, "Okay?" I just nod.

He's handsy as he takes me into the office, and I don't mind that a bit. That's how I know I'm okay, that I don't actually have a concussion. If I did, I wouldn't remember my insane attraction to my best friend and co-manager.

I park myself in my office chair and Elliott kneels in front of me. "You sure you're okay?"

"Yes," I say.

"I want to drive you home."

Maybe dreams do come true after a slip and fall. "Okay," I say, because sometimes arguing with Elliott is futile. My phone bleeps and sings the whole way to his car, and once he's got me in the passenger seat, he takes it from me and goes around the front of his SUV.

My head hurts, but I don't want to tell Elliott that. He'll have to come back to the store and close up by himself now, and I try not to feel bad. I fail, but I try. I reason with myself that he's closed up Paper Trail plenty of times. I'm only causing a problem for him, and I'm horrified when tears burn in my eyes.

"Your momma is begging you to come for Christmas." Elliott gets in the car and sets my phone in the middle console. "She's asking about a date again."

"What else is new?" I sniffle and wipe my face really quick. "She's relentless."

Elliott doesn't ask me if I'm crying. He doesn't press me for more details about how I feel. He simply drives me home with the radio on low, his car smelling like vanilla and musk and everything male-delicious.

He walks me into the Big House, where Tahlia is curled up with a book with the TV on. "Hey," she says over her shoulder. Then she does a double-take. "Elliot. Ry? Are you okay?"

"She slipped where I was mopping," Elliott says. "I'm just gonna go put her to bed."

I nod at Tahlia, who'll come check on me later. That's just what she does. She's a couple of years older than me—than all of us here at the Big House—and she mothers us really well. "Okay," she says. "If you're sure..."

"I'm fine," I tell her, though I feel weak, like a baby bird who's tried to fly and fell out of the nest instead. I sure do like the way Elliott's body heat has melted into mine, and the weight of his arm around my waist makes my heart beat faster and faster.

Or maybe that's just me climbing the stairs to the second floor. "I'm all the way—"

"Down on the end," he says. "I know." He smiles at me, and I swear it lights up the whole hallway. Oh, almond and coffee and peanuts. Some of my favorite M&M flavors, but also me pseudo swearing in my head.

Elliott can't look at me like that. He can't have that dazzling twinkle in his eye, and that dimple in his left cheek, and that smile that's just so dang handsome. And now, he's leading me into my bedroom.

"Go on, Ry," he says. "I know you sleep fully clothed." He peels back the comforter on my bed, because while I feel like a mess most of the time, I actually do make my bed every day.

I slide under the blanket and let him tuck me in. "My phone," I say.

"I brought it." He hands it to me. "But I don't want you looking at it." He takes it back and plugs it in for me, setting it far away on the edge of my nightstand. His eyes sweep that, taking in the packages of candy there, and then he trains that brilliant grin on me again.

"Ry."

I roll over, because I've started to cry again. To my great surprise, Elliott slips into the bed behind me. He wraps me up in his strong arms and says, "I think you're hurting more than you've said."

"Yeah," I say, my voice high and tinny and filled with that emotional pain.

"Is it your head? Or your heart?" He's whispering, his breath barely touching my neck. I shiver anyway, because this is Elliott, and I've been crushing on him hard lately.

"Both," I say.

"I can fix them," he promises.

I turn toward him, and this moment is soft, and wonderful, and if I was brave enough, I'd turtle out my neck and kiss him. But I'm not, so I just look at him. "I need a boyfriend. Don't you have any friends you can hook me up with?"

A fierceness enters his expression. "Absolutely not."

"Why not?" I ask, almost desperate now. "You talk about Carver all the time. Is he dating anyone? Actually, I don't even care if he is. I can just tell my parents I just started seeing someone, and I think he's The One, and I'll take him home for Christmas. Then, they'll get off my back, maybe I can enjoy the holidays, and then I can just text them in January that we broke up."

My chest hurts, and Elliott is too beautiful to look directly at for so long. I close my eyes and take a deep breath. "I need some Tylenol."

"I'll be right back." Elliott slips away from me and leaves the bedroom. I sniffle and weep a little more, but I'm mostly dry-eyed when he returns with a bottle of Diet Coke and the pain medication.

I sit up and take it under his watchful eye, then set the

cola on my nightstand and lay back down. He joins me again, and I sigh back into his chest. We simply lay there for a few moments, and it's wonderful and warm and everything I want.

My pulse starts to beat against my bones, and the words I want to say to him pile up behind my tongue. I don't actually want to say them. If I tell him I like him, and he rejects me? I'll have to share an office with him every day forever. No, I'll have to quit. I can't face him after that.

He's never serious about anyone, I remind myself. *And you don't want a play-baby.*

I really don't. So the words sink back into my stomach, and my pulse steadies slightly.

"I'll do it," he says.

"You'll do what?" I turn my head slightly, and his breath wafts across my cheek. Oh, buttered biscuits and bacon. He's *close.*

"I'll be your boyfriend and go to your parents' house for Christmas."

Every cell in my body goes into a frenzy, and I flap the blanket back as I sit up. "You'll what?" I stare down at him, my chest heaving.

He simply gazes up at me, the picture of calm, cool, cute, and collected. "You just said you need a boyfriend. I'll do it."

I scoff, my mind racing. "No," comes out of my mouth, and I want to chop off my own tongue. The man of my dreams—my best friend, who I could totally convince my momma is my boyfriend—has just offered to be my fake boyfriend, and I say no?

I really did hit my head hard on that tile floor.

"I'll figure something else out."

"Why can't I do it?" he asks. "I'm a good boyfriend."

"Yeah, that's why you've been out with seven different women this year."

Pain and regret streams through his expression, but he blinks, and it's gone. Shuttered away where no one can see it. Except I did see it.

"We're friends," I say. "We work together. I don't want it to be—weird."

"Why would it be weird? It's not real."

"What if you have to kiss me?"

His eyes drop to my mouth, and crunchy cookies and chili nuts, his tongue darts out and wets his own lips. Like he's preparing to kiss me right now. This second.

My heartbeat is a big, bass drum in my chest, and I scramble to the end of my bed and off it. "I think you should go."

Elliott gets to his feet. "I could kiss you."

"Sure, you could, but you aren't going to." I fold my arms over the hideous blue polo I have to wear for work.

"Why not?" He steps closer, a teasing smile on his face.

"Elliott," I warn.

"You might like it."

Oh, I'm gonna like it. And then he'll know how often

I've been dreaming of kissing him. I shake my head. "No, it'll be weird."

He takes my hand in his, and my skin rejoices to be next to his. "What if it's not?"

"Can we talk about this when I don't have a head injury?"

His eyes meet mine, and he leans down. I pull in a breath and hold it, my eyes drifting closed. I mean, I have kissed a man before. Not one that smells like the woods, and paper, and maybe a little of the lemon from the mopping.

Elliott is pure male, and oh, I want to sink into him and let him kiss me, call me his girlfriend—fake or not—and parade him around the family holiday festivities.

"Yeah, this probably won't work," he whispers, his lips actually catching on my earlobe. The house is going to combust into flames from the heat between us. Can he feel that? Is it coming from him too, or just me?

"Yeah," I say.

"Because we can't both be gone at Christmastime." He pulls away, and when I open my eyes and look at him, he's wearing a knowing smile. The glint in his eye tells me he felt all that heat, and he knows it's coming from me.

He continues to back away from me. "I'll come pick you up in the morning for work."

I nod, and he does too. Then he turns and leaves my bedroom, and I huff out the breath still lodged in my lungs. I look at the bed where he lay, and I take his spot, trying to find his scent on my pillow.

It's barely there, and I listen to him say, *You just said you needed a boyfriend. I'll do it,* in his husky, tender, cell-vibrating voice as I close my eyes.

"How do I get him to offer again?" I whisper to myself, and I immediately start to make a plan to get that to happen. "Maybe at Friendsgiving," I tell myself, and then I give in to the pain meds and the headache and the phantom warmth of Elliott's body behind mine.

CLAUDIA

LAUGHTER ECHOES THROUGH THE BIG HOUSE, because as it turns out, Beckett Fletcher is hilarious, and all of my friends love him. I'm laughing too, but I'm not oblivious to the fact that Beckett has pulled out every charm he has.

He's wearing a polo the color of pumpkin flesh, and it strains along his biceps and seems to be made of that dry-slick-semi-Spandex fabric that clings to every line of his body. He's wearing jeans, something I've literally never seen him wear before. This morning, while we walked the dogs, he wore a pair of bicycle shorts with a super-short pair of running shorts over them.

A layered look that kept me looking, let me tell you.

We've both had our initial interview, and mine went amazingly well. Beckett reported that his did too, and we both have a second interview this week. Winslow, Mike, and the mayor are planning to announce the position earlier than planned, so the new City Planner will have a couple of weeks with Mike before he retires.

My pulse skips every time I think about the job. I automatically look over to Beckett, who seems a little flushed as he lifts his flute of grape apple cider to his lips. I've never seen the man drink, but we've never talked about it. I wonder if he has some trauma about alcohol in his past, or if he just takes don't-drink-and-drive very seriously.

"It's time for the nickel game," Tahlia announces, breaking up the party. "Everyone back to the kitchen table!"

"The nickel game?" Elliott asks, and Ry starts telling him about it. Several others break out into chatter too, and I link my arm through Hillary's as we stand up. She and Liam are here for the full week, and she's back up on the third floor, in her old bedroom.

Aaron is Liam's best friend, but he's walking with Emma. He runs the hardware store next door to her flower shop, and they seem Mighty Flirty tonight, just like they were at Halloween. But when quizzed, Emma denies anything between her and Aaron.

Ry's admitted her crush on Elliott, but again, as far as I know, there's nothing actually happening there. He did bring her home last week after she hit her head at work, but I've been extraordinarily busy with the Christmas Festival, and if Beckett and I aren't going over it at work, we're unpacking the boxes that have started to fill one of the conference rooms in our dingy trailer, and next week is set-up.

The festival runs from Wednesday to Sunday, and while I've really enjoyed putting it together for the past few months, I'm also ready to have it behind me.

I detour over to pick up a few glasses that have been left behind, because then Tahlia won't have to. She takes such good care of us, and I like to help her out if I can. Beckett does the same thing, and as everyone else flows through the wide, arched doorway and into the kitchen, I cut Beckett a glance I hope is flirty and fun.

"So you're a real comedian."

He picks up a couple of empty glasses and moves down the coffee table to get more. "I have a couple of funny stories. I probably should've saved them for my sister's." He smiles at me. "I'll be empty by then, and you'll realize how boring I am."

"I've never been bored with you, Becks."

Noise and chatter fills the kitchen as we enter it, and this nickel game with twelve of us should bring the roof down. We all have a plus-one here tonight for our Friends-giving, where Hillary made twice-baked potatoes with more bacon than I've ever seen in one place, and Tahlia made candied ham and smoked turkey.

I bought rolls, biscuits, and pies for our pie buffet later, and Ry made her special gourmet veggies with a stuffing topping. Emma provided our centerpieces for today, and she provided a roll of nickels for everyone for this game.

Last but not least, Lizzie, who brought my brother and my nephew as her plus-one-two after avoiding all kinds of questions about her co-workers or other friends she might bring, made the sausage gravy to go with my store-bought biscuits, along with the white cheddar mac and cheese I can't get enough of.

In fact, I migrate over to the leftovers after putting the glasses in the sink. I fill a plastic cup with a couple of scoops of the mac and cheese before facing the table. Tahlia borrowed some chairs from the middle school where she works, and we put both leaves in our table to make it big enough to hold all of us.

"All right," Tahlia says from the head of the table. "This is an easy game. You roll the dice and you use a nickel to cover that number. If your number is already covered, it goes to the next person, so if you 'take' the number, you have to say, 'I'll take it.'"

"I'll take it."

"I'll take it."

"I'll take it."

"I'll take it," goes around the room, and Tahlia is used to dealing with teenagers, so she simply smiles.

"Everyone sit," Tahlia yells above the giggling and talking, and I move to get a spot next to Beckett. He's already sitting next to Aaron, and as I approach, I hear him say, "Yeah, I mean, she hated me until a few months ago. Not that I harbored any soft feelings for her."

He laughs like he's just told a joke on par with Jerry

Seinfeld, who I know is one of his favorite actors and comedians. But my blood turns to ice. Only a moment later, it roars with flame and fire, like lava erupting from a fissure in the earth.

I put both hands on his shoulders and lean into him. He turns his head toward me, and oh, this would be sexy and awesome if I didn't want to wrap my fingers around his throat. "Who's talking about who now?" I murmur into his ear, and then I slide behind him and take the open seat next to him.

I hold my head high as Emma passes me a roll of nickels and Ry puts a game mat in front of me. It's in a sheet protector, and I read the rules at the bottom of it, ignoring Beckett as he says, "Claude."

"All right," Tahlia yells. "I'll start, and you'll pick it up. It's super easy." She throws the dice, watches them bounce and roll, and says, "Four. I'll take it."

I grin across the table to Lizzie, and we say together, "I'll take it," before we dissolve into giggles. Beckett puts his hand on my knee under the table, and I barely turn my head to look at him. He must get the hint that I don't want to be touched right now, because he removes his hand a moment later.

He hasn't said anything too terribly rotten about me, but it's the principle of it. He's gone Diva Cat on me twice —*twice*—because of things I've said about him "behind his back." I can be upset if he's off bro-gossiping.

The dice go around; we cover our numbers; people get

skipped; doubles get rolled. I'm sure no one is ever going to win. I only have an eleven left, but it seems like any time anyone gets close, they'll roll a seven, and that means they have to take off one of their nickels.

Finally, Emma rolls an eleven, but she doesn't need it. Aaron doesn't need it. Beckett doesn't need it. I look at him, realizing what's happening. I pluck a nickel from my pile and say, "I'll take it!" and lift both hands into the air. "I win!"

A cheer goes up from everyone around the table, and I high-five with Hillary and Liam, then across the table with Ry and Lizzie. When I turn to my right, I meet Beckett's eyes, and he pulls me into his side, his smile-guns blazing. "Good job, baby." He presses a kiss to my temple, and I can't help but lean into it, my own smile etched in place.

"Who wants to play again?" Tahlia asks.

Ry gets to her feet, her face flushed as she holds up her phone. "I have to go call my mother. Play without me." She exchanges a glance with Elliott, and he goes with her.

"I'll start getting the pie buffet out," I say as I stand. "Then I won't win again." I grin around at everyone, and then I turn away from the table. Some of the pies are refrigerated, but some have been waiting on top of the fridge or in the pantry for this very moment.

"I'll help her," Beckett says, and I give him a look he surely understands as I hand him the pecan pie from the top of the fridge. "Where are these going?" he asks over the noise from the game.

"Living room," I say. "We're using the credenza behind the couch." I give him the buttermilk pie, and then turn to open the fridge for the key lime and the banana cream.

The living room sits in relative silence, and while I love the life having people at the Big House brings, I also need a break after a couple of hours. "Just set them there," I say. "We'll bring out plates and forks and cut them into squares."

Beckett looks at me with that sexy brow cocked. "Squares?"

"Then you can have some of everything," I say. "Small pieces. A couple of bites of this one, then a couple of that one." I slide my pies next to his. "Don't worry. If you've never had pie in the shape of a square, your feelings might change after you try it."

I raise my eyebrows at him and turn to go back into the kitchen.

"Claudia," he says after me. He's not usually one to back down from a challenge, so I'm not surprised to find him right behind me in the kitchen.

"I'm not sure you should be armed with a knife," he murmurs to me.

I scoff and give him a side-eyed look. "Take the plates and napkins out." I jam them into his chest. "I have a couple more pies to get." A chocolate chess one, a raspberry cream one, and a delicious lemon meringue. So three more. I can't carry them all, so I wait for Beckett to come back into the kitchen, and I give him two more, then I take the lemon meringue with the sharp knife, throwing a look to my friends still rolling dice at the table.

Ry and Elliott haven't come back in yet, and no one else seems concerned about me having a knife. As I join Beckett and the seven pies in the living room, I bend over to start cutting them. "I never hated you, you know."

"I know that."

I'm not sure what to say next. Doubts and irrational thoughts fill my head. Things like, *Maybe Beckett and I just won't work.*

I finish with the chocolate chess pie and look at him. "Do you think we'll be okay?"

"Claudia." He rolls his head slightly, as if his neck is tight. "I think we're doing great."

"We seem to be walking on eggshells every other day." I sigh, tuck my hair behind my ear, and move down the line to the next pie. I pick up a napkin and wipe the knife, so I don't get chocolate in the key lime.

"Do we?"

"I think you like the conflict," I say.

"I think we have different definitions of conflict." He slides his hand along my waist, and I blame my body for reacting the way it does. Beckett seems to know it, and he puts more effort into his touch and pulls me closer. "I really like you, Claudia. Eggshells, no eggshells, all of it."

I cuddle into his chest and let him hold me tight.

"Don't you like me too?"

"Yes," I say. "You know I do."

"A man would like to hear it every once in a while."

I pull the knife out of the key lime and look at him. He glances to the knife and back to my face. "I like you, Beckett," I say right to him, my eyes locked on his.

"Still falling?"

"Yes," whooshes out of my mouth before I can censor it.

"Good." He presses a firm kiss to my mouth. "Me too." He steps back and hands me another napkin when I need it to clean the knife between the key lime and the pecan. With that done, we work in silence, only because we agreed not to talk about work today.

Just as I finish cutting the seventh pie, an eruption happens in the kitchen. "Someone won," I say as we both look that way. A man bellows, and that can only be Liam, as my brother can be loud but he wouldn't do that here.

Sure enough, I hear Hillary telling him to be quiet. He laughs, and that makes me smile. "We need some little serving spatulas." I go to get those, and add, "You stay here to guard the pie buffet."

"Guard it?" he calls after me. "From who? What does guarding it mean?"

I don't answer, because I don't need to throw Lizzie and Ry under the bus. They're notorious for sneaking bites of pie before the buffet begins, and I put the knife in the sink and get the tiny spatulas we've been using for our pies for a couple of years now.

People have already started to stand from the table, and I start waving them into the living room like their airplanes. "This way to the pie buffet," I say. "Plates, napkins, and forks are out there. I've got the serving spatulas, and we will not be mixing them up this year. Y'all can wait in line like civil human beings!"

No one is listening to me, and if I don't get out there, they'll steamroll right over Beckett and the next thing I know, they'll be using plastic forks to pick up their pie bites.

Beckett is standing at the end of the buffet closest to the kitchen, and he's got both arms out wide. "Line up here," he says. "Claudia is going to tell us about the pie bar."

"It's a *buffet*," I say, with plenty of eyerolling in my voice as I step around Aaron and arrive at Beckett's side. "Let me tell you what pies we've got, and I've got prizes for those who take a square of each one and vote for their favorite."

"Don't worry," Beckett chimes right in. "She didn't make them, so there's no competition." He looks at me with that brilliant, sexy smile. "Any vote is a good vote."

"But you have to try them all," I say as if we've rehearsed this, and as I look away from him and take in my roommates, my best friends, my brother and nephew, and others I know and have grown to love and appreciate, I see them all looking back at me with soft-sigh-like smiles, knowing looks, and a general sense of they're so stinking cute together.

And maybe we are.

But as Beckett and I move out of the way, and I grab the voting sheets and pens from the front drawer of the table in the foyer and make it to the end of the buffet before Liam—who said he got to go first through the line because he won the nickel game—makes it through all seven pies.

I glance over to Beckett, who's standing there with a goofy grin on his face, and while I do like him, and when we get along, we get along amazingly well. It's the times we don't get along that nag at me still, and I tell myself, *We have time. We're three months in. Give yourself more time. You haven't even met his family yet.*

But I will—in only three more days.

BECKETT

I DON'T NORMALLY DRESS UP QUITE SO NICELY FOR Thanksgiving, and my sweats cry to me as I pull on a pair of joggers I know I'm going to be hearing about all day. Claudia will mention them and most likely ask me where I got them.

They're a dark brown, almost like a pair of khakis. In fact, the company I bought them from claims I could wear them to work as dress joggers. I pair them with a gray t-shirt with a giant turkey on the front. Claudia says she's never seen me in a t-shirt, and I've decided today is the day.

I can't help that the turkey tee came from the same shop as the joggers and the browns and beiges in the two pieces match exactly. I turn away from the mirror, annoyed at myself for thinking of my clothes as "pieces."

I grab my wallet and the leashes for the dogs, and then

I turn back to them and thrust the leashes at them. "You will not pant the whole time. It's an hour-long drive. An hour, Duke. Claudia is going to be in the truck, and she doesn't want you licking her neck or sniffing her ears. And the panting. My word, can you just *not*?"

Duke sits down, his tongue rolling out of his mouth as he starts panting.

"Of course." I straighten and look toward the back door. "Okay, we better get going. If we're even one minute late, Liv will be calling." And my sister has been laboring over Thanksgiving dinner for days, I'm sure. I don't want to cause her any more grief than necessary.

Half an hour later, Aunt Jill sits in the backseat and I'm playing chauffeur as I pull up to the Big House. "I guess you'll be waiting here, Your Majesty?"

"Oh, you." Aunt Jill laughs, which I take for a yes. Not that she'd be walking up to the door with me to pick up Claudia.

About halfway to the door, it opens, and Claudia comes out. She's wearing a gorgeous dress in golds, oranges, yellow, and brown. It reflects the sunlight and throws rays around, and I want to whisk her off to a castle somewhere and be her prince.

For she is a princess.

"Wow," I say, and I whistle next, though that's a total wolfish thing to do and Aunt Jill would be mortified if she heard me. I grab onto Claudia as she reaches the sidewalk in those sexy ankle boots—which happen to match her autumnly-leafy dress. "This is an incredible dress on an incredible woman."

I don't care if her roommates are watching through the window or that Aunt Jill is probably filming this for my momma. I lean down and kiss her, because it feels like a long time since my lips have touched hers.

We've been working like dogs, ordering in lunch *and* dinner this week to get everything unboxed and categorized, organized and checked off on Claudia's clipboard.

"Beckett," she whispers against my lips, but I stay right where I am as I fall, and fall, and fall. Now, I just have to hope Claudia doesn't end everything with me when I finally tell her all I've been up to this month.

———

"WE'RE HERE," I call as I open the door for Aunt Jill and hold it so she can shuffle-limp through it. She's not carrying anything, but I've got her bowl of cookie monster salad while Claudia has a case of miniature bottles of sparkling cider. She also had me load up a case of grapefruit-essenced water, claiming she's going to make mocktails for everyone, including my sister's kids.

"Uncle Becks! Uncle Becks!" a little boy cheers, and my smile can't be contained.

"Careful," I yell to Denver, my sister's oldest child. "Aunt Jill doesn't walk real well. Give her a gentle hug. Gentle."

Denver comes to a stop and looks up at Aunt Jill with sober eyes. "Auntie Jill, you okay?" The four-year-old has a real soft spot for anyone he thinks might be hurting. He's sweet with his almost-two-year-old sister, who is riding on my sister's hip as she comes around the island in her kitchen, her smile wide and warm and wonderful.

"Hey." I lift my free hand and turn back to Claudia, who enters like the queen she is. My life with her in it is so much more than I ever thought it could be, and I swivel my attention back to Liv so I can judge my sister's reaction to my girlfriend.

Her eyes drink her in, widen slightly, and then her smile grows and grows and grows. She bends and sets Robin on her feet, saying, "Let me help you," as she hurries forward.

"Where's Daniel?"

"Oh, the neighbors tried to deep-fry a turkey, and he got called down there to put out a fire."

"Like, a legit firefighter call? Or a panicked text?"

"It was a *very* panicked *call*," Liv says. "He promised he'd be back as soon as possible." She takes the case of apple cider from Claudia and sets it on an end table. "You are the most gorgeous woman in the whole world." She opens her arms. "Do you hug hello?"

"Sure." Claudia speaks in a warm voice and her smile curves up her mouth, which she's glossed in the last ten minutes. She's told me several times that she's nervous to meet Liv and Aunt Jill, but she's a professional in everything she does. Meeting her boyfriend's family notwithstanding.

"This is Claudia Brown," I say as the two women embrace. "Claude, my sister, Liv. Liv, Claudia. Please don't embarrass me."

"You do that well enough on your own." My sister shoots me a look as she steps back. "This dress." She fluffs up Claudia's wide, billowy sleeves. "Where did you get it?"

"My roommate is a model," Claudia says. "It's one of hers, and it just happens to fit me."

Like a glove, I think but manage to keep dormant.

"It's like Thanksgiving and autumn in cloth," Liv says. She turns her gaze on me. "I see you've decided to be festive this year too."

I puff out my turkey chest. "Claudia wanted to see me in a t-shirt. You want me to dress for the season. This does both."

"I've never seen him in a t-shirt," Claudia says. She picks up the cider and heads for the kitchen. "Baby, will you get the rest?"

"Yes, ma'am." I watch the women as they congregate in the kitchen, and there's so much about seeing them there that makes me so happy. Claudia obviously stands out, because she's dark-haired and skinned and eyed while my sister and my aunt are lighter, fairer, like me.

When I'm bordering on stalker-staring, I duck back out the front door and head to my truck to get the dogs and the rest of the sparkling drinks. "Come on," I say to Duke and Rocky, and I stand back while they jump down. Duke barks out his excitement, and my little nephew calls to them from the front door.

"Come on, Dukey!" Denver yells. "I have a bone for you!"

My sister has a fenced backyard, so I leave the leashes and grab the grapefruit sparkling soda.

"Hey there," someone says behind me, and I turn to find my brother-in-law headed my way. Daniel's wearing a pair of jean shorts and a polo in brown and white stripes. I'm sure Olivia picked that out for him, and I smile at him.

"Hey."

"Got everything?"

I nudge the door closed with my foot. "Got it all. Thanks."

"How was the drive?" Dan takes the case of soda from me.

"Just fine. Not too busy."

"I mean with Aunt Jill and Claudia in the same car." He grins at me. "Did she ask all those embarrassing questions she usually does?"

I chuckle and shake my head. "I told her if she did, I'd turn around and take her home."

Daniel laughs fully and turns toward the house. "So threatening her works. Good to know." He's got a full beard like me, and he lets his hair grow long. Apparently he can do that as a firefighter, but sometimes I wonder how he gets it all under his helmet.

"Daddy!" Denver yells like he hasn't seen his father in weeks and weeks, not a few minutes. "You're back."

"I'm back." Daniel ruffles his son's hair as he moves by, and he adds, "Come on, Baby Princess. The party's in here, not out there," for his daughter.

I follow him inside and scoop Denver into one arm, which causes a squeal of delight to come from the boy. I grab Robin with the other, and she giggles and laughs too. "How are you guys?"

"Look my bows." Robin reaches up to her blonde hair, which my sister has put into two piggy tails, complete with bright orange bows. She touches them, which I'm sure Liv won't like.

"They're amazing," I tell the little girl.

"I got a new soccer ball," Denver says. "You wanna kick it?"

"I know, buddy," I say. "I sent you the soccer ball for your birthday, remember?"

The boy blinks, and I grin at him. "Oh, yeah." He squirms to get down, and I bend to get him closer to the floor before I drop him. Thankfully, that doesn't happen, and Denver lurches forward on his feet, already running into the kitchen.

"Momma, I kick the ball?"

"No, buddy," Liv says. "We're eating dinner now."

I switch my gaze to Claudia, and she's watching me

with my niece in my arms. She probably saw me with Denver too, and I wonder what she sees. As I approach the island, I see the dark depths of desire in her eyes, and it doesn't upset me.

"Did you meet Robin?" I ask, looking at the tiny girl. "She'll be two just after the New Year, huh, baby?" I press a kiss to the little girl's chubby cheek.

"Two," she says, and Claudia's smile blooms to life on her face.

"That's great," she says sweetly. "What do you want for Christmas?"

"Choc milk," she says, and Liv goes, "Chocolate milk. She wants it for everything." She smiles at her daughter and pulls out a pan of yellow Jell-O from the fridge.

"You made Mom's Jell-O salad," I say.

Our eyes meet, and I can feel Claudia's gaze on the side of my face too.

"Yes," Liv says diplomatically. "That way, it's almost like she's here."

But she's not *here*, I want to say. But I'm not going to be the one to start a fight today. It won't be a fight anyway. Liv and I don't always agree, but we don't fight either. I press my teeth together for a single moment, and then I say, "Come on, Baby Princess. Let's get in your seat, because your momma says it's time to eat."

"Momma, I kick ball," Denver whines, and Liv starts herding him toward the table too.

"Dan," she says. "Can you carve the turkey? I think

then I can get everything lined up." They scurry around the kitchen while I help my niece and nephew and Aunt Jill to their spots at the table. My sister is a goddess, and she put me next to Claudia, and I stand out of the way with my arm around her.

"So?" I whisper. "What do you think?"

"I think they're amazing," she says.

"Yeah," I say. "I do too."

"You're..." She looks at me despite the chaos of Robin banging her plastic spoon on her tray and Denver asking Aunt Jill if he can go out and kick his soccer ball. "You have a lot of different facets."

"Most people do," I say as Liv says, "Okay, we're ready." She looks over to us, then past us to the table. "You kids hush up." She raises her voice a little, and she marches over to Robin and takes her spoon from her.

The little girl blinks and then starts wailing, and Denver climbs up on his seat and says, "Where's my soccer ball?"

I look at Claudia as Liv and Daniel descend on their kids to try to get them to play nicely now that dinner is ready. She grins at me, and then she moves over to Denver and pulls him onto her lap. She bends her head, her long, dark hair falling down over her shoulder as she speaks to him.

I take Robin from Liv and hand her back the spoon, and my sister runs her hands through her hair, and I don't dare tell her that now she has a little bit of turkey grease on her face. She blows out her breath and looks over to Daniel.

"Let's pray while they're quiet, because we're only going to get these five seconds."

———

HOURS LATER, after pie and coffee and the beginning of *White Christmas*, after dropping off Aunt Jill, and after throwing the ball to the dogs for a few minutes, I settle onto the swing with Claudia.

She smiles at me, brings her feet up and tucks them under her as she cuddles into my side. "That was really fun."

"Well, we survived it anyway." I curl my arm around her, liking this physical closeness. "What did Luke do today?"

"He's got new bros in Liam and Aaron, and Dylan is at his mother's, so I'm pretty sure he went over there."

"That's where the others went too, right?"

"Just Ry, Emma, and Hillary," I say.

"Which is half of you."

She doesn't argue back with me, which is my first clue that she's a touch irritated. The moment is quiet, and I can practically hear everyone who already knows about the job in Beaufort—which is everyone except Claudia—yelling at me to *Tell her already, Becks.*

It's time to tell her.

"So." I clear my throat. At my feet, the dogs pant. The sun has gone down. The porch swing drifts back and forth. "I've got an interview on Monday morning, so I won't be in the office."

The words scrape my throat, but they come out.

Claudia sits up. "You got a third interview?"

"No," I say carefully. "I have an interview down in Beaufort." I clear my throat again. "I'm not going to get the City Planner job, Claude."

"What?" She narrows her eyes. "Why won't you get it?"

"Because—"

"Beckett." She holds up one hand. "I do not need you to concede this to me. In fact, I will be *up-set* if you do that."

"I'm not conceding."

"You're interviewing somewhere else. What do you call that?"

"Trying to keep you," I say.

She blinks and scoffs, scoffs again and shakes her head. "That's ridiculous."

"You—you don't even know the rules." I shake my own head, because I'm tired of being perfect today. Perfectly dressed. The perfect gentleman during dinner. A perfect driver, with two side-seat and back-seat drivers in the truck with me. The perfect dog-dad. Boyfriend perfection. All of it.

I get to my feet and say, "Let's talk about this later."

"Later?" Her eyes blaze with black fire. "What's the job in Beaufort?"

I whistle to the dogs and say, "Come on, guys. It's time for bed." I head for the house, trying to figure out a way out of this that doesn't end with her stomping into the Big House in that phenomenal dress.

"Beckett."

The full name. I really am in trouble.

"Claudia, forget I said anything, okay? I'm too tired to explain this tonight. We'll talk about it later." I open the back door and let the dogs in, then turn to face her. "Let me take you home and kiss you good-bye, and we'll talk about it later."

She studies me in the light pouring out of the kitchen.

"Please," I say.

She huffs, pushes past me into the house, and continues toward her leftover bottles of cider. She swoops them up into her arms, and I look up toward the ceiling as a sigh flaps between my lips.

"Why does every conversation have to be hard?"

CLAUDIA

I stew in my ire from Beckett's house to mine. When he pulls up, I look over to him. "Do you really think every conversation between us is hard?"

He gazes at me evenly. I shouldn't have asked, but I can't help myself. "No," he says. "I think we've been doing great at work with the Christmas Festival."

"That's work."

"We've had plenty of personal conversations that aren't hard."

I nod and turn to get out of the truck. He copies me and meets me at the hood. "Claudia, please."

I can't deny him when he begs like that. "Kiss me, Becks." I lean into him and somehow gather enough of his collar to fist, drawing him closer.

His arms come around me, his gaze lighting up with desire. "Did you like my t-shirt?"

"Yes," I whisper. "It's adorable."

"Adorable?" He quirks his mouth at me. "Your dress is stunning."

"You're wearing a turkey tee," I tell him. The ground we're standing on is a little shaky. But he lowers his head and kisses me like we're rock solid. Maybe I'm the only one with doubts right now, and I shove them away, because we've had such an amazing day up until now.

"I'll call you tomorrow," he says huskily as he pulls away. He tucks my hand inside his and takes me all the way to the door. I can't seem to look straight at him, and he hugs me as he adds, "Thank you for an amazing holiday."

"Thank *you* for an amazing holiday." When I step back, I expect a smile, but I don't get one. Beckett really has dozens and dozens of facets, and I picture him with both of those adorable little children in his arms. They could've been his.

But not mine. I'm way too dark to have blonde babies like those children were. Still, seeing him with them showed me another polished side of him that I really like. I smile at him quietly and open the door behind me. Then I slip inside and close the door while Beckett turns to go back to his car.

I sigh, already reaching to undo the gold leaf earring in my left lobe. "Definitely a mistake wearing these," I say to the quiet, dark house. They're too heavy. I grab a piece of leftover pecan pie from the kitchen and take it up to the third floor.

For two beats, I forget Hillary's here this week, and I startle toward the end of the hall where music softly plays from her bedroom. I go into my room and shed my dress and unzip and kick off my ankle boots.

I've barely pulled on my ratty tee before Hill knocks on the door. "Yeah," I say in a tired voice.

She comes in as I pull on my sweats and sink onto my bed. "Well?"

"Amazing," I say with a sigh that says otherwise.

"Uh oh." Hillary joins me on my bed and reaches over to unclip my hair. "They loved you, I'm sure." She smiles at me the way only a very, very good friend can.

"They seemed to." My chest shakes as I breathe in. "I loved them."

"You love Beckett."

I shake my head slowly and look down at my comforter. "No, I don't."

"Not yet."

I meet Hillary's eyes, a storm whipping through me body, soul, and mind. "Hillary."

She peers at me, pure concern in her face. "What is it, sweetie?"

I don't know how to put anything in words, so I shake my head again. I just have to open my mouth and let the story come out, even if it's talking about Beckett behind his back. Hillary's always been the easiest for me to talk to, and she's always helped me riddle through problems, work, personal, or family.

"Beckett's interviewing for another job down in Beaufort," I say, and from there, everything I know pours out of me.

———

MONDAY MORNING, I show up at the office, expecting to see Beckett's dark doorway. I do, and I immediately tear my eyes from it. We haven't spoken much since Thanksgiving evening. He didn't come dog-walking with me this weekend. Hillary did, and I feel like crying all over again, just like I did last night when she and Liam left for the airport and California.

I hold my head high as I say, "Good morning, ladies," to Tabby and Sybil.

"Morning, Claude," they chorus back to me. "Oh, Claudia." Sybil jumps to her feet and follows me into her office. "Mayor Garvin wants you to call her."

"Really?" I set my bag on my desk and turn to look at Sybil. "When did she call?"

"About ten minutes ago. I said you'd be showing up any moment." Sybil looks especially birdy today, as her blouse actually has birds all over it. Blue birds and red birds and yellow birds. Primary color birds. "She wanted you to call the moment you could." She hooks her thumb over her shoulder. "Should I get her on the line?"

I haven't even sat down yet, but I nod. "Sure. Thank you, Sybil." I round my desk as my secretary leaves my office. My breath catches going down and coming back up, and I cough to clear my throat.

My desk chair feels two sizes too small as I sit, and I wait for my phone to ring. It only takes another few seconds, and then Sybil says, "Line one, Claudia."

"Thank you." I take a breath and let the oxygen run through me. Then I pick up the receiver, press line one, and say, "Mayor Garvin, good morning," in a voice as bright as the sun. "What can I do for you, ma'am?"

"Claudia," she says. "We'd love to see you over at City Hall this morning if you've got time."

I think of the empty office next door to mine. "I've got time," I say.

"We know you're working every moment possible on the Christmas Festival, but this is also urgent."

"Yes, ma'am," I say. "I can just grab my purse and head over now?"

"I'll rally the troops here."

"Great." The call ends, and I suddenly realize I don't know where "here" is. Mayor Garvin's office? Winslow's? My other two interviews have been in a conference room down the hall from Winslow's—and where the new City Planner will be housed—and I reason that I'll surely go there again.

As I leave the office, my traitorous mind thinks, *Maybe Beckett had a third interview this morning and he lied to you about it. Made up some story about Beaufort.*

"Headed out?" Sybil asks, and I spin back to her.

"Yes," I say breathlessly. "I guess I'm going over for another interview right now. Wish me luck." I try to smile, but it feels pasted on wrong, and I don't want to show up looking like a house with bad wallpaper.

So I take a moment in my car to get put back together. I pull out my lip gloss, and my interview shade is actually called Boss Babe, and I try to adopt that mindset as I walk into City Hall.

I curse myself for not looking for Beckett's truck in the parking lot, and then I chastise myself for thinking he lied to me. The truth is, Beckett and I have a relationship like a yo-yo. Sometimes it's up, and sometimes it's down, and sometimes it's been thrown all around. Right now, I don't know where we are, and when I have to face him this afternoon, I have no idea how that will go.

Those feelings of uncertainty drive me nuts, and I shelve them as I peer around the corner into the usual conference room. There's no one there, but my binder-portfolio sits at the head of the table, so I know I'm in the right place.

No one's ever announced me before, so I enter the room and move over to my binder. I flip open the front cover, expecting to see my cover letter, the one I labored over meticulously to outline why I'm the perfect candidate for this job.

But it's not my letter sitting there. The piece of paper there isn't even in a plastic sleeve, something I immediately rebel against. It does make it far easier to lift out of the binder, and as my eyes slide from left to right, and then down a line, and left to right again, my pulse increases and increases and increases.

"I wholeheartedly endorse Claudia Brown for the city government position of City Planner in the municipality of Cider Cove." My voice doesn't sound like my own, because I can barely hear it above the gonging of my pulse.

The room spins, because I'm not breathing properly, and I sink into the chair at the head of the table as if I'm the mayor herself.

This letter is really, really nice, but it's completely unfamiliar. So, before I finish, my eyes drop to the bottom, where a flourish of a signature sits, and this guy thinks he's a doctor, because no one can read that.

Which is fine, because he's typed his name below it.

Beckett Fletcher, Deputy Director over City Development, Cider Cove, SC

Every thought vanishes.

All emotions flee.

I can still hear, and see, and feel, and taste, and smell, but there's nothing there tickling those senses.

That's when I realize I have tears pricking in my eyes, and now they're sliding down my face.

Beckett Fletcher has written me the most complimentary letter of recommendation known to mankind.

My eyes fly to the top of the paper, where the date sits. October twenty-ninth.

I even say it out loud: "October twenty-ninth?"

He's known for a lot longer than a few days that he's going to walk away from this job. Walk away from Cider Cove.

Walk away from us.

"Ah, there you are," Winslow says. "Sorry, we got caught in a call."

"It's fine." I drop the letter like it's toxic waste and now I have it on my hands, flip the binder closed, and get to my feet, all in a single, sweeping motion. I duck my head and wipe my tears, and when I face him, Mike Bowing—the current City Planner—and Mayor Winslow, it's with my Boss Babe face securely hiding anything going on beneath the surface.

I have no idea what's about to happen, but after that letter, I know I better be ready for anything.

Dead Salmon and *Caliente* and *Barbie Dreamhouse Pink* run through my mind, and let me tell you, combining those three colors would be putrid. I can only hope this interview will be the opposite of that.

BECKETT

I FAKE-LAUGH MY WAY OUT OF THE BRICK BUILDING IN Beaufort, keeping my smile and positive expression hitched in place until I'm in my truck and driving down the block. Then my face falls, and I glance over to my briefcase bag riding shotgun in the passenger seat.

"Well, I mean, it went well. I think they liked me." I need to practice what I'm going to tell Claudia once I get back to the office. Surely she'll have questions, and I can just hear her saying, "It's later, Beckett. Time to talk."

She might even make me close my office door.

I have one more stop to make before I head out to the drab trailer bordering the rail yard, and I tell myself that the building in Beaufort is way better than the Public Works trailer. "Yeah," I mutter. "If only it wasn't in Beaufort."

Because if I get that job—and I really think I will—I'll

be moving. And I'm moving to keep Claudia in my life. But then, Claudia and I will be long-distance dating, and that's no picnic. Most couples don't survive that.

My thoughts swirl like cotton candy going round a stick, and they feel as thready and lightweight too. Before I know it, I've arrived at City Hall. I glare at my briefcase bag, though it's not its fault it's been carrying a letter around for a couple of weeks.

It gets heavier and heavier every time I pick it up too, and it's time. I open the flap and take out the letter. It's printed, dated, signed, ready to go. I just have to walk into Winslow Harvey's office and hand it to him. I don't even have to do that.

I glance up to the fourth floor, where his office is. I can just give it to his secretary. I can leave it on his desk. I don't have to personally hand him the letter. We don't have to have a lengthy conversation about it.

"Go," I tell myself. "Do it." Still, I wait, almost hoping someone will call me or text me, delay me a little.

I've missed Claudia these past few days, and if anything, her silence has proven to me that I'm doing the right thing. She's going to find out about all of it really, really soon, and there's nothing I can do to slow that tide.

But it doesn't matter. All I can do is what I've done, and now, I have to hope that we're strong enough to weather the water. I don't know if I can survive Hurricane Claudia, but I sure am going to try. Because I've missed her *terribly* these past few days, and I need her in my life forever and always.

She probably thinks she's punished me this weekend, but the reality is, she's only given me more clarity. She's proven to me how hard I need to dig my heels in. "She's going to filet you alive with one of those pie spatulas."

That thought gets me out of the truck, because before I die a painful pie-death-by-tiny-spatula, I need to turn in my letter of resignation.

CLAUDIA

"THAT'S WHAT I'M SAYING," I say to Ry, who's called me on her break. "And he's not back yet. How long can an interview in Beaufort be?" I glance left and right through the parking lot, but there's only one way in and one way out. Beckett won't be able to get by me sitting on the steps either.

"Let me get this straight. He wrote you a letter of recommendation after all," Ry says. "And turned it in with his own application—days before you turned in yours."

"Yes."

"And now he's interviewing other places for other jobs."

"Yes." This time, the word is a whisper.

"And Mayor Garvin said to your face that you're going to get the City Planner job."

"Shh," I say, my eyes sweeping left and right again.

Ry giggles. "I'm standing in my office with the door locked," she says. "This place is like a metal trap. No one can hear me."

"She didn't say it in so many words. She said to expect to get a letter by the beginning of next week, following the Christmas Festival."

"But you're going to get it."

A half-smile twitches against my lips. "I'm ninety-nine percent sure, yes." I sigh, my smile slipping to the pavement. "But Ry, don't you see what that means? Lizzie was right. There's a loser here, and it's Beckett." I don't even want to say what's percolating in my head now. "Maybe he's planning to quit and move to get away from me."

I drop my head and frown at the ground near my feet. "I just need to talk to him."

"No," Ry says. "And you listen to me real good now, Claudia. You don't need to talk to him. You need to *listen* to him."

"I listen to him."

She snorts, and I can just see her incredulous look. The wide eyes. The raised eyebrows. "Promise me you'll *listen* to him."

"I do listen to him. You should see how much I've listened to him over this Christmas Festival."

"Claudia," she says, and now she's using her Firm and Authoritative Voice. "You're in love with this man, and you need to admit it. Once you do that, you'll do the right thing."

"I am not—"

"My break is over," she yells over me, and the line goes dead in the next moment.

I blink, sure Ry's breaks have never been so short. I even check my phone, and sure enough, she's hung up on me. I fist my phone and look out into the parking lot again. It's not exactly warm sitting in the shade on these metal steps, but I don't dare move.

I have to see Beckett. I have to talk to him.

I have to...listen to him.

So much hinges on what he'll say to me, and I wish he'd hurry up and get here. I twist my hands together and scan the parking lot. Every sound the breeze makes through the trees or along a bush causes me to jump.

And then, like the silent black panther Beckett is, his truck turns into the lot. I get to my feet, my mouth suddenly so, so dry. Which is fine, because I'm not going to say a word. Beckett gets to do the talking; I am going to listen.

I am.

He sees me way before he even finds a parking space, and he takes his sweet South Carolina time getting out of the truck and gathering his briefcase, his lunch, and his jacket. That's slung over his forearm, with two brown bags of food gripped in the hand balancing it all, and he carries his briefcase in the other one.

He's dressed to the nines, of course, because Beckett had an interview in Beaufort for their City Controller position. Yeah, I looked it up over the weekend. I needed to know what I'm dealing with.

"Hey," he says from several paces away.

"You've been gone a long time," I say. "I was getting nervous."

"You were?" He gives me one of his cocky Co-worker Beckett smiles. "Why? I told you I'd be gone all morning."

"I think you said *in* the—" I cut off when I realize I'm arguing semantics with him. "How did it go?" I ask instead.

He looks up into the blue sky and sighs. "I think it went really well, actually. I think I'll get it." He moves past me and says, "It's too cold to stand in the shade, baby. Let's go inside."

"Beckett," I say as I hurry to follow him. "Sweetheart, wait."

He turns back to me in the middle of the metal stairs, his eyebrows practically on his hairline. "Did you call me sweetheart?"

"Yes." I step up onto the stair he's on. "I... Can you please tell me everything that's been going on since October twenty-ninth, when you decided to write me the nicest, bestest, most amazing letter of recommendation in the world?"

I lightly touch his forearm, and he looks down where we're connected. "Please?" I ask.

He meets my eye. "Bestest is not a word."

I grin at him, my tears already close to the surface again. "You made me cry."

He sighs and does that head rolling again. "Oh, no. That wasn't the goal." He gathers me close, the way I need to be held. He always seems to know exactly how to hold me. "The goal, baby, was to make sure you got the job."

"I didn't—"

"Because you're the best person for it," he says over me. "I realized about the time I kissed you for the first time that I'd rather have *you* than any job, ever, anywhere."

I pull back enough to look at him. Our eyes search and search the other's. "And it took you *two months* to write me the letter of recommendation?"

He tilts his head back and laughs, the sound joyful and flying up toward the heavens.

"Can we please go eat whatever you brought in those bags in your office?" I ask. "I really want to hear everything."

"Yeah, come on." He's still chuckling as he leads me inside, and we walk side-by-side down the hall and into our department. He casts me a look that says he hasn't made anything official yet, and I will not say a word until he does.

"Ladies," he says, facing them again. "I have an announcement."

Tabby and Sybil look up, but their expressions are exact opposites. Tabby knows; Sybil doesn't.

"I'm going to be leaving Cider Cove city government

at the end of the year," he says in a smooth, clear voice. This is his Presentation Voice, and it used to rub me entirely the wrong way. Now, I'm beaming at him. He glances at me, and I nod in answer to his unspoken question. "Claudia is going to get the City Planner job, so we're both going to be gone."

"Beckett," Sybil says as she rises to her feet. "Really?"

"It's the best move for me," he says. "See, if I stay here, Claudia and I will have to disclose our relationship. She'll be my boss, and there'll be all this paperwork. She hates paperwork, and she hates people looking at her and knowing her private business."

He focuses on me, and every word he speaks makes more and more pieces fall into place. "I thought I might lose her if we had to go through that. I thought she might feel too bad by beating me out of a job that she wouldn't want to be with me. And see, I can't lose her. I'm trying really hard not to do anything that would cause her to not want to be with me."

Beckett takes a breath and looks at the secretaries again. I do too, and Tabby is smiling that female smile that says, *Awwww.*

I feel it moving through my soul too. Sybil has one hand pressed against her heartbeat, her mouth open in an O.

"So." He exhales heavily, his shoulders going down with the release. "I'm applying for jobs anywhere within a fifty-mile radius of Cider Cove. I interviewed in Beaufort today, and—" He turns toward me, his hands still gripping two bags of food and his briefcase. "I turned in my letter of resignation just before I came into the office."

I gasp this time too, and I'm frantically trying to find any hint of untruth in his gaze. There is none. "Beckett."

"I'm quitting, Claude," he says. "To be with you. So you can just move seamlessly into the job you were born to do. On your own terms. And I can leave on *my* terms. Find a job that's right for me—and hopefully, even if it's in Beaufort, we can still make this work."

Tabby approaches, and she takes everything out of Beckett's hands, like they've perfected this dance over the years they've worked together. He gives speeches; she takes his things when he needs her to.

"Because I'm in love with you, Claudia Brown," he says next, his voice husky. It reminds me of Warm Honey, which is a wonderful, warm, golden yellow, perfect for sunrooms and porches and even kitchens. It's cheerful and bright and filled with everything good. Everything worth having.

That's what it feels like to be loved by Beckett Fletcher.

"You don't have to say it back," he says as he leans closer. "I know you will when you're ready, but I just want you to know why I'm doing what I'm doing. It's for you, but it's for me too. Because I want to be with you. I never want our jobs to come between us again, and I will never *ever* take another bet of yours."

He grins as tears fall down my face.

"You didn't lose that bet," I whisper. "You didn't have to write that letter."

"Baby, I am totally lost when it comes to you, and I will write a hundred letters to make sure you get what you want." He brushes away my tears and adds, "So don't cry, my Midnight Beauty," just before he kisses me in front of our department.

BECKETT

I TAKE A FOUR-FOOT SPRUCE FROM THE BACK OF THE trailer and turn to place it on the ground. I can carry two at a time, something I've done a couple of times now. And bonus, I already know where these go, as Claudia has already given me my instructions.

We have a whole crew here with us in the downtown square today, as it's set-up day for the Christmas Festival. Vendors have until ten a.m. tomorrow to have their tents filled and ready, because that's when the Christmas Market opens.

It'll actually run all the way through Christmas, while the Festival only lasts through the weekend. The ice skating rink will be here all month too, and Mobile Adventures has been in town for the past couple of days, prepping the area.

They have three men here working right now, and

Claudia stands in the middle of the park, her jeans like painted denim on her body and a cute little red puffer jacket covering her top half. I can look at her all day, but I focus on putting the baby spruce trees where they go in Santa's Village, where his sleigh has already arrived.

The groundskeeping crew from Cider Cove is here today too, and they've clearly been working on the park for days. The city building across the street drips with icicle lights, and the church across from it hosts pure white lights and a star on the steeple to contribute to the ambiance.

The businesses that line the other two sides of the street have donned their windows with holiday trimmings, and any that hadn't, we've arranged to hang wreaths and lights for them. Mayor Garvin wants the most festive square in all of the US, though I'm not sure how she can possibly measure that.

I arrange the trees and pick up the light string I'd left behind last time. The grounds crew have cleared the park. They've hung lights in every tree, along every branch, and they've hung garland along the fence around the statue, leaving space for the ice skate rental booth, and as I look over to the monument in the middle of the square, I watch as someone I should probably know from the Public Works Department hangs an enormous wreath of mistletoe from the hand of one of our founders.

He's pointing toward something as he looks over his shoulder, and right below the mistletoe is a spot on a narrow sidewalk in the gardens surrounding the statue where a *lot* of kissing is going to happen this holiday season.

The worker calls down to someone else, and they lift their hand in a thumbs-up. More and more comes off the trailer and gets put where Claudia wants it. As the morning progresses, Santa's Village comes together completely. The tents for the Christmas Market get set up, the white flaps tied back and open.

I finally catch up to Claudia near the amphitheater in the corner of the park, where she and Larry are reviewing the schedule for the Living Bethlehem performances that begin tomorrow night and run for the duration of the festival.

"There you are," she says. "What are you doing?"

I glance over to Larry. "The village is done. All we need is Santa and our photographer to show up."

"Excellent." She'll walk the whole park before we go home tonight, making checkmarks on her clipboard. *Check, check, check.*

"Mobile Adventures is starting the rink." I nod over to it. "Mistletoe is hung. Garland and lights. Christmas Market only has two more tents." I look over my shoulder to the church. "I need to go talk to the pastor over there about hosting a hot chocolate station, and I need to call the theater and make sure we're set for this weekend."

"That's what I was going to ask you," she says, consulting her clipboard for a moment. "Nancy called from the theater, and I told her I'd send you down to her."

"Sure." I lean down and kiss her quickly. "Should I bring back coffee?"

"Not if you're going to drive all the way to Legacy." She gives me a look that says, *You don't have time to do that, Becks.*

I chuckle and say, "No, I was just thinking of stopping in the diner over there and grabbing some."

"Then yes."

The mayor provided lunch for us today, as well as the other fifteen people still working in the park, but my stomach still growls as I decide to tackle the closest problem and cross the street to the church first.

I secure the area there, which will be easy to get to and offer somewhat of a shelter from the storm of the festival, and as I come out of the church, I pause and really drink in the Christmas spirit as it spills out of the park.

The streets around the square are closed today, and they'll remain that way until we tear everything down next week. So the "reindeer rides" will circle the block, and music will pipe over everything, and in the evening, when it's dark... I see perfection, lit up in Christmas lights.

My eyes travel to Claudia, and she's bent over a box, digging through it for something. What, I don't know. I just know that whatever it is will be placed perfectly, and that Claudia's attention to detail will all pay off.

This Christmas Festival is going to be the best one Cider Cove has ever seen. I bask in the glory and warmth of the Christmas spirit as it flows out of the square and down the streets of the town. This town I love.

A hint of sadness accompanies me down the block to the old movie theater that's been in town almost as long as Cider Cove has existed. My resignation has been accepted. My last day will be December twenty-ninth, and I hope to start another job in January. I haven't heard anything from Beaufort City, but I just interviewed there yesterday.

As I open the door to the theater, I come face-to-face with Elliott, Luke, and Aaron. "Hey, fellas." I scan the three of them, as we're semi-friends. They've been at the same parties at the Big House or Liam's place as me in the past couple of months. "What's happening here?"

Luke holds up a couple of tickets. "They're almost out of tickets for Saturday night."

"Couples night?" I ask.

Elliott grins and nods over to Aaron. "Ask him who he's taking."

Aaron scoffs. "Please. Ask *him* who *he's* taking." He glares at Elliott, who simply keeps grinning and then over-acts as he puts his tickets in his back pocket.

I smile over to Luke. "Who are you taking?"

"I asked this woman at the bakery I stop by some-times." He doesn't seem embarrassed by it at all, and when I look at Elliott, he says nothing.

"So I'm getting nothing from you two?" I grin at them. "I better get my tickets for me and Claude."

"You have to buy them?" Elliott asks. "I thought you'd get them for free."

"I'm sure I'll get some from Nancy." I edge by them to go find the manager of the movie theater, so I can make sure she has everything from us that she needs for this weekend, because *I* need things this weekend on couples' night to be absolutely perfect.

———

THE FOLLOWING AFTERNOON, Claudia and I finally stop obsessing over every pine bough that might be bent wrong, and we wander in front of a row of white tents selling things like churros, puzzles, Tupperware, hand-stitched tea towels, and hot roasted nuts.

"This is incredible," I say in a loud voice. "Whoever put this together is a genius."

"Becks." Claudia giggles and cuddles into my side. "Stop it."

"Did you see them ice skating?"

"You've asked me that four times."

"But did you *see* them?" I grin over to the rink, which seems fairly full, and there's a line of people waiting to get skates. My phone rings, and I tug it out of my pocket and see a number I don't know.

My brain fizzes at me, and I swipe on the call. "This is Beckett Fletcher," I say, because I do get some cold calls about work sometimes.

"Beckett," a man says. "This is Craig Biggs. From Beaufort."

"Of course, Beaufort," I say, looking over to Claudia. "It's great to hear from you Craig. From Beaufort."

Claudia stops walking, pure anxiety on her face as she watches me. I have to admit that my pulse might be racing a bit too fast.

"Well, we all loved you, Beckett, and I got the great job of calling and offering you the job of City Controller here in Beaufort."

"Wow," I say, a smile painting across my whole face. I feel like one of the Christmas bulbs, pulsing out joy and light and happiness.

Claudia swats at my chest. "Say yes," she hisses.

"Yes," I blurt out, so many thoughts running through my head. "I mean, I'm—I'd love the job. Thank you."

"And you'll have that office we showed you on Monday. The one with the window that looks over the bay."

"Great," I say, though that office needs some serious love. No one's been using it, as I was told on Monday, and it definitely felt like it. Unused. No spirit.

"Great," Craig says. "If you come in next week, since I know you're swamped with your Christmas Festival this week, we'll get the paperwork started."

"Paperwork," I say, grinning at Claudia. "I love paperwork."

Craig laughs, and the call ends. I calmly and quietly

stow my phone in my back pocket, and then I meet Claudia's eyes. "You're being incredibly—"

I throw both hands up into the air, my hands balled into fists, and bellow, "I got the job! In Beaufort!" I hold onto the last word and howl it like a wolf while I expect Claudia to shush me and tell me to be quiet.

She doesn't, and when I lower my arms and look at her, she's grinning. "Did you get the job in Beaufort, Beckett?"

I sweep her into my arms, and she squeals as I turn her around right there in the park. She hates the spotlight, but I don't care who's watching. The Christmas Festival has started without a hitch—knock on wood—and I got the City Controller job in Beaufort.

We laugh together as I set her back on her feet, and she brushes her hand down my chest. "Now, I just need to get the job here."

"You're going to get it."

"I hope so." She takes a big breath, nods like she's steeling herself to summon up another reserve of patience. "Come on, you promised me a hot dog from The Weiner Wagon." She links her arm through mine and aims me toward the northern street which we designated for the food truck rally.

"Claude," I say. "The office they're giving me is next-level bad. Like, so bad."

"What do you mean?'

"I mean, it hasn't been used in a while, and it's—brace

yourself." I glance over to her, and the way she watches me lights me up from within. She's interested, hanging on my every word. "Beige," I mock-whisper. "I'm really gonna need someone who can pick out the *perfect* paint color."

Her eyes widen for a moment, and then her expression dissolves into one of pure joy. "Well, it's a good thing you have an amazing girlfriend who can pick the exact-right paint color for any room."

"It's a government building," I say. "What if they don't let us paint?"

"Beckett, I will not let you go to work every day to a *beige* office." She shakes her head. "Nope, no way. We'll get this sorted before you start, don't you worry."

I pull her close and gaze down at her. "With you at my side, Claude, I don't worry about anything."

"But getting me a hot dog before I gnaw off my own arm."

"But getting you a hot dog before you gnaw off your own arm." I grin at her and touch my lips to hers. "I love you, Claudia."

She kisses me back, which surprises me given the location. Then she says, "I love you too, Becks," and my joy is complete.

CLAUDIA

"How do we look?" I ask as I put my foot down into the living room.

Tahlia chokes on her sip of Diet Coke, and Lizzie whistles. "Dang, girl," she says. "That is taking the little black dress to a new level."

"She's going to make the rest of us look bad," Ry says as she joins me in the living room, but she has no room to talk. She's wearing a gorgeous red gown with sequins sewn into the sheer sleeves and sparkling even in our boring living room lights.

She's going to knock off Elliott's socks, and the man won't know what hit him. She's told me fifty times that it's not a date—that Elliott just wanted to go to couples' movie night tonight, because he's sick of staying home alone on the weekend. He's normally pretty social, and the fact that he hasn't had a girlfriend for a couple of months has only fueled Ry's crush on him.

She claimed Elliott would be dressed up, and she couldn't just show up in her pajamas. He waited until the last-minute to ask her, but Lizzie still had something for her in her closet. And the dress looks like it was made for Ry, though she slides her hands down her midsection.

"Stop that," I hiss at her. "You look amazing."

"I'm stress-eating candy until he arrives." Ry holds up a bag of peanut butter M&Ms and moves around the couch to collapse into it. The doorbell sings in the next moment, and she pops back to her feet.

"I'll get it," I say.

"No, no, no, no-no-no-no." Tahlia jumps up, and she's wearing thick, padded socks. She loves them and owns several pairs. They have rubber bits on the bottom so she doesn't slip, but this must be an old pair, because she yelps as her front leg slides out in front of her.

She drops into a near split, and then she groans loudly. "I—help." She looks up at me, and I don't know what she thinks I'm going to do. I'm wearing a tight tube studded in black jewels and heels that are an inch higher than normal.

Thankfully, Lizzie drops to her knees and helps Tahlia to her feet. Meanwhile, the doorbell rings again, and Ry huffs as she gets to her feet to go answer it. Emma's already off on her date for tonight, and I scurry after Ry as she rounds the corner.

"Ryanne," I hiss. "Let me get it for you."

"What if it's Beckett?"

"It's not my first date with Beckett."

She reaches for the handle and pauses. "This is not a date." She rolls her eyes and adds in a much quieter voice, "Elliott only told me that four hundred times."

Before I can stop her, she opens the door. Sure enough, Elliott stands there, and he's wearing a smile as wide as the ocean. When he sees Ryanne, his smile drops right from his face. He swallows, and his eyes travel down the length of Ry's dress, past the hem to her matching shoes, and when they come back up, they move slower than ever.

He clears his throat, and I step to Ry's side. "Good evening, Elliott," I say with a diplomatic smile. "As you can see, Ry is ready." I pluck the bag of candy from her and hide it behind my back. I nudge her with my elbow. "That jacket is amazing, Ell," I practically yell.

Elliott startles as if he's just-now realizing that I'm standing there too. "Thanks." He drinks in Ry again. "Ry, you look absolutely amazing. Stunning. Gorgeous." There's not a smile in sight, because he's dead serious.

Ry says nothing, and I elbow her a little more forcefully. She huffs and glares at me, and I try to indicate Elliott with only my eyes. "Doesn't he look great too?" I ask her. She hasn't dated in a long time, and surely her crush on this good-looking man has addled her brains.

She blinks and turns woodenly back to Elliott. "Yes," she says. "You do look great too."

"There you go." I practically push her out of the house. "You two have fun. I'm sure we'll see you at the movie." I close the door behind her to give her some privacy, and I return to the living room, where Lizzie is leaning over the arm of the couch to hand Tahlia an ice pack. She places it in her groinal area, and I pause.

"Are you okay?"

"I'm fine," she gripes at me. "That must've been Elliott."

"Yep." I cock my head at her and then Lizzie. "You might need to take her to the hospital."

"Yeah, right," Lizzie says as Tahlia goes, "I'll just refuse to go."

"You might be hurt," I tell her.

"I'm thirty-four and did the splits." She shakes her head. "I'm *fine.*"

I want to argue some more, but I don't. I'm learning to listen to those around me instead of trying to impose my will on them, so I simply nod. "Okay," I say. "But if anything changes, text me, okay?"

"Sure," Tahlia says in a monotone, which means she could be nigh to death, and she won't interrupt my evening. The doorbell rings, and we all look toward the archway.

"I can answer the door for my own date," I say. "See

you guys later tonight, okay?" I make strong eye contact with Lizzie. "Lizzie?"

"Yes," she says, and she might actually call me if she thinks Tahlia is in real trouble. I pray she won't be as I open the door and find my handsome boyfriend standing there.

He's holding a bouquet of roses in a deep, dark, crimson, and the leading paint supply chain would call that—

"Bewitched," I say out loud.

"Oh, I am," he says, his gaze traveling down my body. Beckett steps up onto the threshold of the house with me, one hand expertly sliding around my waist and the other still gripping those flowers. "Do we have to go out tonight?"

"Yes," I whisper against his throat as I fiddle with his tie. It's red and green plaid and oh-so-festive for the holiday season. "This is what we've been waiting for all week." I look up at him. "You don't want to go?"

"Not with you in that dress," he murmurs.

I smile at him and say, "Thank you."

"Is it a rental?"

"I own this one."

"Hmm."

"Oh, *you're* humming now?" I grab onto his tie as I lean back a little more, because he keeps crowding in close to me, and I can't see him. "What did that mean?"

"What did it mean?" He gives me a mock-innocent look. "I didn't even realize I was doing it."

"It sounded judgey. You don't think I should own a dress like this?"

"It meant I'm glad you own that dress, because maybe then I'll get to see you in it again. And be able to take it—"

"Claude?"

With a flushing face, I drop Beckett's tie and turn back to Lizzie. "Yeah?"

"Sorry, uh—hey, Beckett."

He drops back to the porch, and that four inches both vertically and horizontally makes all the difference. "Hey, Lizzie. You look smashing tonight."

She looks down at her pj shorts and white tank top. "Thanks?"

"Lizzie," I say. "What's going on? Do you really think Tahlia will be okay?"

"What happened to Tahlia?" Beckett asks, but I hold up a hand in a signal that he should just wait.

"It's not Tahlia." She motions me closer to show me her phone. "It's Aaron," she hisses as she tilts the device toward me. "He said his date fell through and he wonders if I might want to go to the movie with him tonight."

I read the texts quickly and look at Lizzie with plenty of disbelief running through me. "Aaron Stansfield?"

"Yes," she whispers, and she's clearly excited. I thought she had a crush on a guy at work and then Elliott, but the razzle-dazzle in her eyes says different. "Should I say yes?"

"What about Em?" I ask.

"She's out with Taylor," Lizzie says, but her whole demeanor fades. "I should say no. She'll be upset."

"Does she like Aaron?" Beckett asks, and I pull in a breath, because I'd semi-forgotten he was standing only a few feet away.

"We think so," I say. "She hasn't said as much. There's been some flirting. I mean, you've seen them at the parties."

He looks totally confused, so I decide to put a wrap on this. "Go out with him, Lizzie. Emma's a big girl." I pick up my purse and smile at Beckett. "Let's go, baby."

He takes me back downtown to the magic of Christmas. The theater is just down the block, and the lights, the music, and the spirit of it reach me as I get out of his truck. I take a deep breath of it and look up into the sky.

"We did a good job on this festival," I say as I release my breath.

"Yes," he agrees as he comes to my side. "We did."

"We make a pretty good team."

"I'll agree," he says.

I nudge him with my hip as we start toward the theater, where several other couples are headed too. "What do you think about marriage?"

He takes my hand in his and lifts it to his lips. "We've talked about marriage."

"No we haven't."

"Haven't we?"

"No."

"Well, I'm not the date-forever type," he says. "I want to get married."

"To me?" I challenge, trying to hear something in his voice or in his words. Something.

"Yes, Claude," he says with a grin. "To you, okay? I want to get married to you." He opens the door of the theater and pauses to look at me. "What about you? If you marry me, you won't be able to live in the Big House."

There are so many things that would change. Heck, just having Hillary gone is a big shift, and when she comes back, she'll marry Liam and be gone for good.

But I heard Beckett say he isn't a date-forever type of guy. "I'd get married," I say. "To the right man."

He grins, clearly picking up the piece I put down, which had been part of a previous conversation about children, actually. "How do you know when you've found the right man?"

"You just know," I say as I move past him and into the theater. The whole thing has been transformed, as white Christmas lights beam down on movie-goers from the ceiling. Waiters loiter around every few feet, holding trays of pink champagne, and chest-high tables are filled with people drinking, chattering, and laughing.

An enormous Christmas tree takes up the spot in front of the big windows, and an electric fireplace crackles from the concessions area. "That fireplace is perfect," I say with a sigh. There are even stockings hanging from it.

"A genius definitely thought of that," Beckett whispers as he leans in close. "How soon would you want to get married?"

I smile to myself and duck my head. I don't have an answer for him, because I'm not one who really rushes into much, and certainly not matrimony.

"Chocolate-covered strawberry?" someone asks, and I reach for one. I pick up a glass of pink champagne too, and after I bite off the end of the strawberry and eat it, I grin at Beckett. "This is amazing. One of the better ideas anyone's had for a town event."

"Ladies and gentlemen," a woman says, and I know that's Nancy. "We're ready to begin seating now. Please have your tickets out and ready to speed us through this process."

I stick close to Beckett, not knowing where his seats are. When we reach the scanner, it's Nancy, and the older blonde woman takes us both into a hug. "This has been such an amazing day," she tells us, her face alight with that Christmas glow.

"I'm so glad," I say at the same time Beckett says, "All because of you, Nancy."

We head inside, where Beckett has great seats high enough to see the movie. And they're on the end, bless him. Mocktails are being served in here, along with small bites of food. We get goat-cheese-stuffed mushroom caps and tiny beef Wellington and pear tartlets before we take our seats.

Everyone here seems to be enjoying themselves, but I don't see my brother, and I don't see Emma or Lizzie. People are still coming in, and I lean into Beckett and say, "I've always wanted to get married in the warmer months. Spring or summer."

He nods, his Very Serious Beckett expression on. "This really is an amazing event, isn't it?"

"It is," I say. "Though it's not really about the pear tartlets."

"It's about who you're with." He gazes at me with that soft, filled-with-love expression, and I want to dive into his eyes and bathe there for a while. "I'm so glad I'm with you, Claudia."

"Me too, Becks." I curl one hand around his strong jaw and touch my lips to his. "I love you."

"I love you too."

———

Oh how I love Beckett and how he tells Claudia how much he loves her. I hope you did too!

Read on for a couple of sneak peak chapters at the next book in the Cider Cove series - **A VERY MERRY MESS** - and meet Ryanne and Elliot.

Get new free stuff every month, access to live events, special members-only deals, and more when you join the Feel-Good Fiction newsletter. You'll get instant access to the Member's Only area on my new site, where all the goodies are located, so join by scanning the QR code below.

SNEAK PEEK! A VERY MERRY MESS
CHAPTER ONE: RYANNE

I HAVE NO IDEA WHAT TO DO WITH THE STARES. Everyone seems to be looking at us, and I can't decide if it's me in this designer gown, or Elliott in his sport coat that used to be his grandfather's, or the awful combination of us.

Almond, peanut, chili nut, peanut butter. I recite the nutty M&M flavors to try to maintain my sanity, but it doesn't seem to be working. Everyone just keeps staring and staring and staring.

"Don't they have their own problems?" I mutter to myself.

"What?" Elliott leans his head toward me, but I don't want to explain to him. I just shake my head, and he turns toward me as a couple squeezes by him in this crowded lobby. "Do you want something to drink?"

"Heavens, yes," I say.

He plucks a drink from the tray and hands it to me, no smile in sight. "Is being out with me so bad?"

"What?"

"You look like you've stepped in something foul." He lifts his champagne to his lips and takes a sip. He makes a face and lowers it, and I know he won't taste it again.

"I'm just..." Something. I don't know what. Concussed? I'd have to be to agree to come to this couples' movie night with him.

"Elliott," someone female says before I can come up with an explanation. The woman's face brightens, and she doesn't see me as she moves into brush her lips along Ell's cheek. No one ever sees me, so I'm not sure why this tall blonde should. Or why it irritates me so much that she's now introducing her girlfriend to him.

Not that they're dating. They just came to this together, which is single-white-female code for, "I'm single, Elliott. Do you want to go out with me sometime?"

I take another sip—much bigger than Elliott's—of my drink and wait for her to walk away. "She was flirting hardcore with you."

"She was not." His smile drops, and I seriously don't know why he's so annoyed tonight. *He's* the one who asked *me* out.

"Was," I say, and not two seconds pass before another woman says, "Elliott Hutson? Holy gators and cattails, it *is* you!" Squealing happens, and this woman full-on hugs the man I can't drive from my mind no matter how many M&M flavors I recite, or how many bags of candy I eat.

I stand politely silent and invisible while Elliott chats up yet another woman, and then turns into me once more. He looks a little flushed, which only pushes all my buttons in the wrong way. "I want to go home."

He blinks at me, his expression going blank. "What?"

"In case you haven't noticed," I say. "And why should you? I'm invisible to everyone, including you. I always have been." My chest rolls left and right like a big ship on stormy seas. "I'm just standing here while you chat it up with all your potential girlfriends. Is that why you brought me? So you'd have an excuse to come and meet women?"

"Whoa, whoa," Elliott says, holding up both hands. "I'm not here to meet women."

I snort-scoff and look away. "Sure. That's how it totally seems." I drain the last of my champagne. If he doesn't want to take me home, I can call a ride. It's not that hard. "I'm leaving." I head for the door, and Elliott is right at my side.

"Ry," he says. "You don't want to see the movie?"

I push out of the theater, and the cooler air out here clears my head slightly. My face still feels too hot, and the alcohol still burns down my throat. Me and drinking is never a good idea, and I feel my tongue getting looser by the moment.

"I do," I say. "But it's just—it feels weird to be here with you."

"Why?"

"Because." I stop and stare right at him. "Can't you feel it too? It's just weird. I shouldn't have to explain it to you."

"Try."

I breathe in through my nose and out through my mouth, as if I'm in an active military unit and have learned to control my thoughts and emotions through breath. I have not.

"It's weird, Elliott, because everyone here is a couple. It's *couples'* movie night, with pink champagne." I wave my arm to make this a big deal. "And chocolate covered strawberries, and oh, we'll be passing out blankets because the theater gets a little cold." I sweep my arms left and right with each—romantic—thing.

I glare at him. "And yet, you've told me at least fourteen thousand times that this is not a date." I indicate my gorgeous dress. "But I'm all dressed up. Claudia curled my hair. I'm wearing eyeliner, Ell. Eye. Liner." I sigh when he still stands there, mute.

"And you look so...so amazing in that jacket. And it somehow goes with that silly t-shirt and those—" I look down to his pants. They're not really jeans, but they're not really khakis either. He has to wear black pants to work, and they're kind of like that, but a washed out blue.

"Pants," I finish lamely. "So it feels like a date, and it's weird, because we're *not* dating, but I don't want to have all this datey stuff so you can chit-chat with other women." I wipe my hand across my forehead, and oh, Claudia is going to be so mad at me. She spent a long time in hair and makeup with me, and I'm smearing it everywhere.

If I go home now, Lizzie and Tahlia will have a million questions. Everywhere I turn, I run into some major roadblock.

"Let's go walk around the Christmas Market," I say. "Maybe we can get into the Living Bethlehem on stand-by." I start walking toward the town square, and Ell comes with me.

He doesn't touch me, and he doesn't address anything I've just said. I wonder what it would be like to simply blow away. Will anyone notice? Will he?

I could duck between the theater and the diner, and I wonder how long it'll take before Ell realizes I'm not sauntering along at his side.

My chest pinches, and I pull in a breath to try to stem the hurt now blitzing through me. I'm so tired of being invisible, especially to him. To my parents. To everyone.

Technically, I know I'm not. My roommates see and love me. I want more, and maybe that makes me selfish. I'm not sure.

My phone zings, and I don't even bother to look at it. "That'll be my mother." She doesn't listen to me either.

"Yeah? Is she still asking about the Christmas party?"

"Several times each day," I say. "My sister is probably going to get engaged, and Momma says I need to be there." I sigh as my phone chimes again, and we pause on the cusp of the square so I can take it out and read her texts.

"Ry, it's December seventh. I must book airplane tickets in the next couple of days. I'm happy to pay for yours and a guest. Please let me know immediately what I should do." I look over to Elliott, and for the first time since he showed up on the porch at the Big House, he looks like himself.

Dazzling eyes, with that hint of mischievousness in them. Half-smile, slightly crooked. Adorable dimple. Straight, white teeth, and all the dashing and debonair of a true Hollywood heartthrob.

"Let me see." He holds out his hand, and I pass over my phone the way I have plenty of times before.

I look away and spot a hot chocolate station. Because of Claudia, I know more about this festival than the average attendee, and that hot chocolate is free. "I'm going to get some hot chocolate. Want some?"

"Sure."

I walk away, wishing I was dressed more like those who've come to the square tonight. Jeans, sweaters, even a scarf or two, probably just for festivities sake. I wait my turn, then fill two paper cups with hot chocolate. It's steaming and thick, and the first thing I have to smile about tonight.

I approach Ell and we do a trade—he takes the hot chocolate; I take back my phone. "What should I tell her?"

He calmly takes a sip of his hot chocolate. "I answered her for you."

My heartbeat thrashes against my ribcage. "What now?" He's never done that before. He reads my texts and tells me what to say. He doesn't actually type it out and say it.

"Yeah, yep," he says, and that makes me pause and blink. *Yeah, yep.* That's what Elliott says when he's nervous.

"Well, what did you say?" I lift my hot chocolate to my lips and blow gently. I like things hot that are supposed to be hot, but I like my taste buds to function too.

I start to take a sip, and oh, yeah, that's rich, full, and the perfect amount of chocolatey flavor.

"I told her you needed two tickets," he says calmly. "One for you and one for me."

The hot chocolate in my mouth spews out—all over his father's jacket, that funny tee, and those sexy pants.

He stands there and takes it, not moving a single muscle. When I can get a breath, I pant and say, "What? Do you know what this means?"

Elliott finally blinks, and he reaches down to the hem of that shirt and lifts it to wipe his chin and neck. In doing so, he's completely flashing me his abs and chest, and raspberry birthday cake with fudge brownies, the man has muscles.

"Yes, Ry," he says. "It means your momma now thinks we're dating."

WATCHING MY BEST FRIEND SPUTTER IS ACTUALLY kind of funny. I hide my smile for now, because she won't appreciate it. I'm feeling lucky I just got sprayed with hot chocolate, because with something like this, Ryanne could skewer me with that sharp tongue of hers.

And there I go, thinking about her tongue again. Her mouth. Her eyes. The shape of her body. The way she laughs with me and the other employees at Paper Trail. The way she brings in a birthday treat for everyone at the office supply store we co-manage. The way her roommates love her. The way she loves M&Ms. The way her momma pushes all the wrong buttons inside her.

"I can't—this is unbelive—how could you do this?" She finally rights her phone and looks at it. Oh, the text is there. In fact, Ry's momma has already replied how "delighted" she is to meet me, though, technically, we've met before.

"I told you weeks ago I'd be your boyfriend," I say smoothly. I have to put on this act or Ry will know why I've not started dating anyone else—it's because I want to date her.

I know, I was as shocked by that as anyone. Not because Ry isn't amazing. She is. It's not because she's ugly. She's one-hundred-percent not.

It's not because she's my best friend, and I'm terrified I'll lose her. She is, and I'm sure I will, so fine, maybe that's part of why I was shocked. I don't have many friends, and Ry is my very best one in the whole world.

But it's really because she's too good for me. It's because she wants long-term, and I just can't give her that. It's because she's a bad liar and won't be able to do the fake-dating thing.

"We can call this a date," I say. "Our first one."

"Are you out of your mind?" She shoves her phone under the strap of that stunning red dress, and oh, it's no fun to be jealous of an inanimate object. Ry looks left and right like we're doing something illegal. It sort of feels forbidden and dangerous, and I'll admit, that's part of the allure of the text I sent.

She folds her arms as her gaze comes back to me. "This is not our first date. First dates are supposed to be magical. Amazing. You spent the first twenty minutes flirting with other women."

"I did not." I glare at her. "I spoke to them like human beings, but you know what? I don't want this to be our first date either."

"Why not?" she demands.

"Because you spit hot chocolate all over me." I raise my eyebrows and look down at myself, as if we both don't already know where the sticky drink landed.

"You flashed me your *abdomen*." She whispers the last word like it's dirty.

I grin at her. "Can we start over?"

"Start...over?"

I reach out and take her hot chocolate from her. Then I take her hand in mine. "Yeah. I'll run home real quick and change. We'll go to dinner somewhere far away from here. Just me and you." I swallow, because I know how smart Ry is. "On a date. Our first date, so we can get things right for your family party in a couple of weeks."

She looks down at our hands, but she doesn't pull away. "Get things right."

"Right," I say. "Your family will want to know why and when we started dating, how it's working out with work, blah blah blah."

She pulls in a noisy breath through her nose, almost like those cute little snorts she makes. "Work," she blurts out. "Paper Trail. We can't date." She pulls her hand back, and I wish I had better ninja reflexes so I can keep it in mine. Unfortunately, I don't, and she even backs up a step as she does that left-right, left-right sweep for federal agents.

I chuckle, because Ry is always a little too serious. "Ry, honey, no one at Paper Trail cares if we date."

"Corporate does."

"I seriously doubt it."

"We're co-managers."

"So at least it's not someone in a position of power over the other."

She narrows her eyes at me. "You have an answer for everything, don't you?"

"No," I say.

She opens her mouth to argue again, then realizes what I've said, and closes it again. But given a few moments to think, she comes at me with, "Why do you want to do this?"

"Because." I sigh and look across the street to the market. "I hate hearing how sad and upset you are when-ever you hear from your momma. This is an easy fix, Ry."

Liar! screams through my mind, but I ignore it. Yes, Ry is sad and upset when her mom and dad text her about who's she's dating—no one this year that I know of—and they've been pressuring her about coming home for Christmas for months.

But the real reason I want to do this is because I have real feelings for my best friend. Real feelings that I have no idea what to do with, and this feels like a safe way to stick my toe out of the friend zone, something I've never done before.

She stares at me, and I'm having a hard time holding her gaze. Her eyebrows are thick and perfectly sculpted, and they frame her eyes in a sexy way I can't describe. She's a beautiful woman, and I've always thought so.

"I see you," I say next, and I hate myself the moment I do.

Because Ry crumbles right in front of me. Just simply falls apart, her perfectly made-up face plummeting as she starts to cry.

"No, shh." I gather her into my arms, wondering why I have to say such stupid things. "I'm sorry, Ry. Don't cry." I keep her close to my chest, not caring at all about my t-shirt getting mascara stains on it. Now, this jacket... That's another story, but I know a good dry cleaner, and I'm not sacrificing this moment of holding Ry in my arms for a sport coat, even if this one has sentimental value.

"Let's go," I say quietly, and she doesn't argue with me about leaving the square. I help her into my SUV as she sniffles, and I head for my house. "I'm just going to change," I tell her when we get there. "Do you want to come in or wait here?"

"What are we going to do next?"

"What do you want to do next, Ry?" I ask.

She looks at me, and I manage to look back at her. "I'll take you home so you can change, and we can just...be together."

She nods, and I'm not sure what that means. I have no idea where I'll take her after she shimmies out of that dress. Maybe she doesn't even want to change, or maybe after she does, she'll just want to crawl into bed and forget tonight ever happened. I honestly have no idea.

I also can't believe I brought her to my house. See, I don't exactly live alone, and while Ry knows my mom lives nearby, she doesn't know it's in the bedroom just down the hall.

Momma looks up as I slip in through the front door. "Elliott?" She's on her feet in less than a second, before I can wave her off, even.

"I'm fine," I say in a tired voice. I'm so sick of telling people I'm fine, or it's fine, or everything will be fine.

Sometimes things aren't fine, you know?

"I spilled some hot chocolate down me. I'm just gonna change and head back out."

My mother looks from me to the door. "Where's Ry?"

"Momma, leave her be!" I yell as I hurry out of the main part of the house and down the hall to my bedroom. "I'll be two minutes!"

Sometimes I trust my mother explicitly, but in this case, I change as fast as possible and head back down the hall while I'm still pulling my new tee over my head. Because my mom might have gone outside and invited Ry in. Or at least shown herself.

Thankfully, she's sitting on the arm of the couch, her

eyes on the TV. She does turn toward me when she hears me coming, and I give her a smile. "I'll be back later."

"Okay," she says. "You're okay?"

"Fine, Mom." I don't want to be rude to her—she's given up a lot to be here with me—but I don't want to talk about my co-manager and my feelings for her.

"Wear your night-driving glasses!" she yells after me, and irritation spikes through me. Of course I know to wear my driving glasses, especially at night. I let the door say what I want to as it closes loudly behind me, and I jog down the steps to the SUV.

Ry looks over to me as I get back in. "I do want to go home and get out of this dress."

My fantasies go wild, but I press my teeth together and keep everything inside. I've been doing that for a long, long time, and it gets easier every time. Except with Ry, I feel like I'm starting over at square one with everything.

So I almost let something slip like, *I'd like to help with that.*

But my one-liners that might work with other women will never, ever work with Ry. If I want to blow everything with her, then sure, I should let my mouth run wild. But for some reason, I don't want to do that.

At the same time, there's no way we can be together long-term. Thus, this fake-boyfriend-for-the-holidays fits the bill nicely. I suppress my inward sigh, because I'm too young to even be thinking "fits the bill nicely."

I take her back to her house—which she and her friends call "the Big House," where she looks at me fully for the first time since I got back in the car. "Do you want to stay here? Should we go somewhere else?"

"I'm following your lead, Ry."

She tilts her head to the side. "That's obviously not true. My mother has asked me about fifty-five questions since you texted her, and she's already got the tickets booked." She makes a face that displays disgust and irritation at the same time. "An eight-ten flight, Ell. Do you know what that means?"

"Yes, I do," I say.

"This is your fault."

"I'm sorry," I say. "You always just sound so frustrated by her, and I wanted to help."

"I think you wanted a free trip to New York City." She gives me that sexy smile that has kept me up at night for the past couple of months.

"Yeah, in the dead of winter," I say, returning her smile. "You caught me."

"You're such a soft Southern boy."

"I'm thirty-three years old," I say. "I'm not a *boy*."

Ry grins at me, and there's the best friend I know and love.

"Go change," I say. "And I'll take you to that gourmet street taco truck that is a total contradiction."

"They have pork belly, which is total gourmet, in a taco. It's the best thing you'll put in your mouth."

I laugh, because she says the same thing about the veggie taco—and I'm not even sure something can be labeled a taco if there's no meat. "All right, all right," I say. "Do you want to go in that gorgeous dress, or...?"

"No, I already said I wanted to change."

"But you're just sitting here." I lean my head back and gaze at her. She really is beautiful, and the whole office at Paper Trail smells like warm cinnamon toast and fruit champagne, which is the body spray Ryanne loves so much.

It's called Fairy Woods. I know, because I ventured out of my usual buying routine and went to the mall to get her some for her birthday last year. To me, she's a fairy tale, a princess in a tower I'll never have.

I want to be with someone long-term, but I won't doom them to my fate. So I've put on the player hat, and I'm never serious about anyone. I date a lot, because who wants to stay home with their momma when they're thirty-three years old?

Sometimes, I feel completely trapped in my life, and Ry has always been an escape for me. Maybe I acted a little rash tonight by texting her mother. Maybe this will be the worst Christmas in the world. *A very merry mess*, I think.

But then my eyes drop to her mouth, where her lips shine with something pink and tasty-looking, and my thoughts flip. Maybe, just maybe, this will be the best

Christmas ever, and I'll finally get to kiss my gorgeous, kind, and hard-working best friend.

Maybe I'll even get to do it tonight. For practice purposes, of course.

"I'll be right back," she says, and Ry slips from the SUV. I watch her go, my plans for a good-night kiss swirling and taking form as she walks away from me in that sexy dress.

"You're in trouble, Ell," I whisper to myself. "Remember who you are. Remember what your life is." There's more for me to tell myself, but I don't say it out loud.

Remember, you don't want to hurt Ry.

So maybe there won't be any kissing tonight after all.

————

Sometimes the holidays are messy...

PREORDER **A VERY MERRY MESS** today by scanning the QR code below.

BOOKS IN THE SOUTHERN ROOTS SWEET ROMCOM SERIES

Just His Secretary, Book 1: She's just his secretary...until he needs someone on his arm to convince his mother that he can take over the family business. Then Callie becomes Dawson's girlfriend—but just in his text messages...but maybe she'll start to worm her way into his shriveled heart too.

Just His Boss, Book 2: She's just his boss, especially since Tara just barely hired Alec. But when things heat up in the kitchen, Tara will have to decide where Alec is needed more —on her arm or behind the stove.

Just His Assistant, Book 3: She's just his assistant, which is exactly how this Southern belle wants it. No spotlight. Not anymore. But as she struggles to learn her new role in his office—especially because Lance is the surliest boss imaginable—Jessie might just have to open her heart to show him everyone has a past they're running from.

Just His Partner, Book 4: She's just his partner, because she's seen the number of women he parades through his life. No amount of charm and good looks is worth being played...until Sabra witnesses Jason take the blame for someone else at the law office where they both work.

Just His Barista, Book 5: She's just his barista...until she buys into Legacy Brew as a co-owner. Then she's Coy's business partner *and* the source of his five-year-long crush. But after they share a kiss one night, Macie's seriously considering mixing business and pleasure.

———————

Bonus for newsletter subscribers! Just His Neighbor, Prequel: She's just his neighbor...until his dog—oops, his brother's dog—adopts her.

Get this book by joining my newsletter here: https://readerlinks. com/l/3887964 **or scan the QR code below.**

A Very Terrible Text, Book 1: Sometimes the thumbs slip...

She's finally joined the dating app everyone in Cider Cove is raving about...when she accidentally sends a message about wanting to meet up for a first date to her enemy.

A Very Bad Bet, Book 2: *Sometimes a wager only makes things more fun...*

She's got seniority over the obnoxious grump next door, and she's determined to beat him out for the top job in their charming hometown. But a bold bet spins their rivalry into a flirty attraction that could change everything.

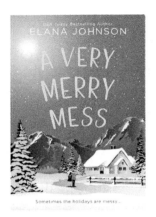

A Very Merry Mess, Book 3: *Sometimes the holidays are messy...*

Christmas is the season of joy, mistletoe, and, unfortunately for Ryanne, the pressure of bringing home a date. When she vents to Elliott, her best friend and co-manager at the small-town office supply store, he impulsively grabs her phone and texts her mother that they're dating.

Date. Ing.

Elana Johnson is a USA Today bestselling and Kindle All-Star author of dozens of clean and wholesome contemporary romance novels. She lives in Utah, where she mothers two fur babies, works with her husband full-time, and eats a lot of veggies while writing. Find her on her website at feelgoodfictionbooks.com.